Buckskin and Satin

Buckskin and Satin

A Novel by
Romain Wilhelmsen

SUNSTONE PRESS

SANTA FE

Sunstone books may be purchased for educational, business, or sales promotional use. For information please write: Special Markets Department, Sunstone Press, P.O. Box 2321, Santa Fe, New Mexico 87504-2321.

FIRST EDITION

10 9 8 7 6 5 4 3 2 1

Library of Congress Cataloging in Publication Data:
Wilhelmsen, Romain, 1924–
    Buckskin & Satin / by Romain Wilhelmsen. —1st ed.
        p. cm.
    ISBN: 0-86534-279-2 (hardcover)
    1. Tombstone (Ariz.)—History—Fiction.   I. Title.
PS3573. I4345B83   1999
813' .54—dc   98-38937
                                                    CIP

Published by   SUNSTONE PRESS
                  Post Office Box 2321
                  Santa Fe, NM 87504-2321 / USA
                  (505) 988-4418 / *orders only* (800) 243-5644
                  FAX (505) 988-1025

This book is dedicated to my wife, Jane Bower, whose editing and word processing skills saved me from shooting myself in the foot.

PREFACE

OF ALL THE FRONTIER TOWNS IN THE Old West, one in particular stands out. It was a town too tough to die.

Bordered by the Chiricahua and Dragoon mountains on the west, and the Whetstone Mountains on the east, this silver-mining town within shooting distance of Old Mexico attracted its share of heroes and villains, the famous, and the infamous.

My fascination with the story of Tombstone, Arizona, began one afternoon in the 1940s while poking through years of accumulated debris in the O.K. Corrall. From that time on, I yearned to learn all I could about this town too tough to die.

In this novel, I have delved into the lives of the people who inhabited Tombstone during the turbulent 1880s.

Many of the names are familiar: the Earp brothers—Wyatt, Morgan, Virgil, and Warren; Doc Holliday; Old Man Clanton and his boys; and a host of other colorful characters who came and went.

Less well-known were Frank "Buckskin" Leslie, the handsome bartender and part-time scout for the army during its pursuits of Geronimo and his renegade Apaches; the woman he wanted—the beautiful Nell Cashman—an independent woman determined to experience life on her terms; and Louis Hancock, a big black man whose avowed vengeance for a heinous crime brought him face-to-face with the deadly gunslinger, John Peters Ringo.

The principals brought to life on the pages of this novel lived in Tombstone during that time period. Only in those instances where history is silent have I attempted to create characters and events as they might have been, and perhaps were.

—Romain Wilhelmsen, East Lansing, Michigan-1998

1

FRANK "BUCKSKIN" LESLIE ENJOYED

his coffee. It was army coffee the way he liked it—very hot and very strong. It tasted good with the first cigarette of the day.

He took pleasure in all that was about him, feeling refreshed by a much-needed rest, and comforted by the familiar rustlings of Captain Wirt Davis's thirty-odd scouts. Yesterday's danger was behind him. No Apache would now dare approach this group of hardened frontiersmen. Each man was busying himself with either cleaning his Springfield Carbine—a Trapdoor Model 1873—or reloading his .45 Colt six-shooter. It was a formidable display of armament.

The driving rain had finally stopped. High above the tall pine trees the morning sky was turning a soft blue and the mist was beginning to lift from the earth. Huge mountains materialized out of the haze—not the friendly Dragoons or the Whetstones of Tombstone—but the mysterious Sierra Madre Mountains of Sonora, Mexico.

For all its soldierly appearance, the small group of mercenaries in the pay of the United States Army was but another moving shadow in the pristine wilderness. They kept together. They were a long way from home.

⁂

Tom Horn hunkered down next to his friend, Frank Leslie, who had been left alone to sleep away the misery of yesterday, and listened while Frank retold the story. "Better get it straight now before he gets into town and begins to embellish it," Tom thought. Frank was that way. If a story was good, he'd make it better; but regardless of how Frank told it, the deed was done. General Crook would eventually report to his superiors that Nashville Franklyn Leslie had all alone braved the cunning, almost spectral Chiricahua Apache to carry Captain Davis's report of success in this thankless campaign. Eleven times Leslie had been forced to swim the Bavispe River to escape them.

Tom was proud of his friend, but Frank was even more proud of himself. He knew that by the time the news hit the Tucson and Tombstone papers it would be one hell of a story, and he was right. Crook, like himself, was no shrinking violet when it came to publicity. To read Crook's report to the AAG Division of the Pacific, one would think two major battles had been fought and that the backbone of the Chiricahua had been broken. In reality, there had been but a couple of quick skirmishes resulting in approximately a dozen casualties, most noncombatants.

Nevertheless, during the Davis scout, Frank had lived up to his reputation as being a fast and sure shot. Of the four Apaches brought down, one had fallen between the sights of Frank's Springfield. Tom Horn liked that. He and Buckskin prided themselves on being sharpshooters, and as long as Uncle Sam was handing out free cartridges, they banged away at every conceivable target. They were good. Perhaps too good. Their guns would eventually bring them a lot of trouble.

⁂

They savored the aroma of the campfire, the sizzle of thick-cut bacon and sourdough biscuits frying in the pan, and the smell of coffee, leather and horses. This was a man's world. At age twenty-five, Horn was in his prime. The juices bubbled in his veins. He still had much to see and more to do, and he intended to live his life to the fullest, as his friend had lived his. Tom's problem, though, and he realized it, was that he was a loner. He couldn't laugh and tell jokes, sing, dance or attract the ladies the way Frank did. Only when he had a snootful could he communicate well. He was actually more content alone in the mountains with his rifle for a companion.

Leslie was different. He was older, and the bloom of youth was fading. His reactions had slowed, and not just from age. He'd had too much whiskey, too many blackouts, and too many shootings. Once in a while his excesses came back to haunt him, particularly in his dreams. He had needed a change, and in joining this expedition hoped to be able to put at least some of his demons behind him. The campaign had rejuvenated him. He felt relaxed and re-energized, and best of all he hadn't had a bad dream in over a month. His dreams now were for a better future, and he was glad when the chief scout, Al Seiber, announced they were going home.

⁂

The half-breed scout that Al described as "half Mexican, half Irish, and whole son of a bitch" now joined the two scouts. Mickey Free was quite a sight. He had long, tangled red hair worn in the Apache style, and one eye had been badly mutilated in an encounter with a bear. His castoff army coat hung loosely over his shoulders and breechclout. A Colt revolver nested in the holster fastened to his oversized Mills cartridge belt. He carried a 45/70 Springfield rifle and a Bowie knife, and about his head wore a red band that distinguished him from the hostiles. Like Tom Horn, Mickey displayed the stoicism of the Apache. He had been captured by them when he was just a boy; had lived with them, loved them, and was one of them until liberated by the whites. His services as an interpreter at the San Carlos Reservation, and as one of Al Sieber's scouts, were invaluable. He could easily out-track both Tom and Frank, and some swore he could literally smell a hostile Indian from half a mile away. But his ambition was to be able to shoot with the same accuracy as Tom Horn and Buckskin Frank. No one was better than they were, and whenever possible Mickey traveled close to these two contract scouts in order to learn from them.

Tom and Frank liked their strange companion. For one thing, he had enough white in him to make him more palatable than the other White Mountain Apache scouts. For another, he spoke their language, and had wonderful stories to tell after the teswin liquor loosened his tongue. This he did now as the small group of scouts cinched their saddles and began the long way north to the border and home.

The sun began to warm the countryside. Frank reached into his "bag of possibles" which had been retrieved from one of the pack mules, and pulled out his canteen filled with Old Crow. He had saved it for an occasion such as this, having just four months prior taken its contents from the ample supply at Tombstone's Oriental Bar where he was head bartender. He let the smooth liquid slide down his throat and take hold. It was so much better than the pulque, teswin and mescal picked up when passing through the little Mexican villages along their trail. He took another slug, and then handed the canteen to Tom, who was only too glad for a sip of the good stuff. Frank was about to cork the container, but instead turned to Mickey Free, nodded for him to move up, and handed it to him. As he did, he thought "whiskey sure brings an odd lot of humanity together—

drifters, desperadoes, liars, cheats, sadists, damn fools, Indians, and half-breeds. So be it." He replaced the canteen in the special bag, hung it on his Mexican saddlehorn, and took a biting slug from Free's bottle of mescal. Drinking was strictly prohibited by the army, but what the hell. This wasn't really the army. It was just a bunch of thirsty misfits working for the army. It sure livened up the day and the conversation as the straggly column wound its way through massive expanses of pine forest, gloomy valleys and along game trails. It would be this way for several days until the cactus-filled Chihuahua Desert could be glimpsed occasionally from the heights of the Sierra Madres.

Frank kept his bourbon to himself, but Mickey Free was plenty free with his mescal and his stories. He spoke of the legends whispered over nocturnal campfires by the *Shis Indy* (Men of the Woods) Apaches. He told of grand cities of stone that appeared to be hanging from the mountainsides, great cliff dwellings long abandoned by the Anasazi, and a huge cave in which a giant was said to be buried alongside old Spanish Conquistador armor. He told the story of the large Spanish colonial city of Baroyeca in the Sonora Desert that the Indians overran a century ago, now forgotten, its church bells still ringing in the wind.

Farther along on the descent from the mountains he pointed to a distant mesa rising conspicuously from the desert floor. He said it was the *Cero de Miñaca*, the main geographical evidence relating to the lost Jesuit mines of Tayopa. He cautioned that this area is guarded by the Yaqui Indians, who see all and tell nothing. "Even now we are under the eyes of the Yaqui. They are everywhere. They, as well as the peaceful Tarahumara Indians who live in the deep copper canyons, know everything that is to be known of the Sierra Madre Mountains." It was at this time, as the little band of scouts trudged slowly across the alkaline desert, their boots and their horses totally worn out, and still with some distance to go, that the Chiricahua Apaches made their presence known. Some distance from the rear of the column a scattering of shots was heard. With speed belying their weary bodies, each of the scouts—white and red—came off his horse, scrambled behind it, and almost instantly was on the ground with long guns at the ready. Eyes red with fatigue squinted at the trail over which they had come. Puffs of smoke floated in the air. Then came the distant boom of Sharp's "Big Fifty" buffalo gun. It upheld its reputation as a mile-long range rifle when a couple seconds later one of the supply mules brayed, sagged to the ground, and died. There was silence for a moment. Then nine forms materialized in the distance.

Here was the enemy that Captain Wirt Davis and his band of scouts had been tracking for four months. These opposing forces watched each other for a few moments. Then, with a derisive howl, the Chiricahua swung easily onto their mounts which had been hidden nearby among century plants and Spanish Bayonet scrub trees. They had had their little joke. They rode slowly toward the west, to the Sierra Madre Mountains, with no fear of pursuit because their horses had just been stolen from General Luis Terraza's Santa Clara Ranch, and they were fresh and rested, quite unlike those of the white eyes and their Apache scouts. So sure were the hostiles of their superiority that one of them turned and rode back toward the scouts. He came within shooting distance, shook his fist, spat on the ground, stood on his horse's back, and scornfully exposed his genitals and buttocks to his enemy. He called out to Mickey Free and cursed, calling him "*lo-kohì-sca-'ni-ilgáe o ndi yù-dastin a-atà lick-ind-ye `n' -naltì-i-gi-a net-j-ta-iltcohe te-indì-ndì*" (a crazy, scabrous half-breed bastard with a snake eye and a forked tongue who spies and lies in all things). His fun didn't last long. Buckskin Leslie's Springfield was at his shoulder, and he squeezed the trigger. It was a long shot for this weapon, but the renegade and his horse went down. A cheer went up from the ragged band of scouts, only to turn to disappointment as the Indian rose from the ground, stripped the blanket from his thrashing horse, and hastened after his companions. "Son of a bitch," muttered Frank, as he sent another bullet into the wounded animal. "Son of a bitch," he said again as Tom and Mickey mentally calculated and marveled at the distance of his shot.

So ended the campaign that George Crook had hoped would enhance his reputation with the War Department and the nation. It didn't. So, too, was Frank Leslie's contract with the government officially terminated.

⁂

Tom Horn was to be sent back to Fort Huachuca from Fort Bliss in El Paso, Texas. Frank would eventually take the train from El Paso to Tucson, and then ride his horse home to Tombstone. Mickey Free was already on his way back to San Carlos. Tom and Frank looked one another over. Tom was all cleaned up, and had shaved off four months' growth of beard, but he had kept his long mustache. He was quite the figure of a westerner—a good six feet tall, lean and clean-cut. Frank was somewhat shorter, but he was handsome and had the presence of a professional actor. His mustache curled at the ends, and he had pale blue eyes which never betrayed his emotions. With his rakish demeanor, there was something of the devil in Frank "Buckskin" Leslie.

The two men had much in common. While still in his teens, Tom and twenty-one unemployed scouts and packers from Fort Huachuca had joined Frank, and they prospected the Dragoons just west of the Fort. On occasion, they joined up with Ed Schieffelin. It was in that area that Ed made his momentous discovery of the immensely rich silver mines that brought Tombstone, Arizona, into being. Leslie was going back to Tombstone and his prosaic job behind the bar at the Oriental. The fun and games were over, or so he thought.

Frank and Tom clasped hands. Tom turned back to the army post, and Frank swung aboard the train.

With a swoosh of steam, the Southern Pacific heralded its departure. Frank settled in, closed his eyes, and was soon asleep, dreaming of the future.

But nothing in his dreams could compare to what actually took place when he was once again back in Tombstone.

2

JOHN PETERS RINGO HAD A BAD
night. By his own recollection it was one of the worst in a long history of bad
nights. He'd had them on and off as long as he could remember. He was plagued
by a dream in which a gun was fired so close to his face that he was blinded. The
reverberating boom would fill his head, and a piercing scream would follow.
He'd always wake with a terrible headache, trembling and covered with a clammy
sweat. Though he tried, he just couldn't get to the source of the dream. Once he
thought it might have something to do with the James Cheney shooting. It hadn't
been the most even-handed one he'd ever experienced, but he always rational-
ized that since it had taken place during the Texas Hoodoo war, near Burnet
down Lampasas way, he needn't have any guilt over that. Then why this utterly
terrible nightmare repeating year after year after year? His head throbbed. Relief
came only after some long pulls from a bottle of whiskey. He kept one close at
hand, and would soon have to replenish it—like today, at Murphs.

He sat up in his hotel bed, slipped his feet into hightop calfskin boots, and
with the inside canvas loops pulled them up snug. At this hour he wasn't going
anywhere, but who wanted to step on a scorpion, or worse yet a vinegarroon that
had sneaked in from the cold? Besides, with Texas boots on a man stood tall and
above it all. He'd never be mistaken for a sodbuster or a storekeeper. He clomped
over to the window, the only one in this very basic hotel room. Though the wind
had died down, he could feel the cold December air seeping through the poor-
fitting frame and into his longjohns. But the air felt good on his flushed face.

❦

Outside there was a full moon unobstructed by any clouds. A light snow
earlier had painted the desert an eerie white, and here and there balls of tum-
bleweed cast strange shadows. Several giant saguaro seemed to beckon with their

thorny arms to the lone figure looking out the window of Safford, Arizona's second-rate hotel. He studied the heavy growth of palo verde and catclaw trees and the tangle of mesquite around them. Except for a big, brown tarantula lumbering from one growth to another, the night seemed devoid of motion. Illuminated only by moonlight, it seemed a scene from another world. It appeared dead, as dead as the wasteland which was his soul. If Ringo were inclined to feel sorry for himself, now would be the time for it; but he wasn't. He turned to the rickety table beside his bed and drew his .45 Colt from the Mexican loop holster which hung from a nearly full cartridge belt. He checked the cylinder, then removed the chair which he had placed as a barricade against the door, and opened the door cautiously. He stepped quietly into the still, cold night, holding the gun in his right hand.

From somewhere came the mournful howl of a coyote. Ringo peered around the corner at Safford's main street: a muddy route for reaching its two saloons, a mercantile store, the sheriff's office, and other nondescript places of business. One store, he noted, had a Christmas wreath hung on the door. For some reason, this bothered him. He pulled back, fumbled at his longjohns, and relieved himself.

Returning to his room, he again placed the chair against the door and slipped his gun into its holster. This so-called hotel furnished no kerosene lamps, so he lit the solitary candle on the table and with the same match fired up a thin cigar. He was really feeling the cold now, so he slipped back into bed, boots and all, pulled the blanket to his chin, and reached for the papers which he'd placed beside the bed. One was the October 1879 *Police Gazette*. He'd read it before, and now he would read it again. He liked the story about the recent Lincoln County War in New Mexico, and he really fancied the vivid accounts of young Billy the Kid. They reported how Billy had stood up to the oppressors of his friends, and how the Kid had cleared the range of the big cattle companies, companies owned by rich New Yorkers and others from big cities in the east. "Served those New Yorkers right," he said aloud, "just like we took care of those damned Dutchmen in Texas." Ringo was not merely interested in the way the press was writing up the Kid—he liked it. Along with the *Police Gazette* he had also collected several back issues of the *Messila Valley Independent* that were following the exploits of this "hero of the Lincoln County War." He read all of them again, then stubbed his smoke out on the table, pinched out the flame of the candle, and put his reading material back on the floor. He finally managed to doze off.

A scorpion soundlessly crossed the floor, paused on the newspapers containing the reports on Billy the Kid, then made for the space beneath the door and the comparative warmth of the sun as it began to rise on still another day.

Murphy's Bar, called Murph's, was where most of the serious drinkers went. It was across the street from the hotel. Right next door, which was a good place for it, was the sheriff's office. Forty-Rod was the only whiskey available at Murph's, but no matter. Neither Murphy nor his patrons were all that particular anyway. A favorite expression was "Drink enough Forty-Rod, and forty rods down the road you're off to bye-bye land." For those less bold, there was beer, and plenty of it, served up in large mugs. Murph's wasn't a fancy emporium such as those now being built in Tombstone just a hundred miles southwest, but it was all that was wanted here: a fair-sized room with a twenty-foot bar, several tables and chairs for the card players, and a faro layout with all the goodies. Only Pat Murphy handled the faro boxes. When he wasn't there, which was quite often because he worked the little spread he owned up in the valley, the game shut down. But there were plenty other things to bet on in this little bar room.

Pat was a Catholic Irishman and didn't allow the "ladies of the night" on the premises, even though it cost him business. He'd say, "I've got enough sins to atone for already. If it's hanky-panky you want, go across the street to Harrisons. John don't care what you do there. What can you expect of a Scotch Episcopalian?" But his morality didn't extend to the drinking, blasphemy and gambling that went on in his establishment almost eighteen hours a day because, as any good Irishman would tell you, "When the thirst is on a man, it's got to be served."

The bar had opened at six in the morning, as usual, and early business on this day was particularly brisk. Pat, having already made a good profit for the day, was relaxing in the back room in the late afternoon when occupants of two stagecoaches and their escort of a dozen troopers, enroute to the silver diggings at Globe and the San Carlos Reservation seventy miles east, stopped to wet their whistles. They had continued on, and now only a few regulars sipped beer and talked away the day while their wives were home doing the chores.

The tall, lean Texan from the hotel was back at his favorite table, drinking whiskey, as he had been doing the last few days. The previous week he'd brought in a few cows and sold them to Fred McSween of the Blue Jay Ranch. McSween wasn't particular as to where his stock came from, and never questioned their origin. Now the Texan seemed determined to drink up his profit. In this sparsely-settled country, with the Apaches still around, most men carried a weapon. This stranger wore a six-shooter Texas style—low on his hips—a fact which had drawn the attention of the drovers and farmers who passed through for their morning eye-opener. Along toward evening when the bar was beginning to fill, he'd leave his table in order to palaver with the patrons and swap a few lies. By that time he was generally pretty well soused.

Louis Hancock, a big, muscular Negro, entered the saloon. The oil lamps flickered and sent shadows dancing around the room as he shut the door against the cold. Hancock worked a few head of cattle at his homestead along the San Simon, where he lived in a small ranch house with his pretty Pinal Apache wife. They were a devoted couple, and had won the respect of the Safford community. The men would joke, "He might be a squaw man, but with a squaw like that I sure wouldn't mind being in his moccasins once in a while." Louis knew they gossiped about him, but it didn't bother him. He'd come a long way since his army days, and he knew what he wanted out of life. Right now he wanted a beer.

He bellied his two-hundred-plus pounds up to the bar and accepted a cool mug of Murph's finest, "just brought up from the cellar." Pat liked serving this man. He was quiet, good-natured, could give and take a joke, feared no man, and didn't stink up the place as so many of the others did. He was good for a couple stops every week, an hour of talk with the locals, no more than two beers, and then home to his wife. He was a "no problem" man. "How's the little one?" Murph asked, and Louis was off and running. He dearly loved to brag about his three-year-old daughter.

A few feet away, John Ringo was engaged in loud talk with a couple of Texas cowboys with whom he had a lot in common. They had come all this way with John Slaughter's herd of longhorns, and were headed for Douglas along the Mexican border, traveling in easy stages. Slaughter was in the process of moving his ranch operations from Texas to Safford. The cowboys were waiting for the foreman, John Roberts, who had just delivered a herd of steers to the San Carlos Reservation. The younger of the two was nineteen-year-old Billy Claiborne. He fancied himself another Billy the Kid, and was pleased to hear John Ringo speak so nicely of the Kid. A lot of whiskey was going down, and the talk was getting a bit too loud for Louis Hancock, so he picked up his beer and moved down to the far end of the bar.

Ringo, drunk or sober, was always alert to the placement of the people around him, and he didn't like Hancock's move. His "curly wolf" was rising as he sneered, "What's the matter, boy, too proud to drink with a couple of Texans?"

Louis had been this route before. He finished his beer, wiped his mouth, and moved to go home.

Claiborne fueled the fire rising in his new friend, goading him with, "I know damn well Billy the Kid would never let a nigger turn his back on him!"

Ringo grabbed Louis by the shoulder and swung him around. "You!" he shouted. "Have a man's drink with us. Murph, bring him a glass."

Louis jerked away and in a slow, measured tone answered "I don't know you boys, and I don't drink whiskey. I'm goin' home."

"The hell you are," Ringo snarled, and faster than anyone there had ever seen, he had his six-shooter out and was making to club the big man's skull. He'd have done better to pull the trigger right then. Louis deflected Ringo's gun with his arm, and smashed his huge black fist into Ringo's face. Louis saw the hate in his eyes as Ringo's six-shooter exploded between them. Ringo went down. Not by a bullet from his own gun, but by Louis's one-two punch that sent him sprawling onto the floor. Murph quickly wrenched Ringo's gun from his hand as a spittoon went flying and spilled its contents all over Ringo, who looked up at Hancock now bleeding heavily from wounds to his ear and neck.

The big man drew his old army Remington and looked at Claiborne. The would-be Billy the Kid backed off with both hands in the air, crying "I'm out of here."

The sheriff arrived after the trouble was over, as did half the townsfolk. Hancock had bound his wounds with his neckerchief. He was all right, but shaken. The sheriff learned enough to put the irons on Ringo.

"No need to do that," Hancock said in a steady, unnerving voice. "He goes out of town tonight, or I'll kill him tomorrow." Hancock knew from the expression in Ringo's eyes that he'd have to bushwhack the son of a bitch in order to do it. He refused to press charges against the obviously drunk Ringo, and would only repeat to the sheriff, "Get him out of town."

The sheriff knew the townsfolk wouldn't stand the cost of keeping Ringo in jail until the Circuit Judge came by, so he fined him twenty-five dollars for discharging a gun within the city limits, and whispered a word of advice: "Move along tonight. That big fellow is a man of his word."

Ringo had been around long enough to know it was time to move on. He paid his fine, rounded up his gear, bought two bottles of Forty-Rod, checked out his Winchester, then mounted up and rode south into the night with the other two Texans. On the release form of his arrest sheet he had written after "Destination": Tombstone.

3

NELL CASHMAN WAS A BEAUTIFUL
woman. To many in Tombstone, Arizona, she was the prettiest thing they'd ever seen. She was just over five feet tall, and possessed a perfect figure. Men thought she was one delectable handful, but those who tried to lay a hand on her never succeeded. She had dark brown hair and dark, flashing Irish eyes which seemed to beckon and reject at the same time. Everyone loved her and appreciated her sense of humor: the cowboys, the miners, the prostitutes, the lawmen, and even the society matrons. Those elegant snobs gossiped that Nell used lip rouge, that she pinched her cheeks to give them a rosy look, and that she buffed her fingernails with pink powder. But still they all agreed with Mayor John Clum who printed in his newspaper, the *Epitaph*, that Nell Cashman was the Angel of Tombstone.

She had come from Tucson, where she owned the successful Delmonico Restaurant, at about the same time as Clum. Before that, she had prospered in the boom camps of Virginia City, in British Columbia, and way up in the northwest snow country where she had expertly handled malamute dog teams. Nell and her sister Fannie had originally come from Queenstown, Ireland, to escape the potato famine and the political troubles there. They had settled in Boston with other Irish immigrants, and it was there that Nell had succumbed to wanderlust.

She sat now at her desk in the back room of the Arcade Restaurant and Chop House, to which she had recently acquired ownership, and opened a letter just received. She was intrigued by the letterhead: SISTERS OF MERCY AT ST. VINCENT'S ACADEMY, Savannah, Georgia. A feminine hand had penned the following message:

September 11, 1880

Dear Madam Cashman:

You have been suggested to me by the Catholic Appeal Service Organization of which I understand you are a member.

I am a maiden of thirty years, and am about to enter as a Novice the Order of Sisters of Mercy. There is but one affair that I feel I must clear up before leaving society and taking my final vows.

I have been attempting to locate, or at least ascertain if he is still alive (God forbid he might not be), a dear cousin of mine whom I understand is somewhere in the territories. We have corresponded much of our lives, but a year ago his letters ceased. He is known to have a lung disease.

The last address I have for him is Prescott, Arizona. At that time he had written he was considering settling in Tombstone.

Would you please ease a young woman's mind, and attempt to locate for me Doctor John Henry Holliday? He is a dentist of good family.

Thank you so much.

Most Sincerely,
Mattie Holliday

(Soon to be Sister Mary Melanie)

Nell was familiar with lung disease. She was a good friend to the miners, those grimy men who grubbed for twenty-four dollars a week in the Lucky Cuss, Contention, and Tough Nut mines. She knew their families, and she personally tended some of their broken bones, their powder-burned faces, and the dreaded lung sickness that overtakes most all men who work beneath the surface of the earth.

She felt great compassion for this young woman who was about to trade her place in the world for a cloistered life of good works. On occasion, Nell had considered it for herself. She also felt sorrow for this Doctor Holliday. In her work in the mines here and elsewhere, Nell had learned of some basic treatment for lung disease, and was able to alleviate pain; but she knew that cures were seldom effected. She would definitely follow through on Mattie's request.

As a two-year resident of Tombstone, Nell Cashman was familiar with most of its inhabitants, but had only heard of Doc Holliday: that he was a gambler and a drinker, that he consorted with prostitutes, and was a gunman. Nell sighed. That was the bad. Surely there must be some good. Just a week ago at Mass, Father Gallagher had spoken about casting the first stone, and she remembered reminding herself that she, too, had played games of chance and called Bingo when raising money for the construction of a church or the miners' hospital.

Her full lips parted in a smile as she recalled how, during her early months in Tombstone, some had thought she was one of the prostitutes, because she was frequently among those unfortunate women on an errand of mercy, counseling a young girl about to embark on a life of hell in the cribs, or on occasion raising money for charity. They realized the true situation in a short time, but the society matrons would never approach those women themselves. Though they sneered at the givers, they always eagerly accepted the money they gave Nell. They were quick to say, "Let Nell do that. She likes those people." And Nell, with a twinkle in her eyes, never let them forget that the red light district, the gamblers, and the whole drinking and sporting crowd, were consistently her biggest contributors. Nell understood these self-righteous people, and knew why they treasured and protected their side, but she appreciated—and really found more of interest in—the other side.

She kept a bottle of good Irish whiskey in her pantry, and relaxed at the end of the day by having a drink and a slender Bull Durham cigarette that she hand-rolled. If the good folks of Tombstone knew that!

Now she prepared to call on Doc Holliday, having obtained his address from Frank Leslie. "An interesting man, this Frank Leslie," she mused as she fastened a red scarf about her neck and shoulders. She'd liked him from the first time they met, when he auditioned for the amateur production of *The Irish Diamond*, which she had organized for charity. She enjoyed listening to his rich baritone voice and his hearty laugh. She liked his clean-cut look, and the way he smelled of Bay Rum and buckskin, but most of all she took great pleasure in the teasing way he paid her compliments. He delighted in making her blush, especially when he'd refer to her as his little Irish diamond. Nell felt at ease in Frank's presence, and though he was some years her senior, she decided he was of a good age.

Nell was aware that Frank was an object of gossip for the good folks of Tombstone. Some even said he was a dangerous man. Perhaps it was because of his roguish attitude toward life, which was in contrast to his otherwise charming and outgoing personality. For all that, Nell thought Frank "Buckskin" Leslie was all man, and she liked the company of men. Though nothing had come from their flirtation, the two became more than mere acquaintances, and Frank frequently took his morning coffee at Nell's Arcade Restaurant where they held long and intimate conversations.

When Nell brought up the subject of Doc Holliday, Frank told her all he knew, or thought, or had heard about him. He seemed surprised when Nell mentioned Doc's cough, and asked if it was in any way connected with the miners' lung disease. He told her, "Doc's cough goes a long way back, but it has nothing to do with the mines. He's never been in one in his life. What he has is consumption, and it ruined his dental practice both in Dodge City and Las Vegas. He's been trying to run away from it since he was a young man in Georgia, but he knows it'll get him eventually, and probably soon. I'm sure there are times when he looks over his shoulder and sees death coming, and then takes to drink to forget; also, I'm sure, to deaden the pain. When he drinks he loses his temper, and is quick to go for his gun. He acts like a lost soul."

At the very instant Frank stopped talking, Nell noticed a melancholy expression cross his face. "Except for the consumption, I could be describing myself," Frank thought.

He gave her Doc's address and changed the subject.

Nell's other source of information on Doc Holliday was one of the older girls of the red light district who doubled as a barmaid at the Bird Cage Theatre, and as courtesan for Dutch Annie, the queen madam of the district. Her name was Charlotte "Lottie" Deno. She had a way with words, and long before her demise she penned this epitaph to be carved on her tombstone:

> Here lies the body of little Charlotte,
> Born a virgin—died a harlot.
> For fifteen years she kept her virginity,
> And that's damn long in this vicinity.

When Nell asked her about Doc Holliday she sneered, "If I should step in soft cow manure, I wouldn't even clean my shoe on that bastard!"

As she walked down Allen Street and into the business district of Tombstone, Nell wondered what had happened to bring on such an outburst.

⁕

At ten in the morning the gaming houses were quiet, as were the eateries which were in the process of being cleaned. The sporting crowd was mostly sleeping off a night of drinking, or planning how to get even at the gaming tables come night time. The sky was cloudless and the air was crystal clear. Nell liked Tombstone, especially on peaceful mornings like this, but she also looked forward to the nighttime activities: the whir of the roulette wheels, the shouts after the roll of the dice, the sound of a piano and the singing of a happy drunk. She liked the excitement of a frontier town, often listening to its sounds from the warmth and security of her bed. As she walked, she reached into the muff she carried and felt for some loose dollar bills, wanting them handy in case she was approached by some down-and-outer begging for a meal. She also secreted in it a pearl-handled Remington .41 Double Derringer. It had been with her a long time. She passed the back gate of the O. K. Corral and the assay office, and turned in at Fly's Boarding House and Photography Studio owned by Camillus Sidney Fly, who preferred to be called C. S. or Buck. Nell couldn't fault him for that.

Mollie Fly, Buck's wife, a dignified lady no taller than herself, rose from a large, overstuffed ottoman as Nell entered. She had been separating photo proofs and negatives. The two ladies were well acquainted, as both traveled in the best of Tombstone's social circles.

"Good morning, Nell. No doubt you've come for our contribution to the charity ball. Buck has already dropped it off at Martha Kine's house." The ball to which she referred was being given to raise money for the Irish National League, of which Nell was treasurer.

Always one to get right to the point, Nell replied, "You must know it's not about the ball that I have come, Mollie, since I sent my card announcing that I'd be by to see Doctor John Holliday. I have an important message for him from his family back east."

Mollie said limply, "I forgot about that." But she hadn't. When Nell's card arrived the day before, Mollie had wondered what the devil Nell would want to see that drunk for, and was hoping for some juicy gossip to pass on at her card party that afternoon. She was disappointed that Nell wasn't going to share any news with her.

"Doctor Holliday has room four right down the hall," she said haughtily.

"Thank you," Nell replied with a smile. "I look forward to seeing you and Buck on Saturday." She then sashayed down the hall and tapped on Doc's door.

When it opened, Nell was surprised. The consumption hadn't taken nearly the toll she'd been led to believe. He stood tall and erect. At not quite six feet, and one hundred and fifty pounds, he merely looked lean for his height. He had a nice frame, blond hair flecked with gray, and a neatly trimmed mustache. He wore an immaculate white shirt with a hint of ruffle at the open collar, a long dress coat over a pearl-gray brocade vest, and black trousers. Nell thought he looked every inch the gambling man everyone said he was.

Holliday seemed amused as Nell looked him over. Accepting his hand, she said, "I am Nell Cashman. It's good of you to see me."

Doc bowed slightly, and replied in a soft southern drawl, "The pleasure is mine, Miss Cashman. I've heard about you. Everyone in Tombstone must know you. You're reputed to be the brightest light in this benighted city."

He released her hand and guided her by the elbow to a plush chair at a small round table, made sure she was comfortable, and pulled up two more chairs.

Nell then became aware that someone was sitting on a divan in a corner of the room which was partially obscured by heavy, dark red draperies. Doc motioned, and an attractive woman rose and joined them at the table.

"Miss Cashman," he said, "please meet Mary Katherine, my dear friend and confidant, whom I call Kate." Kate immediately extended her hand to Nell and said, "I'm pleased to meet you, Miss Cashman." Nell noticed a European accent.

Kate, who had been born in Budapest thirty-one years before, didn't seem to Nell to be the kind of person anyone would have expected to see with this man. There was an air of quality about her, and obviously at one time she had the sensuous beauty such as was found in women who came from the Steppes of eastern Europe. But now her face bore a drained look, and she had some wrinkles which probably shouldn't have been there. Even though she and Doc were impeccably turned out, there was an aura of decay about them.

"Doctor Holliday," Nell said, "I've come to deliver this letter which came to me from Tucson. It is self-explanatory." She handed the letter to him, and Doc stiffened noticeably when he saw the handwriting. He excused himself and read the letter through, slowly. Then he read it again. He sat in silence for a moment, then handed it to Kate.

Doc knew he was dealing with the cream of Tombstone society, and as he gazed steadily into Nell's eyes said, "I regret I have no refreshments to offer you for your trouble in seeking me out. However, a good host must provide something for his guest. Therefore, Miss Cashman," he continued as he rose and walked to a small table, "if you would care to join Kate and me in a glass of Mr. Thistle Dew's fine whiskey, we would be delighted."

Nell saw two full bottles and one half-full bottle of the Kentucky whiskey on the table, and knew it wasn't the best to be had. She thought she detected a note of sarcasm in his voice, but also noticed the sparkle in his eyes, and felt he could be merely teasing her. Though she considered it much too early to be drinking, she answered without hesitation, "I do thank you for your offer Doctor Holliday, but the only spirits I occasionally partake of are those which come straight from the land of my birth. Would you by any chance have a bit of Irish whiskey?"

Doc smiled, took a healthy swallow from the glass he had poured for himself, and said, "You catch me short, Miss Cashman, but next time you won't, and I'll drink to that." And so he did—another stiff one. Kate had finished her first glass, and watched in silence as Doc walked Nell to the door.

"Trust me," he continued, "before the week is out a letter will be on its way to my cousin in Georgia. I must do something before she takes the drastic step she threatens here."

As Doc, adding more profound thanks, closed the door, Nell glimpsed Kate filling her second glass. But this was not her concern any more than was the condition of Doc's lungs. She knew that now.

As Nell left the studio, she nodded to Mollie Fly, who was deep in conversation with a well-dressed man. She'd passed him on the street before, and had considered him to be one of the most handsome men she'd seen in the territory. He carried himself very erect, and exuded self-confidence in every move of his well-built body. His eyes as he returned Nell's gaze contained no warmth, and no hint of mirth. He nodded almost imperceptibly to her. As she turned toward the doorway, she heard Mollie say, "You may go in now, Mr. Earp."

4

JOHNNY BEHAN HAD A WAY WITH THE

ladies, and he knew it. He was a man who got what he wanted, whether by fair means or foul, and right now he wanted the innocent eighteen-year-old Josephine Sarah Marcus. He was thirty-four. Johnny liked the odds. He prided himself on his ability to make a woman desire him, even though this attitude had, on occasion, gotten him into trouble. The records of the District Court of Yavapi County contained ample evidence of that, as in the case of *Victoria Behan vs. John H. Behan*:

> . . .The said defendant disregarding the solemnity of the marriage vows, has within the past two years at diverse times and places openly and notoriously visited houses of ill fame and prostitution..., and more particularly the said defendant in the month of December 1874, at a house of ill fame. . .at which resided one [woman], commonly called Sada, a woman of prostitution and ill fame, did consort, cohabit, and have sexual intercourse with said [woman]. . .openly and notoriously causing great scandal. . .

His marriage had been dissolved then and there. Though saddled with alimony payments, Behan had reflected, "I'm free now to do what I want."

The ladies kept falling all over him and under him, and his persuasive charm took him to the top of frontier society. He was appointed sheriff of Prescott, Arizona, by the Democrats, and he had hoped this would be a stepping stone to the governorship. But when the following article appeared in the *Miner*, Behan instead became a laughing stock because of his incompetence:

> Hon. J. H. Behan had occasion to call at the Chinese laundry this P.M., when a controversy arose, leading to some half dozen of the pigtailed race making an assault on him with clubs. He tried to de-

fend himself with a revolver, which unfortunately failed to work. He received several severe cuts about the head. Four of his assailants were arrested and lodged in jail.

Worse yet, John Behan, a Democrat, had to be rescued from the sing-songing Celestials by his constable, a Republican by name of Virgil W. Earp. The story was too good to ignore, and many a man would thereafter put fingers to eyes, slant them, and chime out, "ching, ching Chinaman" as he passed the sheriff on the street.

While the rougher element of Prescott might look the other way, and even admire Behan for his antics in the bawdy houses and saloons, they were also quick to turn against this pretender to fame when he became the butt of a joke. Thus John Behan lost out on his dream of becoming the Governor of Arizona.

Now, late in 1879, hoping to regain some respect, Johnny decided to join up with a posse tracking three Mexicans who had robbed a stage on the LaPaz-Prescott route. None other than that crack Apache tracker, Al Sieber, was heading the group, and success therefore seemed assured. Nice to have him along, too, because the Apaches were once again up to their deadly tricks. On this very route eight years before, Apache-Mojave Indians had ambushed a stagecoach and killed seven passengers in what became known as the Wickenburg Massacre.

The posse rested its horses. There was desert as far as the eye could see. Not the sandy landscape of the Sahara, but an open, alkaline plain abounding in cactus, shrubs, and—as a result of the recent heavy rains—a multitude of blossoms. The Vulture Mountains lay to the south, and to the west through which the stage had traveled, the Harcuvar Mountains rose above the horizon. And right there, all alone in the desert, stood a stagecoach—team of horses and all.

"*Mein Gott*, they are sitting ducks," muttered Sieber as he lowered his field glasses. He ordered Bob Paul to take four men and immediately ride down to the stagecoach, saying he and the other three men would follow shortly at full gallop. His strategy was to draw out any Indians that might be around, but it proved unnecessary. There were no Indians anywhere. What they did see was that everything was intact, and that the Concord coach was occupied by seven young women.

The driver and expressman excitedly explained that when they had seen the dust raised by the posse, they were afraid it was caused by hostiles, and pulled up to determine if they should turn about and make a run for it.

Behind the leather curtains, vastly relieved, was part of the Pauline Markham troupe of actresses en route to Prescott to perform their musical *Pinafore on Wheels*. The stunning Pauline stepped from the coach and the dusty posse gaped. They shifted their gun belts, shuffled their feet, and steadied their horses. This was the first time these men had encountered a beauty such as Pauline—a flamboyant, theatrical woman both on and off the stage. Her long duster swung open to reveal an hourglass figure in a skin-tight, black leotard. She wore makeup; not heavy stage greasepaint, but a definite color on her eyelids, high cheekbones, and generous mouth. Just enough to enhance her natural beauty. In spite of the makeup, the men knew instinctively that she was not a loose woman, but a lady. She spoke impeccable English, learned from her stage experience at Niblo's Garden in New York, where she listened in awe from the wings to the thunder of Edwin Booth's *Hamlet*, and to the flawless diction of Lawrence Barrett's *Cassius*. Bob Paul said under his breath, "That woman is prettier than any I've seen in the *Police Gazette*."

"Gentlemen," Pauline purred in her soft, melodious voice, "In San Francisco we were told we'd have to contend with a rough and rowdy lot, but obviously that is untrue, and I will certainly correct that misconception when I return there. I will tell how you honorable men rescued us and saw to our safety as you escorted us on our journey through this savage-infested land. On behalf of my troupe, I thank each and every one of you." She looked down the long trail stretching out before them, and continued, "Please, as you ride with us, do so in such a manner that the dust kicked up by your mounts doesn't blow on us."

She threw a kiss to the smitten posse and resumed her seat in the coach, saying to the driver, "You may proceed."

The driver arranged the ribbons, spoke softly to the six horses, and kicked the brake lever. Meanwhile, Johnny Behan leaped from his saddle, stole a look into the Concord, and got a glimpse of women the likes of whom seldom graced these parts. He drew back as the stage lurched ahead, saying quietly to himself, "Some better than others," but there was one he knew he'd have to see again. She was dressed, surprisingly, as a boy, and had the most impish dark eyes he had ever seen. He was positive she'd smiled at him.

Al Sieber grinned at his men. He didn't have to say a thing. Let someone else catch those greasers! This escort duty just might turn into something really worthwhile. And so the stage to Prescott rumbled on. Nine rough-and-tumble men dutifully followed behind, in order to assure they didn't create any dust to disturb the ladies.

The Arizona sun had almost completed its unparalleled, brilliant descent behind the little caravan. Ahead the lights of the Wickenburg stage station came into view, and several horsemen, armed to the teeth, galloped out to greet them. They were all business, quickly guiding the coach into an adobe compound consisting of four five-foot-high walls with a large, wooden gateway. It had the look of a small fortress.

Sieber swung easily from his horse and was greeted by the station agent, a man by the name of Sam Atkinson. "Al, what're you doin' here?" he asked. Sieber then related how he and his men came to be with this bevy of beauties.

"Well," Sam stated matter-of-factly, "they're gonna have to stay here for at least a couple days. Victoria has busted loose from the reservation. He and some of his mavericks have been raidin' all up and down the line in this very area. The word's come down that everyone stays put 'til the soldier boys can get here and escort the stages into Prescott. It's happened before, but we allus make out okay. Rooms in town ain't all that good, but they be a heap better'n bein' stretched out on a ant hill by the Apaches."

The ladies emerged from the coach. Due to lack of luggage space, on this journey each had worn a mixture of street clothes and stage costumes. Despite their makeshift outfits they managed to look extremely feminine, so much so that the men who had gathered around let loose an appreciative cheer, and gave the little troupe a big round of applause as the ladies bowed in thanks.

Pauline, apprised of the situation, took it in stride. She knew she had a captive and most attentive audience and quickly decided what to do. It was her decision-making ability which had elevated her from the chorus line to a management position. She turned to her new friends and declared, "If you gentlemen will see to our comfort and can bring us some musicians, my troupe and I will perform for you this evening, and afterwards we'll dance with you and turn this delay into a delightful experience for all of us. We'll have what you folks call a Fandango, and with that she clapped her hands above her head and did a little jig.

The men hooted and hollered, and when the word went out just about everyone in Wickenburg assisted in the arrangements for their unexpected guests. Every girl in the ensemble was treated with the utmost respect, and they showed their gratitude by giving an outstanding performance.

The last of the seven to leave the stage was she of the impish eyes and boyish costume: Josephine Sarah Marcus. Johnny Behan had been waiting for her. He had mentally evaluated the others as they moved about, but this pixie was the one he was waiting for.

In contrast to the seemingly shy and self-conscious men around him, Behan stepped boldly in front of Sarah. Removing his hat, he said, "My name is John Behan, and I am sheriff of Yavapi County. I am at your service, and will do all within my power to make your stay here as pleasant as is possible. We have a miner's hotel that will provide you more comfort than is available at the stage station, and you'll have privacy there. Furthermore, I will personally guarantee you and your sisters complete safety."

He made good on his word, and soon the performers were ensconced in sparse but adequate quarters in the rooms above the saloon which constituted the miner's hotel. And so it was that the folks from Wickenburg and the Wells Fargo station came upon a time they'd never forget.

Choice cuts of range beef, hog meat, prairie hen, venison, onions, potatoes and other foods were prepared for cooking on spits arranged over the fire which had been built in a pit within the Wells Fargo compound. The ladies of the small community, delighted to have a break from the monotony of frontier life, primped and put on their Sunday best.

Lanterns were placed strategically around the perimeter of the compound. A couple barrels of beer were hauled from the saloon in town, and a makeshift bar made of several roughhewn plans was set up on carpenter's horses. It soon held several bottles of Forty-Rod, that staple of the southwest. Nearby, a half barrel filled with soapy water became the sink in which the dirty dishes would be washed.

Soon the delicious aroma of meat and vegetables cooking over the mesquite fire permeated the air, and sounds of laughter mingled with happy conversation. Seven fiddlers began to tune up, and were joined by a couple young men who played Spanish guitars. An old prospector playing a pair of spoons, and several men with mouth organs and a Jew's harp, completed the makeshift orchestra. Boot heels pounded against the hard ground to the beat of the music, and the swish of gingham and creaking leather were heard as singles and couples alike began to dance. The party was on.

The props with which Pauline Markham's troupe usually worked had been sent ahead the week before, so she and her girls made do with what they had with them. They sang, flirted, joked, and did their version of the new and naughty dance that originated in France: the Can Can. They turned their backs to the audience, bending forward and lifting their frilly skirts to display colorful bloomers. Then they quickly turned about-face and kicked as high as they could with those gorgeous, long legs made all the more provocative by black mesh stockings. They showed more leg than had ever before been seen in public in Wickenburg.

The food was as tasty as it smelled, and there was plenty for everyone. Most came back for seconds, and a few really hearty eaters came back for thirds. There was a lot of drinking, but no roughhousing, and no one was hauled off to be chained to the tree—Wickenburg's infamous outdoor version of a jail. It was a fun night, and it lasted until the first golden rays of the sun peeked over the horizon the next morning.

Pauline Markham watched over her girls, who were singing and dancing with an abandon most had not heretofore shown, partly from the effects of a little Forty-Rod, but mostly from relief at being away from the cramped quarters of the stagecoach and that lonely, Apache-infested trail. They were grateful to the men who had helped them.

Though there was a stolen kiss here and there, Pauline made sure her girls remained ladies. She wanted them to have fun, but within established limits. Surprisingly, she didn't object to the obvious, single-minded attention that Sheriff John Behan showed to Sarah Marcus, the youngest member of her troupe.

Sarah, a born performer, had joined the troupe in San Francisco just a few months earlier. She'd left her very wealthy family in order to do that. She had an adventurous spirit usually not seen in well-bred girls her age. Pauline, a childless woman with a mothering streak a mile wide, took particular pride in Sarah, becoming her surrogate mother and teacher. She was particularly pleased when the dark-haired, dark-eyed young beauty nearly brought the boisterous festivities to a standstill with her solo dance as the cabin boy in *Pinafore*. Not once, but twice, she was brought back by thunderous applause to repeat the hornpipe. John Behan beamed.

Johnny and Sarah talked as the party wound down. She liked the way he deferred to her, and felt honored that he had obviously, because of her, taken the time to clean up and shave before coming to the gathering. When he had ridden out of Prescott he'd had no thought of attending a social affair, and wasn't dressed as he'd have liked to be. But he had brushed the dust from his chaps and his dark blue shirt, tied a clean white handkerchief at the neck to cover the soiled collar, and cleaned off his Stetson by slapping it against his thigh. Now, as he stood leaning against an adobe wall, with the flickering embers occasionally lighting up his features, he was to Sarah the most exciting man she'd ever met, and she was all the more glad that she'd left home.

There was a romantic streak in Johnny Behan, but it wasn't at all in the same vein as Sarah's. In truth, Johnny was infatuated. He'd been so before, but this time he felt there was a difference. Sarah was like a new toy—something to play with—but at the same time he envisioned her as always at his side as he climbed the political and social ladders. He figured she was someone he could control, and who would live only for him.

The next morning after breakfast, and throughout the rest of the day, Sarah and Johnny talked. And Sarah fell in love.

⁂

Al Sieber and the posse left early that day to continue their pursuit of the Mexican bandits. They proved to be an elusive trio, and it wasn't until two and a half months later that Bob Paul managed to track them down, get the drop on them, and bring them to justice. Johnny Behan was missing from that posse. He had more important business to take care of in Wickenburg, namely Josephine Sarah Marcus.

⁂

Pauline's troupe continued on to Prescott the following day, escorted by troopers of the Fifth Cavalry, and Johnny Behan. He rode right alongside the Concord and was rarely out of sight of Sarah. She loved it.

The show was a great success in Prescott, and so was stage-door-Johnny Behan's courtship of Sarah Marcus. For a sheltered young girl used to the fog-bound evenings of San Francisco, twilight over the Arizona mountains was as an aphrodisiac. Her whole being thrilled to the sight and sound of Johnny as he gazed across the landscape and told her of his plans, plans which included leaving Prescott. He didn't tell her about his nasty divorce or the ridiculous escapade with the Celestials.

"There's more opportunity in the south than here," he confided. "Prescott has had its day. People are flocking to the mountains of silver and gold. At least fifty claims are being filed every day in the new city of Tombstone."

Sarah was reminded of her own father's rise to power and eminence in northern California.

Johnny warmed to his subject. "A new county is being spoken of, and Tombstone will be the county seat. In time the riches of that town will make it the capitol of the territory." Then he said softly, "Sarah, I've held many important positions in the Legislature in Arizona. I'm well-liked. I see nothing which would prevent my rising to the political top." She shivered as he spoke of the governorship of the territory, and was positively awash with love as he hinted at Washington, D. C. and maybe—just maybe—the White House.

At the urging of a sympathetic Pauline Markham, Sarah sat down and wrote a long letter to her parents. She told them in glowing terms of this inspired man who had asked for her hand in marriage, outlining his plans in ways she knew would impress her father. She told them that she longed to see them, to pray with them again in the synagogue at San Francisco, and that she loved them. She also hinted that a little financial assistance would be most helpful in establishing her new life with her husband. She finished by telling them she'd be returning home almost immediately to receive their blessing, and that Johnny would be coming out in a couple of months, after he got settled in Tombstone. "Then you'll see what I see in him. You'll love him as much as I do."

5

A COLT .45 SIX-SHOOTER HAS ITS OWN

distinct sound—a very loud, reverberating boom—quite unlike the sharp crack of a Winchester or the swooshing roar of a shotgun. Add to that the whooping and hollering of a dozen or so men in the clear, cold, midnight air of Arizona's desert country, and it is one frightening sound for law-abiding folks to experience.

Such was the commotion that filled the air on Allen and Sixth streets in Tombstone the night of October 27, 1880. Gunshot after gunshot was heard, and muzzle blasts could be seen everywhere. Behind the well-lit and very busy bar at the Oriental, Buckskin Leslie checked the loads in his revolvers.

In a neatly furnished, small room in the Arcade Restaurant which had closed its doors a couple hours before, Nellie Cashman turned over and reached for the little Remington Derringer on the night stand next to her bed. She slipped it under her pillow.

In a new, two-room adobe house, Johnny Behan and his friend and roommate, John Ringo, uncorked a bottle, grinned at each other, and took a drink.

A block away in Billy Owen's saloon, a man was checking out the gambling in progress. He was about to pull up a chair and put his money down when all hell broke loose outside. It always happened when the cowboys tired of the action at Evilizer's Saloon in Galeyville, or at the Clanton ranch along the San Pedro, or in the bawdy house across the bridge in the smelter town of Charleston some eight miles away.

This night, instead of the boys making a quick ride through town, as was usual, the disturbance continued, as though they were challenging those inside. The gambler looked out the door, but beyond where the lights of the saloon reached there was nothing to be seen except darkness. He could hear more shots being fired down the block, and then the angry voice of his friend, Marshal Fred White.

As he walked briskly toward the group of men in the center of the furor, he spotted two others crouched alongside the chimney of a nearby cabin, and was relieved to see they were his brother, and his friend Fred Dodge.

"You got a gun, Morg?" he whispered.

"Yeah, but I might need it."

"Here, take mine," Fred said, and handed over his Colt.

As they crept along the side of the cabin, some of the cowboys involved in the assault on Marshal White spotted them and stepped back in surprise. Then another volley of shots rang out from a nearby *arroyo* and splatted harmlessly against the adobe walls.

"Damn cowboys never could shoot worth a damn," Morg grunted.

The marshal, his face flushed with anger, stood facing a big, swarthy man whose expression mocked the lawman. He wore a sheepskin-lined leather vest over a faded-blue homespun shirt. Two full gun belts and two Colt .45 six-shooters hung low, Texas style, over his leather chaps.

The marshal shouted at his smirking antagonist, "I am an officer of the law. Give me your pistol."

Curly Bill Brocius glanced at his companions, who goaded him on with catcalls and the Confederate war whoop. No question about it, these men were Texans. He put his right hand on the handle of his gun and drew it out of its holster. Then, unexpectedly and to his complete surprise, Curly Bill was grabbed from behind and his arms were pinioned. Fred White repeated, "Now, you goddamn son of a bitch, give up that pistol!"

As he and Brocius fought for possession of the gun, it suddenly exploded. "I'm hit!" the marshal groaned as he fell to the ground with a slug burned into his groin. So close was it discharged that his pants caught fire. The blaze was quickly extinguished as Brocius looked on, a satisfied smirk on his face; but the look disappeared as a gun barrel was brought smashing down on his skull. He was struck again, and blood gushed from his nose as he sagged to the ground.

"What've I done? I haven't done nothin'," he cried out as he looked up at his assailant. He never forgot the look on that face. It was the look of a predator, and he didn't like it one bit. He wanted to never see it again.

"I am Wyatt Earp," the man announced, "and I am a deputy sheriff of this city. You're under arrest for the attempted murder of the marshal."

He swung around toward the crowd, made sure his brother Morg was standing by, and that Fred Dodge had taken the guns away from the groggy prisoner. The three men leveled their revolvers at the crowd, and it began to disperse.

Someone said, "Well, anyway, Curly Bill got that bastard White. He won't bother us no more." And then the crowd was gone.

"Why'd you buffalo him, Wyatt? You should've killed him," Morgan said to his brother, loud enough for Curly Bill to hear. "Hickock would've done it. Luke Short, too."

Wyatt didn't answer, but roughly pulled Curly Bill to his feet.

Virgil, Wyatt's older brother, came hustling up from Vogan's bar, and directed that Fred White be carried to the doctor's office.

More townsfolk gathered, and when they realized what had happened, there was some ugly talk about lynching that backshooting, son-of-a-bitching cowboy.

⁂

There existed in Tombstone a loose-knit group of men, mostly businessmen, who had joined together as the Law and Order Committee to protect their property and their families from the gunslingers and troublemakers. Shootings and robberies had gone unpunished because of lax law enforcement, and these men meant to fight back. They blamed all of the problems on the cowboys living on the outlying, isolated ranches, who'd come into town to flex their muscles, play buck the tiger, and relax after a roundup. To these cowpunchers, this committee was nothing but a bunch of old sourpusses out to spoil their fun.

Curly Bill knew he was considered one of the leaders of the cowboys, and that many here were looking for any excuse to string him up. Never mind that more than one of those self-righteous, bible-thumping, pious hypocrites had bought cows from him and Clanton, knowing full well it was stock they'd rustled out of Mexico. If he was dangled, they'd never have to worry that he'd blow the whistle on them. Old Curly would be out of their lives forever, and that is exactly what was being planned. A rope was already on its way.

But Virgil Earp, a county marshal, called for a street posse to round up the cowboys responsible for the shooting. Several were caught as they mounted their horses at the Dunbar and O. K. corrals, and hauled off to jail. More ropes were brought out by the gathering mob.

Virgil, Wyatt, Morgan and Fred Dodge stood together and faced the hostile crowd which was now demanding a lynching. "We'll have none of that," Virgil shouted. "A bunch of wrongs ain't going to make a right." He grinned at his partners, pleased with himself for what he considered a display of his knowledge of the scriptures.

The muzzles of five heavy-caliber guns in the hands of four determined men were enough to convince the mob to go back to what they'd been doing, and leave well enough alone.

One man stood silently in the background, taking it all in. He should have involved himself, but didn't. It was his duty as sheriff of Tombstone to handle this sort of thing. But Johnny Behan, who'd already thrown in with the predominantly Democrat ranchers, didn't want to upset the apple cart by going after these cowboys. He figured there were more votes to be had from them than from everyone else in town put together. Behan nodded to himself. He felt justified in his decision not to get involved.

Fred White died the next day, and on that day Virgil Earp was appointed Assistant Marshal of Tombstone by the Common Council. His first official request—the prohibition of concealed weapons—was honored by the passage of Ordinance Number Nine. The cowboys didn't like that one bit.

With Wyatt acting as deputy sheriff, the Earp brothers had an inside track on most all of the comings and goings in Tombstone. And Fred Dodge, a good friend of the Earps whom everyone thought was a gambler, was in reality an undercover agent employed by Wells Fargo.

⚜

The Earps had arrived in Tombstone during the first week of December in 1879. They came in three wagons from Prescott, where Virgil had been a lawman.

With Virgil was his diminutive wife Allie, the woman he loved dearly all of his life. Wyatt brought Celia Ann Blaylock, whom everyone called Mattie. They had met in Kansas when he was working the cow towns in the '70s. She'd been a prostitute, and was more than happy to get out of the cribs and throw in with this man, who not only showed interest in her, but who was a giant step above the riffraff she'd been associating with. Wyatt liked her company. James and Bessie Earp came with their son Frank, and daughter Hattie. Morgan joined them a few days later with his beautiful, blonde wife Louisa. Not long after, Wyatt's friend from Wichita and Dodge City, Doc Holliday, arrived with his lady love, Kate.

The Earps and Fred Dodge, with his connection to Wells Fargo, carried a lot of weight in Tombstone. But times do change.

Two weeks after the Fred White murder, Ben Sippy, an inconsequential political hack, was elected town marshal. The disgusted Virgil, having served in Prescott under the ineffectual sheriff, John Behan, resigned his commission as assistant marshal, and Wyatt turned in his deputy sheriff's badge. The brothers were stunned when none other than Johnny Behan was given that same badge. Johnny was on the move.

Behan fulfilled his promise to Sarah Marcus. He had traveled to San Francisco and met and sweet-talked her parents. Sarah had accepted his diamond engagement ring, but to the family's disappointment he had insisted the marriage ceremony take place in Tombstone. He said he needed to go back and prepare a proper house for his bride, and to tie up some loose ends, such as expanding the stable he and Thomas Dunbar had opened. His good manners, his logic, and his charm, soon had Hyman and Josephine Marcus agreeing to everything he wanted, and they offered several thousand dollars for their daughter's future home. Johnny "reluctantly" accepted this generous gift. Before leaving for Tombstone, Johnny arranged for Kitty Jones, a very pretty and vivacious young woman who was also visiting her parents in San Francisco, to accompany Sarah when she made the return trip. Kitty would be going back to her husband, a lawyer who, like Johnny and Thomas Dunbar, was climbing the political ladder.

Johnny, ever the ladies' man, took advantage of his remaining time by squiring Kitty around while Sarah and her mother shopped the City on the Bay for a proper trousseau. They even took ballroom dancing lessons while the Marcus family was occupied elsewhere.

The Benson-Tombstone stagecoach noisily approached its final destination. It had passed the Contention Mill and was nearing Walnut Gulch. Sarah and Kitty could see the distant skyline of Tombstone. Suddenly a horseman appeared, and Sarah's heart skipped a beat. She wanted to cry, she was so happy. There was Johnny Behan, waving his hat and calling her name. She was home!

Johnny rode all the way in alongside the coach, throwing kisses and shouting words of welcome. Sarah was suddenly the belle of the Concord. Passengers patted her on the back, pointed at Johnny, and laughed as she wiped the tears from her eyes. She reveled in the attention. As the stagecoach rolled toward town, the driver urged his team to make the usual last burst of speed to the express station.

Sarah tumbled out and into the arms of her lover. He smothered her with kisses, and even though a little embarrassed, she made no attempt to stop him.

"Here's the little woman I've been telling you about," Johnny shouted proudly to everyone at the station. "She's made it home."

As the man riding shotgun climbed down from his seat, Johnny laughingly introduced him to his "little woman," saying "Virgil Earp here is the best messenger we've got. If anyone could get you through this country safely, he's the one." He shook Virgil's hand, then gallantly assisted Kitty as she left the coach. Sarah was quick to notice that they greeted each other a mite too formally, but forgot about it as Kitty's husband came and whisked her away.

Sarah was also quick to notice the man who greeted Virgil Earp. She was intrigued by the rather austere look on his face, and became even more so as Virgil introduced her to him. "Wyatt," he said, "this is the lovely Miss Marcus that Johnny has been telling us about. She's just in from San Francisco, and is going to be one of us." Wyatt's somber face broke into a warm, friendly smile. He gently took Sarah's hand, nodded ever so slightly, and said, "Welcome to Tombstone, Miss Marcus." Then he and Virgil turned away, and Sarah watched as they passed the O. K. Corral and disappeared into the Wells Fargo office.

6

NELLIE CASHMAN WAS SURPRISED
when Doc Holliday came into the Arcade Restaurant, and for a number of reasons: it was only eight-thirty in the morning, and the gamblers usually showed up much later; Holliday had never been there before; and he was strictly a man of the night. Nevertheless, here he was. He eased into a chair that backed up to the wall. Doc always liked to face into a room, figuring that he wasn't going to let himself get it in the back the way Bill Hickock did a few years before in Deadwood City. He placed a package on the table.

Nell went right over, and as usual was in a playful mood.

"Doctor Holliday," she said with a grin, "getting an early start today? What may I bring you?"

Doc returned her grin. "Ma'am," he answered, "I'd be most pleased if you would bring me one of those scones you're so famous for, and a big mug of your strongest black coffee." He chuckled as he thought how incongruous this was. Coffee instead of bourbon! He added, "And bring me you. I'd like for you to sit with me a spell."

"Done," Nell retorted as she left to bring his order and a mug of coffee for herself. She sat down opposite him.

Doc pushed the package to her. "First things first," he said. "This is for you."

Puzzled, Nell quickly removed the wrapping and opened the box inside. There lay a bottle of the best Irish whiskey to be had in the territory.

"Why, Doctor Holliday," she exclaimed. "How very thoughtful. You certainly are a man of your word. I'll think of you every time I open this."

"Well, Miss Nell." Doc replied. "Think of me now. A little of that would really sweeten my coffee."

Nell noticed several curious patrons looking their way. Though not one to bow to convention, she nevertheless thought it would be prudent not to have them see what was going on. So she stood in order to block their view as she poured the whiskey into Doc's coffee, and hesitated just a second before she poured some into her own.

Holliday enjoyed this little performance, and especially appreciated her generous pour, figuring it had to be at least three fingers. Nell sat down, and they raised their cups in a salute.

So began a unique friendship that only a few in Tombstone were ever aware of. Several times a week Doc would come to the restaurant early in the morning, and the two of them would talk and sip coffee, sometimes for more than an hour. But it was only that first morning that the whiskey was brought out. Nell was no Kate, and Doc appreciated that.

Among the things they talked about was the letter that had brought Nell into Doc's life.

"Mattie and I grew up together in the south," he explained. "We had the best of it: the plantations, the money, servants, and culture. We were young when the war broke out, and all that good life was lost to us forever. When Sherman marched through Georgia, he took away all that was dear to us. Our lives would have been so different. I'm sure if we hadn't been cousins we'd have gotten married. Mattie is the only woman I've ever loved."

He frowned and brought a handkerchief to his mouth to suppress a cough. "Because of the deplorable conditions in Georgia, I came down with consumption. I was told to get a new start in the southwest where the air is clear and the sun might bake away my affliction. I've been running ever since, and guess I've come about as far south and west as a man can go without leaving the country." He reached into his vest pocket and brought out a thin Panatella cigar, commonly called a long nine, lit it, took a drag, and coughed again.

Nell warmed to this seemingly lonely and somewhat strange man over time, and came to really like him. The abundance of maternal instinct within her made her want to save him from himself and help him chase away his demons. She was especially touched when Doc spoke of his association with Wyatt Earp.

"He," Doc said, "is one of the few friends I have in this world other than Mattie, and she has removed herself from it by entering a convent. I'm pleased, though, that she hasn't given herself to another man. But Wyatt," Doc continued, "will stand with me to the end. I pulled his fat out of the fire once in Kansas, and he's done the same for me. I know his brothers don't give a tinker's damn about me, but that's their problem. Wyatt is my true friend."

At times when Doc would get melancholy like this, Nell would touch him gently on the arm and say, "I want to be your friend too, John." He would merely give her a quizzical look and escape behind his handkerchief in another coughing fit.

Nell, too, spoke openly to Doc. She told him of her adventures in British Columbia, and how she had lived with the miners up in that cold country, sometimes mushing behind a team of Huskies to bring them medicine and supplies. She told him about her restaurant, and of some of the characters she'd met.

Doc loved these stories, and in an exaggerated southern drawl at one time said, "My little magnolia blossom, you are indeed an angel to the miners. My Mattie would love you. I've mentioned you in my letters to her."

Nell learned a lot from Doc about the seamy side of Tombstone politics and the two factions which were bitterly fighting for control of the town.

There was the Law and Order Party headed by Mayor John Clum, whose sights were set on the lucrative tax revenues, and eventual power over the whole Arizona Territory. They thought the town belonged to them, and envisioned it as the model capitol of the territory; some figured their time in Tombstone would be their stepping stone to bigger and better political arenas. But the killing of Marshal Fred White was a real smear on the ideal image of Tombstone that they were trying to create.

The opposition was called the Cowboy Ring, and consisted of local cattle ranchers as well as some living as far as one hundred miles away. They knew if real law and order ever came to the town, the selling of cattle rustled from outside the territory would come to a screeching halt, and they'd lose the lucrative contracts provided by the government for beef for the army and the Indian reservations. The cowboys complained that an honest rustler wouldn't be able to make it in this part of the world.

Some of the old-time ranchers didn't like Tombstone at all except as a place to have some fun when the wrangling was done. Law and order got in their way. They had their own brand of justice, and figured they'd been getting along just fine before Ed Schieffelin opened the mines which brought Tombstone into prominence. Most of these cattlemen had come from Texas and were still rebels at heart.

Old Man Clanton, who pretty much headed up this group, lived with his sons on a ranch along the San Pedro. Then there were the McLaury brothers who had a couple spreads in Sulphur Springs Valley. These and a few others controlled just about all of the water holes in this part of Arizona. Curly Bill Brocius was also counted among the leaders. His stock had skyrocketed among the boys when he was acquitted of murdering Marshal Fred White. Even Wyatt Earp had admitted in court that Curly's gun might have accidentally discharged as he scuffled with the marshal. With White out of the way, their man Johnny Behan was in, and the good times were about to roll.

The flies in the ointment were Virgil Earp and his brother. They stuck close to town so they could indulge their passion for gambling, and they also gave assistance to the Law and Order Party whenever possible.

Curly nursed a grudge against Wyatt as big as the goose egg Wyatt had raised on his head. Likewise Tom and Frank McLaury who also had been bloodied and thrown in jail the night White got his.

"Of all these men," Doc told Nell, "the worst of the lot is John Ringo. He's a backshooter and takes pride in it. Texas has put out several waybills on him for murder. He was in the same jail in Austin in '78 as John Wesley Hardin. Hardin couldn't abide him, and asked to be put in a separate cell." Doc paused, then continued, "Ringo is as queer as a three dollar bill."

⁂

On one occasion, while enjoying some coffee and a sweet roll with Doc, Nell mentioned that Frank Leslie had become one of her steady customers.

Holliday shook his head. "Leslie is a strange one. As a marksman he's in the same class as Frank Butler and Annie Oakley, but he's a loner. He mixes a good drink, but not one of us knows what that son of a bitch—pardon me—is all about."

It so happened that Leslie became the town's prime topic of conversation when it was reported in the *Epitaph* that he had shot Mike Killeen. On the surface, there was nothing spectacular about that, considering all the shootings that took place in all the frontier towns; but this one provided some juicy gossip. Frank was sparking Mike's wife.

Mike Killeen was a brawny, Irish brawler and he had a short fuse. It had gotten him into more than one scrape since he'd arrived in Tombstone several months earlier with his pert, raven-haired wife, May. It was his disposition that finally drove May to leave him. The separation didn't bother Mike, though. As bartender at the Commercial Hotel, he was frequently the center of attention of the women who used the hotel's rooms to conduct their business. On a slow night, all Mike had to do was set up some free drinks and he'd have more women than he could handle. He liked it that way, but wouldn't tolerate anyone taking a second look at his estranged wife. He'd confront any man who came near her with his pistol, or his Bowie knife, or his bar club, and warn them to move along. Eventually, most prospective suitors concluded she just wasn't worth all that grief and did just that. Then May met Frank Leslie, who wasn't in the least intimidated by Mike. May was captivated by Frank, and his reputation was sufficient to give Mike pause about confronting him. Frank moved in quickly. Here was, for him, an Irish colleen in many ways like the untouchable Nellie Cashman, but one who welcomed his advances. So far as Frank was concerned, Mike could just go on pouring drinks at the Commercial and be damned.

The reported shooting took place on a balmy night in June. A gala ball was held at the Vizina and Cook Building and May was there. So was Frank. And so was Mike. The two men arrived after midnight when their shifts ended, and they'd had an opportunity to get duded up for the occasion. Frank got there first. May, wearing an extremely low-cut gown that accentuated her voluptuous cleavage, was waiting for him.

Frank waltzed better than anyone else in town, and to May's delight and that of the other dancers, he whirled her 'round and 'round the floor until she finally begged for fresh air. She suggested they walk over to the nearby Cosmopolitan Hotel where they could enjoy the moonlight and the starry sky from the porch.

"We can have a lemonade and be away from the crowd for a while," she exclaimed happily.

They settled themselves onto the porch swing and Frank placed his big Colt on the adjacent railing. They'd gone beyond hand holding, and Frank was getting down to serious business with the ecstatic May.

Suddenly, and without warning, a shadow loomed. Mike Killeen bellowed, "Take that, you son of a bitch," as he let go with a heavy-caliber six-shooter. The bullet grazed Leslie's head, and he sprawled between two wicker chairs. Mike took another shot and parted Leslie's hair.

Frank's hands had been in the wrong place at the wrong time. He grabbed his gun and tried to cock it as Mike lunged at him. To Frank's dismay, the firing mechanism stuck. Mike stepped back, enjoying the moment as he aimed his pistol at Frank. But he took a mite too long. With a smoothness and speed of motion that amazed Mike and the panic-stricken May, Frank reached around to his back, pulled out his hideaway .38 caliber revolver, and sent a ball clean through Killeen's chest. He gasped, "Oh, my God," fell, and died within seconds.

Leslie claimed self-defense. His friend, George Perrine, who was there when the shooting took place, testified that Mike Killeen had threatened Frank's life on this and several other occasions. Frank's only other witness was the lady herself. So he went scot-free, and the community accepted this gunfighter and Indian scout back into its good graces.

Frank went to see Nell Cashman. She had been totally appalled that her favorite baritone had involved himself in such a tawdry affair, but she felt the court's verdict was the right one. Being the lady she was, she worried about May Killeen, and when she mentioned that to Frank he told her of his love for May. But even as he spoke, Nell sensed he was really speaking of his love for herself.

On his next visit to the Arcade Restaurant, Frank quietly informed Nell that he'd proposed marriage, and that May had accepted.

John Clum, mayor of Tombstone and editor of the paper, publicly congratulated the couple on their marriage. He wrote that Frank was "...a chevalier without fear and without reproach..." and wished them a pleasant journey over life's troubled waters.

The lovers honeymooned at Frank's small ranch in the Swisshelms Mountains, and were very happy. For a while.

Nell went about her business, but often looked wistfully at the chair Frank had often occupied.

In the nearby smelter town of Charleston, Billy Claiborne grumbled to his friend, John Ringo, "That asshole Frank Leslie jus' married the girl I been droolin' over. I been waitin' for jus' the right time to knock that bully of a husban' of hers outta the way, an' now it's too late. I got shit for luck."

Ringo shot him a disgusted look. "You should've just walked up to him and told him to pull or get out. Do that the next time you've got hot pants for some little twit. Just pull your iron."

7

BOB PAUL CLIMBED ONTO THE DRIVER'S
seat of Kinnear and Company's big Concord coach. He was a shotgun rider for Wells Fargo, and on this run they were carrying a shipment of bullion from Tombstone to Benson's railhead.

Big Bob, at six feet six inches, and weighing in at a hefty two hundred and forty pounds, could hold his own in any situation, and had proven it during the nine years he served on whaling ships. He'd gone around the Horn and been to the Cape of Good Hope. At one time, his bunkmate was Herman Melville, who was collecting stories for his novels.

Bob had been saving his money for a foray into the California gold fields, and when his ship dropped anchor in San Francisco Bay, he headed out.

He worked the sluice boxes during the '49 gold rush, panned the rivers, and explored the hills, eventually amassing some sixty thousand dollars. But he realized the big strikes had already been made, and pulled up stakes to go into the gravel business. He went broke. Then he went into law enforcement.

While a deputy sheriff working the mother lode country, he was instrumental in bringing in the notorious Bell Gang, which was the talk of Calaveras County until the advent of Mark Twain's famous frog.

Capitalizing on his size and strength, he went to work for Wells Fargo riding shotgun into areas known to be especially dangerous. It paid well, and he needed the extra money in order to bring his wife and children from California. So it was that he came to be on this particular run through the Arizona desert.

The whip, or driver, of this run was an old-timer by name of Bud Philpot, a man known for his rough ways. But he was honest and well-liked. This particular evening, Bud had a bellyache.

"Somethin' I et," he remarked. Bob Paul volunteered to take over the reins for the ailing driver, so they changed places, Bob moving to the driver's seat on the right, and Bud to his seat on the left.

A full moon brightened the night as the coach pitched and rolled its way north, away from the comforting lights of Tombstone.

Bob was renowned as a raconteur, and he was soon jowl deep into stories of his experiences at sea off the coast of New Zealand. None of his stories was told exactly the same way twice, but they were always true and always entertaining. Bud was so engrossed that he forgot all about his miseries.

They soon passed through Contention, and from the doorway of the Dew Drop Bar a pretty, young Mexican woman, provocatively dressed in a tight skirt and low-cut blouse, grinned and waved her long cigarette at them as they passed by. They waved back and gave her a lusty "Yahoo!"

As they approached the steep incline preceding the descent into Drews Station, a man suddenly stepped out from the east side of the road, shouting "Hold!" He was followed right off by eight more, who quickly took places at both sides of the Concord. Two quick rifle shots boomed out, then several more in rapid succession. Bud Philpot was hit, and he pitched forward and down between the wheels of the coach. He was dead before he hit the ground.

Bob Paul grabbed the shotgun, shouldered it, and cut loose with both barrels. "By God," he shouted, "I stop for no one!"

He dropped the big gun into the boot, brought up his Winchester Carbine, and returned shot for shot as the panic-stricken horses galloped past the startled highwaymen. They hadn't expected such forceful resistance.

The stagecoach careered out of control until Paul was able to leap onto one of the horses and retrieve the reins. Peter Roerig, a passenger who was sitting in the jump seat behind Paul, pitched to the ground, dying from a bullet in his back. Paul raced on toward Benson.

Men came running from Drew's Station and Contention. In the bright moonlight, they could see the fleeing gunmen heading southwest, in the general direction of Old Man Clanton's ranch.

Winchester cartridge casings were scattered all over the scene where Bud Philpot and Peter Roerig had died without a chance to defend themselves. Blood dotted the trail taken by the cowardly backshooters. Wells Fargo had chosen well when they hired Bob Paul. Thanks to him the robbery was thwarted, and at least one outlaw was right now nursing a gunshot wound.

The manager of Drew's Station immediately formed a posse and within an hour some thirty well-armed men were tracking the murderers. The unfortunate victims were rolled up in canvas bags and put aside to be picked up by the next wagon north.

Bob Paul raced on to the Wells Fargo Agency in Benson where he telegraphed Tombstone and reported what had happened. It wasn't long before the bounty hunters came charging down the road from Tombstone. Three posses, an impressive array of armed men, joined in the hunt.

⁂

United States deputy marshal Wyatt Earp felt this attack was an offense against the mail, so he formed his own posse which included his brothers, Morgan and Virgil, and his old crony from Dodge City, Bat Masterson. Bat was in Tombstone scouting for a good gambling-hall site. Wyatt graciously turned the posse over to Sheriff John Behan, who officiously took the lead. He brought one of his deputies, Billy Breakenridge, with him. Behan proceeded to lead them in the wrong direction.

A day went by, and one by one the dusty and deflated manhunters straggled back into Tombstone. They all reported that Behan had told them the trail was cold, and that it would be pointless to spend more time on a fruitless chase. Most of them were just as happy to get back to the gaming tables and their women, anyway. Bat Masterson had to come back because the old filly he was riding played out; but the Earps continued the chase.

It had taken Bob Paul months to track down the Mexican highwaymen involved in the LaPaz-Prescott stage holdup, and he wasn't about to give up on this one now. As a Wells Fargo operative, it was his duty to mind the company's business, but he needed help. He knew there was one man in Tombstone who could give it to him.

He went to his room at the Cosmopolitan, ordered a bath and lathered away the effects of a couple hard days on the trail. Then he poured a stiff drink, fired up a good cigar, and put on his best duds. When his drink was gone, he headed down the street to the Oriental. His timing was right. Frank "Buckskin" Leslie was on duty behind the bar.

"Frank," Bob said, "give me a bottle and two glasses—one for me, and one for you."

"Wells Fargo," Bob began, "has been sorely tried by some cowboys who would make a mockery of our services, and just recently killed two good men. You know the story."

Leslie nodded as he poured himself a drink and lit up a cigarillo. He knew what was coming.

"The boys in the field don't seem to be doing too good, Frank. Behan's got them all discouraged, and they're quitting. He's just got the Earps and a few others hanging on to what they think is the trail. What they could use is a tracker. Someone like you who knows the passes and has followed the Apache. There's more than just a little glory in it, too, Frank," he added, pressing his point. "Fargo is prepared to pay handsomely for any or all of those murderers. They want their stage operations safe; otherwise, they're out of business."

"How do you want them," Leslie asked, "in one piece or any way I can get them?"

"Any way that suits you," Paul replied. "Just make sure you get the right men."

He poured them each another drink, and re-lit Frank's smoke. Frank downed the drink in one swallow, undid his apron, folded it neatly, wiped off the bar, and called to his assistant.

"Al," he said cheerfully, "you're on for a few days. Let May know I'll see her when I see her."

He went to his room behind the bar and closed the door, then took off his white shirt and put on his worn but still good buckskin shirt, breathing in its familiar odor as he slipped it over his head. Next came leather chaps and his scarred and stained riding boots, around which he fastened five-pointed spurs. Then he lifted his gun belt from the back of a chair and checked to make sure all the loops were filled with .44 caliber cartridges which would fit both his Winchester and the big Colt Frontier Model revolver just recently received from the company in Hartford, Connecticut. It was his prize weapon, made especially for him, and had a twelve-inch barrel and carved ivory handles. It was as good a piece as one could get. He stowed a few personal items in his "bag of possibles", along with a couple bottles of bourbon, and then presented himself to Bob Paul at the Cosmopolitan, where Paul had gone to change back into to his trail clothes. They downed another drink and off they went.

Paul sat erect on a huge stallion which fairly matched his own bulk. He had two six-shooters on his belt, a Henry rifle in the scabbard by his left knee, and a ten-gauge shotgun across the pommel of his saddle. Frank was on a smaller, spirited mare. Unlike Paul, he slouched in the saddle. His long Colt hung prominently from his belt, and his Winchester from his saddle. They passed by without acknowledging the cheers of a number of townsfolk who'd gathered to watch as they rode out of town. Obviously, the word was out.

They passed the O. K. Corral, and a woman's voice cut through the sounds of creaking leather and hoof beats: "Frank!"

Leslie twisted in his saddle and reined in his horse as Nell Cashman came running toward him.

"Frank," she cried out again as she reached up and touched his gloved hand. "Bring them back alive. Please!"

He looked down at her, put the spurs to his mount, and galloped away.

⁂

Overlooking Lewis Springs and the San Pedro River was a fortress-like ranch. It had been built, and well, by Mexican laborers who had come north looking for work. Newman Haynes Clanton was proud of the house with its high, foot-thick adobe walls, and he had paid the Mexicans well for their labor. Clanton had chosen this site purposely. It was on high ground and isolated, yet reasonably close to the small town of Galeyville, where folks tended to mind their own business.

At one time, it looked like mining would be big there as it was in Tombstone, but the ore soon played out, leaving little to do other than rustle cattle and carry on in the brothels and saloons. This suited Old Man Clanton, as the locals called him, just fine. Mexico was only a day's ride south, and Clanton and his boys were known to throw a wide lariat. Traffic in ill-gotten goods went in two directions almost within sight of his spread. The Clanton ranch became the headquarters for rustlers, smugglers, bootleggers, horse thieves, and worse.

Curly Bill Brocius was always a welcome guest, as was John Ringo and his sidekick, Billy Claiborne. Pete Spence, Frank Stillwell, and others of dubious reputation came and went. Sheriff John Behan was also known to have taken a few meals at Clanton's table, but it was Old Man Clanton's sons who were his pride and joy. There was Phineas, called Finn, always nearby but a bit to the rear; Isaac, called Ike, loud of mouth and always good for a battle of words; and Billy, the youngest, who was the most game. Of all the boys, Billy was most like the Old Man, and thus was favored by him over the others.

He and the boys were alone in the ranch house when Bob Paul came riding in. Billy quickly slipped out the back door and surveyed the area, calling back, "He's by hisself, pa."

Old Man Clanton reached for his Winchester and went to the door.

"Paul," he rasped, "you're not welcome here. You ought to know that."

As if to back up those words, Finn came from behind the door and stood next to his pa. His hand was on his pistol.

Ike joined them, his flannel mouth chewing the air. "You're on private property, Mr. Wells Fargo man. You'd best git now while the gittin's good." He brandished a double-barreled shotgun, and soon two of their ranch hands came and stood beside him.

There was fight in the air, but Bob Paul didn't back off. "You close your trap," he bellowed at Ike. "By God," he said, turning to Old Man Clanton, "that boy of yours makes more noise with his mouth than he does with his piece. Give me a little information, and I'll be out of here." To Ike he said, "That should suit you, loudmouth."

Ike could see that Paul's hands were nowhere near his guns, and he was further emboldened when he saw Billy come from behind the house, a pistol in his hand and another stuck in his belt. He drew himself up to his full height and made threatening gestures with his scattergun.

"We don't take that from no one," Billy piped up. "Let's rough him up a bit and send him back to Fargo's shithouse where he belongs. How about it, pa?"

"I told you, Paul, you're in the wrong place, and at the wrong time, too. Boys," he grinned, "give him a little taste of Clanton hospitality. Not too much, now. Just enough so's he'll know better'n to be comin' 'round here again."

The ranch hands and the boys began to move toward Paul, but they didn't get far. From out of nowhere a bullet slammed into the dinner gong hanging above Ike's head.

"Shit!" he yelled as he looked frantically around.

"Keep your pants dry," Paul retorted. "That's Frank Leslie out there with his target gun. Don't make a move or he might just lower his sights. He always hits what he shoots at."

He turned toward Old Man Clanton, who was gritting his teeth in frustration. "You know, Newman, my Wells Fargo boys don't only drive coaches. They know how to use their weapons, and there's a whole bunch of them looking at you right now."

Clanton glowered at him. "Okay, okay," he growled, "go to talking." At the same time, he picked up a riding quirt from the porch table and viciously laid it across Billy's face. "Son," he bellowed, "I've told you when you pull a gun on a man, shoot him!"

Frank Leslie rode in a little way and jockeyed his filly around so he could see everything. His rifle was at the ready.

Bob Paul came straight to the point. "I want to know who shot up that stage on the fifteenth of March. I know you boys have too good a thing going right here to be doing a stupid thing like that. It's not my business to know what goes on in these hills, but it is my business to find out who murdered my driver and a passenger. I suspect you've heard something, and I can tell you that Wells Fargo will pay a sizable reward for the capture of the perpetrators."

He turned to Ike and Billy. "You boys could make a couple years' wages in a hurry if you come up with some names. Give it some thought," he added as he and Frank started to leave. "You know where to find me."

Leslie and Paul were certain the Clantons weren't in on the attempted holdup. What was learned from the evidence leading away from Drews Station was that the outlaws had headed their way, but then veered off, going north as far as Tres Alamos sixty miles away. They'd waded across the San Pedro River and also, whenever possible, had used other horses to hide their tracks. There was absolutely no evidence that they'd gone to the Clanton ranch, and Paul knew that. He also knew human nature, which is why he'd planted the idea of reward money in the Clanton boys' heads. He firmly believed there was no honor among thieves.

Paul chuckled, "Guess I had them believing there was a bunch of us, eh Frank? Anyway, unless the Earps come up with something, I've a feeling we did good things here. They'll be getting back to us."

In the distance, they noticed a couple riders galloping away from the ranch in the direction of the McLaury spread some distance to the east, beyond the Dragoon Mountains.

Leslie picked up a set of pony tracks which he said were the same as those seen at the ambush site. They led to the Helms ranch in the Dragoons. Bob decided they'd stop there to water their horses and see what they could find out.

Helms' men seemed genuinely sincere when they said they knew nothing of the outlaws, but they told Paul that Luther King had stopped by briefly and ridden on.

"He was goin' slow," Helms volunteered. "His horse seemed plumb wore out."

"We've got our man," Leslie chortled. "Let's go."

They mounted up, and as they moved out a group of riders came in sight and hailed them. It was what was left of the Tombstone posse headed by Johnny Behan: Virgil, Morgan and Wyatt Earp; Marshall Williams; Billy Breakenridge; and several members of the Law and Order Party.

"Lucky we found you," Behan exclaimed. "We've searched this land all over from Huachuca to the San Simon. Those fellows aren't anywhere near here. Like as not they're down in Old Mexico." He lit a cigar to give emphasis to what he considered the final word on this matter.

"I've suggested to the posse here that we just call it quits and go on home. We've done our duty, and nobody can say we haven't. What do you say?"

Leslie ignored him and cantered up to Virgil Earp. "Virg, I've got a trail. It's one of the stage robbers. I'd bet my shirt on it. He can't be too far."

Virgil grinned and turned to the posse. "Boys, I think Leslie is onto something. Old Frank don't bet his buckskin unless it's a sure thing."

Behan made another appeal. "Men, I tell you I've been out on runs like this many times. I just know there's nothing to be gained by going on. I say it's back to Tombstone, and the drinks will be on me. Come on. What do you say?"

Wyatt looked at Behan in disbelief, then down at the pony tracks, and back to Behan.

Frank Leslie snapped, "I came here to track, not palaver," and swung his horse in the direction of the tracks. As he rode out, the Earps and Bob Paul were right with him. Behan and the rest reluctantly trotted along behind.

Frank's buckskin shirt was in no danger of changing hands. The trail led right to the ranch of Len Redfields and his brother Hank. The Redfields had long been suspected of engaging in stage robberies and rustling. Their spread was too small to support their lavish spending at the gaming tables in Tombstone; but as to the recent holdup, they were in the clear. Their guest wasn't.

Luther King was seen making a dash from the stable to the cow barn. He knew he couldn't outrun these determined men, so he had decided to try and bluff his way out.

Leslie and the others rode right into the barn. There was Luther, sitting on a stool, milking a cow. He looked up, feigning surprise. "Why, afternoon boys. What's on your minds? How's about I get you a tin of fresh milk?"

"Well, lookee here," Virgil gloated. "Len's gone and got himself a new dairy hand. None other than Luther King. But what I'd like to know, Luther, is why you're wearing two six-shooters and two full cartridge belts just to milk old bossie. And why's your horse all lathered up? You been giving it a milk bath?"

Luther was silent, and Virgil continued, "I think we need to have us a little talk."

Sheriff Behan interrupted. "He's my prisoner, Virg, and I'll be taking him in. We'll talk to him in Tombstone."

"Whatever you say, Johnny," Virg replied pleasantly, "but first I think we should take this milk and go inside for a little breakfast." Nodding to the deputy, he said, "Billy, you give the sheriff a hand, and we'll see to the horses. I'll take care of Luther's guns." He undid King's gun belts and slung them over the sheriff's saddle horn.

John Behan, true to his fastidious nature, insisted on scrubbing up before he ate, so he left the barn and headed for the water pump. This gave Wyatt and Morg the opportunity to hustle Luther out the side door of the barn. Wyatt whispered in Luther's ear, "Keep still. We're going to have that talk." Bob Paul followed them out.

Wyatt pushed King to his knees and glared at him. "Where's the rest of them?" he demanded.

King sputtered, "I don't know what you're talking about."

Quicker than spit, Wyatt's Colt slammed into the side of Luther's face. He went sprawling onto the ground, his eyes wild with fear.

"You've got one second or this gun accidentally goes off!"

"Oh, my God," Luther groaned. He knew Wyatt meant what he said.

Frank Leslie, who'd been watching, quickly stepped in. "We'll have none of that, Wyatt."

"He may as well get it here," Wyatt snapped as he pulled the hapless Luther to his feet. "Doc Holliday's woman, Kate, was on that stage and one of the bullets got her in the back. She died just as Holliday got to her, and he's all fired up. He doesn't reason straight when he's mad. Anyone who was anywhere near that stage is as good as dead."

Luther buried his face in his hands. "Honest," he whimpered, "I only held the horses. I didn't do no shooting."

"Anyone near the stage," Wyatt repeated.

Then Bob Paul spoke up. "Look here, Luther, we only want the shooters. You just name some names, and I think I can get you to Tucson without Holliday any the wiser. We just want names."

"Promise you won't let that maniac, Holliday, get at me," Luther whined. "The only names I know are Harry Head, Billy Leonard, and Jim Crane."

Bob and Wyatt had what they wanted. They'd cooked up this little charade figuring it would bring them some answers. Bob wanted a positive report to turn in to the Wells Fargo headquarters in San Francisco, and Wyatt had his own reasons.

He turned toward Frank Leslie. "Sorry we had to fool you, Frank, but I wouldn't have shot him out of hand like that."

"I didn't think you would," Leslie answered. "I sort of made a promise to bring him in alive." He slid his six-shooter back into his holster.

Behan came charging up, demanding, "What's going on here? I said this man is my prisoner."

King looked up at him and blubbered, "I didn't know Doc Holliday's woman was hit on the Benson stage."

"She wasn't," Behan shot back. "She wasn't even on the stage." It was then that Behan tumbled to the fact he'd been outsmarted by Wyatt Earp. He looked very unhappy.

"Your prisoner," Bob Paul said. Then he, the Earps, and Frank Leslie headed for the ranch house, where they eagerly devoured a hearty breakfast of bacon, eggs, biscuits and hot coffee provided by the Redfields.

Behan was plenty disturbed. Before the others were up the next morning, he'd already left for Tombstone with his deputy and his prisoner.

8

SHERIFF BEHAN LODGED LUTHER KING

in the jail. He claimed he wanted to bring him to trial in Tucson, because feelings in Tombstone were running pretty high against him due to the murder of the likable stagecoach driver, Bud Philpot.

Behan deputized two of his political cronies: John Dunbar, his partner in the Dunbar Stables, and Harry Woods. He put them in charge of the prisoner.

It came as a big surprise to some, but not to others, when shortly after his incarceration Luther was reported to have broken out of jail.

The story Behan and his deputies concocted regarding this jail break was so full of holes a Concord stage could have been driven through them. According to Behan, Dunbar was arranging to buy King's horse for his stable. He and Woods had made out the transfer papers, and asked King for his ownership papers. King told them they were in the pocket of his coat, which was in the back room of the jail. On his promise to get the papers and bring them right back, Luther was let out of his cell. According to them, they broke open a bottle to celebrate the deal, but when Luther failed to return they had investigated and determined he'd just walked right out the door and kept on going. It turned out that the horse which was seen tied near the back door also came up missing at the same time.

Tombstone's respected diarist, George Parsons, that night wrote in his journal:

King, the stage robber escaped tonight early from H. Woods who had been previously notified of an attempt at release to be made. Some of our officials should be hanged. They are a bad lot.

He wasn't the only one who thought so. The town was in an uproar. Paul, Leslie and the Earps were still out in the hills looking for Leonard, Crane and Head, and now their only witness had flown the coop.

John Behan's political career was at its lowest ebb, and he hungered to be sheriff of the newly-created Cochise County. Big bucks and big influence came with the title. He figured the Earps and their cronies would ride Paul's coattails if he got the job, and Paul was in line for it. He had to figure a way to stop them.

Behan, John Dunbar, and Harry Woods put their heads together and trumped up an unbelievable story, undoubtedly inspired by the ruse Wyatt and Bob Paul had used to get Luther King to talk.

Doc Holliday had been seen riding out of town the night of the stagecoach murders, and coming back the next morning on a lathered-up horse. If they could somehow involve Doc in the murders, Wyatt, his brothers, and Bob Paul could also be implicated. The only one they didn't point a finger at was Frank Leslie, partly because he hadn't allied himself with either side, but mostly because they were wary of his long gun and short temper.

Woods, editor of Tombstone's *Nuggett*, wrote:

Luther King, the man arrested at Redfield's ranch charged with being implicated in the Bud Philpot murder, escaped from the sheriff's office by quietly stepping out the back door while Harry Jones, Esq., was drawing up a Bill of Sale for a horse the prisoner was selling to John Dunbar. Undersheriff Harry Woods and Dunbar were present. He had been absent but a few seconds before he was missed. A confederate on the outside had a horse in readiness for him. It was a well planned job by outsiders to get him away. He was an important witness against Holliday. He it was that gave the names of the three that were being followed at the time he was arrested. Their names were Bill Leonard, Jim Crane and Harry Head.

John Clum, always a friend of the Earps, wrote in the *Epitaph*:

There is altogether too much good feeling between the Sheriff's office and the outlaws infesting this country.

Two weeks later the Earps, Bob Paul, and Frank Leslie plodded into Tombstone, weary, thirsty, dusty, and empty-handed. They were infuriated when they learned what had happened.

Wyatt realized now how devious John Behan was, and what had prompted his actions when they were out in the field. He knew Behan wasn't to be trusted. Behan had made an enemy. Still, even though Wyatt was burned up about this, he held his tongue in public. Because of his own political ambitions, he didn't want to rock the boat.

Not so Frank Leslie. He stormed into the sheriff's office, and in the presence of deputies Breakenridge, Woods and Dunbar, gave Behan a piece of his mind.

"For two weeks we've been out there busting our asses to catch those murderers, and you turned loose the only man who could link them to the murders. Behan, you're a son of a bitch and a coward! You stay away from my bar, and don't ever call on me to ride out with you again. Never again, Johnny!" he growled as he brushed his fist past Behan's cheek. "I hate your guts!"

Then he glared at Billy Breakenridge, who had looked on in awe at this display of barely-controlled anger. To Woods and Dunbar, Frank said contemptuously, "Flunkys!" and stormed out the door. If he had just made some enemies, he didn't care.

Doc's guilt or innocence was hashed and rehashed for weeks by the gossip mongers, but he was eventually exonerated by the court. He really didn't care much about his reputation; it was already in shambles. But his vanity was bruised.

He asked Nell Cashman over coffee one afternoon, "Do people really think I'm that inept? That I'd have bungled so badly? I tell you, Nellie, my little magnolia blossom, if I had pulled that job I'd have the bullion. Whoever shot Philpot was a rank amateur. He'd have had it if he'd been smart enough to down one of the stage's horses."

⚜

In addition to the excitement surrounding the attempted stage robbery, other events were getting their share of attention in Tombstone. Most notable among them was the fire that took out two square blocks just east of the Oriental. It started when a bartender checking out a whiskey barrel with a lighted match got too close to the fumes, and it blew.

One of the finer establishments to rise from the ashes was the Russ House, partly owned by Nell Cashman, built at the corner of Fifth and Toughnut streets. Nell ran the hotel with the help of her sister, Fannie Cunningham. After Fannie's husband died, she and her five children had come to live with Nell.

Ads for the hotel proudly proclaimed it to have advantages superior to any hotel in Tombstone or this part of the territory. The cost of a room ranged from fifty cents to two dollars a day, and meals from twenty-five cents to two dollars and fifty cents. A typical Sunday menu might include brook trout, lamb with caper sauce, corned beef, pork with applesauce, and veal, in addition to lobster salad, turnips, mashed potatoes, New York plum pudding, and assorted pies. Nell was considered by her customers, including Frank Leslie and Doc Holliday, to be a master chef, and they followed her from the Arcade Restaurant to the new Russ House.

Leslie's love affair with May Killeen was still a hot item, and they were often seen holding hands in Banning and Shaw's Ice Cream Saloon, or whirling around the floor of the newly-renovated dance pavilion at Schieffelin Hall. But Nell had heard that Frank was drinking more than usual, and she was concerned.

The real sensation—the one that had everyone buzzing—was the rumored breakup of the romance between Sarah Marcus and Johnny Behan. Johnny's roving eye lit on every bustle that passed by, including those of Sarah's best friends. Gossip had it that Harry Jones was being cuckolded; that his wife, Kitty, and the smooth-talking Behan—who supposedly was his friend—were being seen in the best dining halls in Tombstone, while Sarah was left at home to look after Albert, Johnny's ten-year-old son by his previous marriage.

Sarah loved the boy, but resented the awkward situation she found herself in just months after arriving in Tombstone. Still, she was determined to get married, even if not by a Rabbi. She'd taken her marriage license with her for talks with the Reverend Endicott Peabody, rector of the Episcopal Church; with Father Gallagher of the Catholic Church; and finally to the city magistrate who agreed to perform the ceremony as soon as Sarah and Johnny set a date.

"If we have to get married on the stage of the Bird Cage Theater, then we'll do it," she angrily told Johnny. "I'm ready!" But he wasn't. He kept putting her off with the time-worn excuse that he wanted to get some more money ahead so they could really get hitched in style. Sarah's father had sent more than enough money to fund a stylish wedding, but it just seemed to evaporate. The truth was, Johnny was a tomcat.

Sarah knew he was spending a couple nights a month with Harry and Kitty. He came straggling home early one morning, as drunk as she'd ever seen him, and crawled in bed beside her.

He'd taken all his clothes off, and instead of going right to sleep, he got amorous, and rough. He climbed all over her, smelling of whiskey and, she was sure, of Kitty's perfume. That was the last straw. She grabbed a six-inch-long crochet hook off the bedside table and let Johnny have it in the butt. Then she gave him another poke where it really hurt. Johnny went flying out of bed, and

Sarah grabbed the pistol she kept on the table, aiming it at his now flaccid manhood.

A flood of Yiddish invectives came spewing out of her mouth. She used all of her father's choice expressions and a few of her own, ending the tirade by shouting at the top of her lungs, "Out, you schmuck!"

She jumped out of bed and prodded him in the groin, then whipped around behind him and goosed him with the gun barrel. Johnny, buck-naked, ran out the door.

Sarah was about to throw his shirt and pants after him, but changed her mind. Just before she slammed the door shut, she said vehemently, "Don't come back!"

Johnny finally gave up begging for clothes, and ran a zigzag path to Dunbar's stable, keeping himself hidden behind whatever was available. His friend and partner showed up later that morning, and laughed himself hoarse over Johnny's plight before bringing him something to wear. He promised Johnny he'd never tell on him, and he never did.

It wasn't long before Sarah was seen walking around town on the arm of Behan's arch rival, Wyatt Stepp Earp.

Another lesser-known so-called romance involved John Ringo and Behan's trusted deputy, Billy Breakenridge. Billy was an interesting man. He talked softly and never went looking for trouble. But still, frontier life had hardened him. In '64, at the age of eighteen, he'd ridden with Colonel Chivington's Third Cavalry into the Cheyenne and Arapaho village at Sand Creek, where they broke the back of Indian power in Colorado. He had knocked about the west ever since. He knew his way around. He was dependable. He was liked. And he liked men.

In the 1880s there was a paucity of eligible women in frontier towns. Except for the likes of Nellie Cashman, who stood in total contrast, most of the women were married or in the cribs. This was especially true in Galeyville, mainly populated by rustlers. Even the prostitutes there left a lot to be desired, and it wasn't at all unusual for some of the men to seek pleasure with their own kind.

Lawmen other than Billy, who as Behan's deputy had the run of the county, avoided any involvement in Galeyville, mainly because they weren't welcome; but Billy didn't because he was. Billy always enjoyed being with the other men there, particularly John Ringo. The two of them had hit it off right from the start. Ringo was really Billy's cup of tea, and they got along famously.

Billy was no fool. He knew who he was and what he was, and how best to achieve his goals. When John Behan suggested, with a wink, that Billy collect the county taxes in the outlying areas, Billy knew how best to do it. He enlisted the help of Curly Bill Brocius.

When ranchers such as the Clantons and the McLaurys saw this pair approaching with their ledgers, they'd happily bring out a bottle, fork over some cash and, as often as not, have a little fun on the side.

Not long after the Benson stage holdup, someone held up the Bisbee stage. Levi McDaniels was no Bob Paul. He figured the better part of valor was to just pull up, hand over the mail sack and Wells Fargo's cash box which contained two thousand five hundred dollars, and stand by while five hundred more was taken from the passengers.

Four gunmen were reported to have been at the scene. When the news reached Tombstone, Billy Breakenridge immediately formed a posse, which included Wyatt and Morgan Earp. It was an easy case to solve. Hoof and boot prints left in the muddy terrain were soon matched to the horses and boots belonging to Frank Stillwell and Pete Spence. It was good detective work, and Billy and the Earps were justifiably proud.

Johnny Behan was mighty unhappy, because Frank Stillwell was one of his deputies.

The court's decision was that there was no case against these men, because the warrant for their arrest had been served by one John Jackson, who was not a legal officer of the court. Both Stillwell and Spence walked away, free as birds.

At the Alhambra, owner Tom Corrigan had just drawn a cold beer for Wyatt and Morgan Earp, when in came Ike Clanton and Frank McLaury. Frank, a handsome, pleasant, open, and very likable man, sported a goatee and a neatly-trimmed mustache. He also had the reputation of being a good shot, and therefore a dangerous man as well.

The McLaurys, Clantons, Frank Stillwell, and Pete Spence were Tom's friends, and he was aware of the tension that existed between them and the Earps. He laid two double-barreled shotguns on the bar and cocked both of them.

"Boys," he said as he gave the guns a pat, "if you've come for a friendly drink you'll get it here, and if it's trouble you're looking for you can get that here, too."

"Tom," Ike blustered, "we're not drinkin' with those two. We've come to give them fair warning."

"Not in my establishment," Tom came back at him. His right hand encircled the stock of one of the guns. "Do it somewhere else."

McLaury had motioned to Ike to take it easy. He'd noticed that Wyatt had slipped his hand beneath his coat, and that he had stepped away from the bar and a little to the side.

McLaury said to Morgan, "We'd like a word with you. Let's go outside."

Morgan looked at Wyatt, who nodded assent. Then Morg followed McLaury and Clanton out the door and onto the boardwalk. Wyatt stood just inside the door.

Will Hicks and his brother were waiting on the walk, and a short distance away stood John Ringo with his pistol in full view.

McLaury said, "Earp, you had no right to arrest Stillwell and Spence. No mail was taken in that holdup, and there's no reason for federal marshals to be poking their noses in it. You're trying to make more trouble for us, and we ain't goin' to stand for it. Stillwell and Spence are my friends, but I'm going to give them a piece of my mind anyway for being taken in by a couple of tinhorn Dodge City gamblers." He turned his eyes to the doorway where he could see Wyatt puffing slowly on his cigar, and directed his next comment that direction. "If you ever come after me, you'll never take me like you did them."

Morgan's face was turning red, and he said to McLaury, "If I ever have occasion to come after you, Frank, I'll arrest you just as I did them. Either arrest you or plant you." His hand was dangerously close to his gun.

Ringo's lean body tensed, and he spit his cigarette onto the ground.

"Gentlemen! Gentlemen!" a familiar voice broke in. "Let's hold our tempers and keep our guns put away. It isn't the time or the place for this."

Billy Breakenridge then stepped right in front of Morgan, and put an end to the confrontation. Ringo was relieved. He'd heard the Earp brothers weren't to be taken lightly.

Billy turned to Ringo. "John, what do you say to a game of billiards? I haven't seen you for a spell."

Frank McLaury glared at Morgan. "You've been warned, Morgan," he said in dead earnest. "You and your brother have both been warned."

He motioned to Ike, and with the Hicks boys walked rapidly to the O. K. Corral where their horses were stabled.

9

GERONIMO WAS OUT! HE JUMPED
the reservation and was on the warpath with a sizable band of Apaches. He was
here, there, everywhere! Tombstone prayed he was south of the border in Old
Mexico. But he wasn't.

People scoured the hills with their binoculars, particularly those living
close to the border and near the crumbling walls of Father Kino's Mission
Tumacacori.

Pete Kitchen ordered extra sentinels to the tower atop his ranch house. It
overlooked *El Camino de Los Muertos*, the road of the dead, which wound past
his ranch and into Old Mexico. He'd fought off the Apaches here for twenty-five
years, and was always at the ready for another raid. Most others in the Arizona
Territory were not so well prepared.

The *vaqueros* of the Mexican pack train that slipped across the border into
the United States in July of 1881 stayed on full alert. They carried seventy-five
thousand silver *dobes* packed away in rawhide *aparejos* strapped to their saddles,
and drove a small herd of Mexican cattle which would be sold to the illegal
slaughterhouses in San Simon for what they hoped would be a handsome profit.
Once there, these riders of the Hoot Owl Trail would convert the silver to United
States greenbacks.

They had made this run through the San Bernardino Valley before. The
Pendregosa Mountains rose to the west, and the Peloncillo Mountains to the east.
Indians could be lurking anywhere. This was a rough region. Scouts were dis-
patched to the east and west of the little column, and reported back that there
were no signs that the Apaches were anywhere around. Everyone breathed easier.
Out came their long, thin cigars, and they resumed the lively chatter and the
singing, joking and horseplay for which the Sonora Mexicans were noted.

They were even more relieved to see a rider approaching, not just because
he was familiar to them, but because he came from the north, which would indi-

cate there were no Indians up that way. Though he was swarthy and rode his horse *a la brida* in typical Mexican style, he was an *Americano*.

"Beelee," they called out happily as they rode to meet him. *"¿Qué tal? ¿Cómo se va? ¿Hay Indios?"*

Curly Bill Brocius gave several of the leaders a warm abrazo.

"'Sta bien," he assured them. *"No hay Indios aqui. No hay nada."* He gestured broadly with his hand, indicating there was no one out there other than themselves.

During this exchange, John Ringo, Frank Stillwell, and Pete Spence came from the nearby *arroyo* where they'd been taking the shade, and joined up with Brocius. They exchanged greetings with the Mexicans, and followed along as the pack train plodded north. Curly Bill casually mentioned, as though it was an afterthought, that he was pretty sure he had a buyer for the longhorns.

The Americans and Mexicans were soon deep in negotiations. Curly and his boys dropped back to "take a better look at them," he told the Mexicans, and then rejoined the column at the rear as they were entering a narrow ravine.

Two Mexican scouts could be seen riding along the rimrock, then suddenly they disappeared. Gun shots were heard, and soon one of the scouts' horses bolted down the trail toward them, riderless.

The Mexicans swung their mounts around and headed out of the ravine, back toward the Americans, shouting, *"¡Indios! ¡Indios!"*

They galloped straight into the rapid fire of Curly Bill Brocius, John Ringo, Frank Stillwell, and Pete Spence, who levered round after round from their Winchesters, and then continued the massacre with their six-shooters.

Another group of men charged the Mexicans from the rear, and others fired from behind boulders and mesquite. It was a perfect ambush, carried out by ruthless killers. The Mexicans hadn't gotten off a shot.

Now joining the four who had been riding with the Mexicans were Tom and Frank McLaury, Ike and Billy Clanton, Joe Hill, Jim Hughes, Rattlesnake Bill, Jake Jauze, Charlie Thomas, and Charlie Snow. Old Man Clanton trotted in from where he'd concealed himself, and grunted his approval. He patted his boy Billy on the head, and gave him a plug of tobacco.

The men rounded up the cattle and stripped the dead Mexicans of their valuables. Their remains were left for the coyotes and other desert creatures to feast upon, and soon there was nothing left of them but their bones, earning this spooky valley the name Skeleton Canyon.

The men had themselves a high old time in Galeyville. For more than a week the prostitutes got plenty of what they worked for, the men got what they paid for, and the merchants rejoiced all the way to the bank.

Old Man Clanton called the men together and announced it was time to get the Mex cows sold. "There's been a lot of talk around the territory about the doings in San Bernardino Valley and Guadalupe Canyon, so's I expect we'd better dispose of them somewhere up north. John here," he said, nodding toward Ringo who was well into his second bottle of the day, "tells me he knows a place up by Safford along the Gila and San Simon where they don't ask questions. He said he'd bulldog the critters up there if we'd furnish a few hands. I figure half the proceeds goes to the ones that gets them there, and the other half to the rest of us. How about it?"

Without waiting for an answer, he said to his boys, "We're gonna put a little of our share aside in case we hit a dry spell."

The boys groaned, because they figured the only worthwhile thing to do with money was to spend it on a good time as soon as they had it in their hands, but none dared dispute their pa.

Frank Stillwell, Pete Spence, and Billy Clanton teamed up with John Ringo to drive the cows north. They hooted and whistled and sang and prodded the cattle along all the way to the Blue Jay Ranch. Fred McSween put them up in his bunkhouse and gave them a grand feed and a grand time.

After a little haggling, a price was agreed on and the deal was sealed in the usual way—with a handshake and a tilt of the bottle. No papers were signed.

The boys drank to everything in sight. They went on a toot that lasted the rest of the week. Then McSween butchered a steer and a hog, and everyone ate 'til they were fit to burst.

They finally began to tire of what they'd been doing, and were thinking of other forms of pleasure.

Billy Clanton staggered up to Ringo. "You been here before," he slurred, "where d'ya find some tidbits? I'm gettin' a itch that I can't scratch. I need a good piece'a ass, an' I need it now."

The rest of the men stomped and yelled their approval of Billy's comment, and began chanting, "We want meat, we want meat," and fell all over themselves laughing at their cleverness. Billy, of course, had asked the wrong man. Ringo had absolutely no idea of where to find willing women, nor did he in the least care to.

Fred McSween began to chuckle. "Boys," he said, "I got an idea. Not too far from here there's the prettiest little squaw you ever did see. She belongs to a big, uppity buck nigger that ain't home half the time. I say we ride over there tonight and do us a little courtin'."

The boys were in motion before he finished what he was saying.

⁂

Louis Hancock was feeling pretty good that afternoon as he sat in Murphy's saloon. He'd just sold eight of his steers for a good price. He'd taken good care of them, and kept them corralled so they'd be plump and ready for the auction block. Now, as he talked it over with Murph, he ordered a second beer.

Louis was always open and above-board. He was genuinely fond of the Irish barkeep, and his feelings were reciprocated. As a matter of fact, this second beer was on the house. Pat just wanted Louis to stay around and jaw some more before he went home.

"I got fifteen bucks a head for them," Louis said proudly. "Top dollar around here, I reckon. Plenty enough so I can add on to my corral and move the privy closer to the house. Nadine's a couple months along now, and I want to make things easier for her." Nadine, Murphy knew, was Louis's Indian wife.

Louis spread a length of bright red cloth over the bar. "Look at this, Murph. I'm kind of celebrating my sale today, and got this so Nadine can make herself a new dress." They both chuckled as Louis added, "She'll be needing a little extra room now, you know."

Louis put the cloth away, and unwrapped a little doll wearing a checkered gingham dress with a white collar. It had a genuine porcelain head.

"Listen to this," he said as he held the doll to Murph's ear. He pulled the cord at the doll's back, and it cried, "Mama."

Murph pulled back in surprise. Louis laughed as he began to carefully wrap it back up. "Don't that beat all?"

"Damn," Murphy answered, "what won't they think of next? I bet that didn't come cheap."

"No, it didn't," Louis replied, "but with all the fussing about the new baby, I figured I'd best get Juanita a little something to show her we still love her." He was speaking of his three-year-old daughter.

"I'm a lucky man," he said as he gently arranged the gifts in his haversack and prepared to leave.

"One more?" Murph asked. "On the house."

"Thanks, no, friend. Two's my limit. Besides, I should be moving on."

As he mounted his horse, he waved to a passerby. The sun was shining. It was a good day to be alive. He hummed to himself as he rode home.

⚜

Hancock's ranch was located along the San Simon River a couple miles west of the small Mormon settlement of Solomon. On a hill overlooking the ranch there were prehistoric ruins believed to be remnants of the large stone house called *Chichilticalli*, which the Indians had shown to Francisco Coronado back in 1541, and it hadn't changed since that time. Travellers along the road could catch glimpses of the ruins for many miles.

Louis liked that old pile of stones. At dusk, when the sky went red with the last rays of the setting sun, it tugged at the big man's soul. He and Nadine often sat on their stoop and watched as night enveloped this relic of another civilization.

Louis hastened past the willow, mesquite, and underbrush that lined the trail to his home. He thought maybe he could beat the setting sun, and he and Nadine could watch it again.

The corral came into view, then the stable, and finally the ranch house itself. Louis was about to call out, but was stayed by the sight of six horses tethered to the porch railing. He knew immediately that they weren't Indian ponies, because they were all saddled. Besides, his wife was an Apache, and her people never bothered them. He removed his old army Remington from the loop on his belt and slipped silently off his horse, keeping to the shadows as he worked his way to the house.

Louis heard loud voices and raucous laughter. Then Nadine's shrill scream pierced the air. Louis cocked his gun, charged onto the porch, and through the door.

The blanket used to separate the parlor from the bedroom had been ripped down. Spread-eagled on the bed was his wife, her arms and legs tied to the four bedposts. She was naked, and blood covered her stomach and thighs. Blood was smeared all over the bellies and crotches of the three naked men who stood over her.

Louis saw it all in the brief second before an ear-splitting explosion thundered through the house. He went down as a bullet smashed into his leg. His gun flew out of his hand and slid across the floor. John Ringo stood in the corner of the room, holding a smoking pistol.

Nadine cried out, "Loo-ees, Loo-ees," and struggled against the leather straps tying her to the bed. Billy Clanton punched her in the mouth, and wiped his bloody knuckles on her long, black hair.

Louis tried to rise and go to his wife, but he couldn't. He tried crawling, but another shot crashed into his shoulder and slammed him against the wall. He was immobile, but conscious and able to see everything going on.

"I like the way you shoot," the weasel-faced Fred McSween said to Ringo. "That ought'a finish off that black bastard. Teach him to come messing around white man's country."

His partner, Harry Kent, possessed a deep, booming voice, and he used it now to call out, "The son of a bitch is watching us!"

He aimed a kick at Louis's head, and the spur on his boot tore Hancock's left eye clean out of his head. "Time for beddy-bye," McSween said, guffawing loudly at what he thought was a good joke. He then stripped off his boots and pants, and mounted the unconscious Nadine.

This was the part that Ringo liked. He didn't want anything to do with the woman; not at all. His ecstasy was achieved in watching these men display their maleness, and then ramming it into the woman's body. The masculinity of it enraptured him. He thrust his hips back and forth, imitating McSween's movements, and so in his own way joined in the heinous orgy.

Louis Hancock was fighting to remain conscious, but didn't miss a thing that was going on. Their mistake was leaving him with one good eye.

Billy Clanton whooped to Pete Spence, "Hey, Spence, how's this squaw compare to your Mexican woman?"

Pete laughed. "All's the same to me, Billy," and he went to work on the dying woman.

Frank Stillwell came in from the kitchen, all bloodied up and grinning. "Never had it so good," he shouted. "I just had me the sweetest piece of meat you ever did see."

The men ran into the kitchen, thinking maybe there was something more for them, but what they saw was Juanita's savagely brutalized and lifeless body sprawled on the table. All of them—evil as they were—turned away. Even Frank. There wasn't enough rotgut in the world to erase this scene from their memories.

Ringo said anxiously, "Let's get a move on."

They took Louis's Remington six-shooter and his big Sharp's rifle, then turned out his pockets and took all of his money. They wanted to make this look like an Apache raid, and figured that's what the Apaches would do. They were smart enough not to take Louis's horses and cattle, because they could be easily identified.

It was about ten at night. Their final act of violence was to throw some coal oil into the room and set a match to it. It had taken them three hours to completely destroy the home and family that gave meaning to Louis Hancock's life.

John Ringo lingered behind as the others mounted up, "to make sure the fire takes hold."

It wasn't just because he wanted to make sure the house burned. He wanted to see the flames. John had always been obsessed by fire.

He walked to the door and peered inside. The fire was blazing angrily, and before long the entire room would be consumed by the flames which illuminated Louis's face.

Ringo started to leave, but quickly realized Louis was staring at him, and it startled him. "I should'a put a bullet in you and finished it," he shouted, "but now I want you to fry. You're goin' to hell anyway."

He jumped off the porch, swung onto his horse and rode after his companions. When he caught up with them they were drinking, smoking, and indulging in silly horseplay. The night resounded with their bawdy laughter as they made their way back toward the Blue Jay Ranch.

Ringo felt another headache coming on.

❧

Back at Louis's ranch, a man darted silently from behind the stable to the burning house, and was followed immediately by several more. One wore a cast-off military coat and a loincloth made from an animal hide. His feet and legs were covered by high, leather moccasins, and he clutched a Model 1873 Winchester rifle. He was joined by another who carried a Springfield Trapdoor Carbine. Each had a revolver stuck in his belt and wore a cloth band around his head to keep his shoulder-length hair in place. Apaches! They belonged to Geronimo.

❧

Forty-three Indians were terrorizing the Gila Valley. Several ranches had been raided and burned, and most of the smaller ranches had been abandoned by their owners who'd gone into nearby towns for protection. Citizens of the territory demanded that General Crook get off his duff and move against the hostiles, but, as usual, he was slow to get his army into the field. As a result, for a short while the Apaches had their way. A score of murders were attributed directly to Geronimo and his band of renegades.

❧

The Apache warriors stood about Louis's ranch and wondered at the savagery of the white man. A few worked their way past the flames and discovered Louis and the bodies of their sister and her half-breed daughter.

Geronimo's mouth was set in a straight, hard line, giving him the appearance of having no lips at all. He issued quiet commands, emphasizing them with gestures from his expressive hands.

The warriors gently lifted the partially burned bodies of Nadine and Juanita and carried them to the *Chichilticalli* ruins a short distance away, where they laid them on a large, flat boulder. The scorched doll was placed between them. Then the warriors put stones over the eyes of the mother and daughter, and left them to the ghosts of their ancestors. In time, the superstitious claimed to see their spirits moving about the ruins in the dark of night.

The barely-conscious Louis looked up into the eyes of the most wanted man in the country. Geronimo's intuition told him this broken being deserved to be saved, if for no other reason than to avenge himself, as Geronimo had done many times.

With gestures and softly spoken words, he directed that Louis be taken from the burning house. Then one of the Indians, known as a *bruja*, or doctor, covered the now-unconscious Louis's grievous wounds with cactus leaves that he and the others soaked in their own urine. Meanwhile, they fashioned a *travois* for him, and with a final word from Geronimo, Louis Hancock was taken away from the ruins of what had once been his happy home.

They traveled southwest through country deserted because of the scare which they themselves had created. They knew the land. It had once been theirs. They passed dangerously close to the Blue Jay Ranch, and that night holed up in the Coronado Forest.

When Louis occasionally regained consciousness, they fed him a bland porridge and all the water he could drink. The livestock they slaughtered before leaving Louis's ranch provided them with plenty to eat.

Another night they camped near the growing metropolis of Tucson, among the majestic saguaros, and continued south the next day. Within four days of leaving Louis's ranch, they reached their destination.

⚜

When the great Jesuit missionary, Father Eusebio Francisco Kino, laid eyes on the Santa Cruz River Valley in 1700, he knew he must build there, and in time the magnificent mission, *San Zavier del Bac*, was constructed, eventually to be taken over by the Order of Saint Francis. The Franciscans had been friendly to the Indians who lived there, to the Spaniards who colonized, and more recently to the Mexicans and Americans who settled in the region. In 1881 it was still surrounded by desert.

⚜

At eleven on the fourth night, after the mission bells fell silent, the vespers had been sung, and most of the good people were in their beds, Geronimo and one of his men soundlessly scaled the high south wall of the mission. They passed through a doorway and down a corridor, halting briefly in the shadows as a gray-robed monk walked by.

They proceeded to the cell of the sleeping Father Humberto Rodriguez, and slipped silently inside. He woke with a start as a callused hand was clasped over his mouth, and others held him down. Geronimo whispered softly, *"Curandero,"* healer, and Father Humberto knew immediately who it was. He had visited Geronimo at San Carlos, and had always been kind to him. He knew Geronimo never forgot a kindness—or, for that matter, a grievance—so the aging priest wasn't alarmed by this visit. He knew his skills were needed.

He nodded his head, and the Indians released their hold. He stood and wrapped his habit around him, then followed them down the halls of the Sacristy, down a wooden staircase, and into the great church. Candlelight flickered faintly in front of the main altar. He motioned for those who saw this strange procession to follow. As the massive wooden doors swung open, Geronimo's man let loose with the call of a coyote. It was answered, and the rest of the warriors came silently out of the darkness, carrying Louis Hancock.

Geronimo spilled out a goodly number of United States silver coins from the little pouch he carried, and pressed them into Father Humberto's hand. He'd stolen them from the whites, and now he was giving them back. He grasped the old priest's shoulder, looked intently at him, and then he and his men were gone, as quickly and as silently as they had arrived.

They lifted him gently, with caring hands, and brought him into the mission.

Father Humberto looked out the small window after the doors had been shut and locked. As he stared into the darkness, he said to his brothers, "We have been visited by the Good Samaritan."

10

THE TUCSON *DAILY STAR* RAN THE
following article regarding the Indian menace:

That the Indian menace is still very real has been borne out by Mr.
Harry Kent and Mr. Fred McSween of Graham County and the Blue
Jay Ranch in the Gila Valley. Last week they reported large numbers
of Apache riding southwest toward Tucson. These hostiles undoubtedly belong to those that left the reservation with Geronimo. McSween
informed the authorities at Safford, who in turn alerted the military, of
a fire and massacre at the ranch of his neighbor, Louis Hancock. The
bodies of Louis's wife and child were found nearby in what appeared
to be an Indian burial ritual. It was reported that she was an Apache.
Mr. Hancock's body could not be found, and it is assumed he was
completely consumed by the fire. We strongly urge all citizens to be
on the alert. If any of you don't have enough ranch hands to adequately
protect and defend your property, by all means come into a larger,
more populated area. We are all in this together.

The Indians were a real threat to anyone traveling outside the town limits,
or who lived in isolated areas, but those living in Tombstone didn't share their
fear. A grand ball had been organized and was scheduled to take place that very
night in the hall of the *Turn Verein*, the German Athletic Club. It was considered
one of the most important social events of the year, and a great deal of effort
always went into these affairs. Let the Apache rage in the hills. Here in the safety
of downtown Tombstone, the dance would go on.

Nellie Cashman, the best in the business, had been hired to cater the affair.
She arrived at the ball dressed in a spectacular gown of ice-blue satin. Her dark
locks were piled high on her head, and wisps of hair outlined her cheeks and

tumbled down the back of her neck.

Setting up the bar across the room was Tombstone's favorite and most jovial bartender, Frank "Buckskin" Leslie. Frank looked up as Nellie came in. He stopped what he was doing and stared, thinking he had never seen Nell look more beautiful or more desirable. The sheen of her satin gown, and its ice-blue color, combined to entice Frank almost beyond his ability to control himself. The vision would be indelibly imprinted on his mind. This promised to be a memorable evening.

Nellie had arranged to be at the club the whole night. This had presented a problem, because her sister Fannie, and Fannie's five children, needed Nell's attention, especially after dark. Nell solved the problem by enlisting the aid of Father Gallagher, who agreed to put the children up in his rectory for the night.

The oldest boy, Mike, was ten. He was a handful, but had a healthy respect for the priest. Besides, his good pal, Carlos Niños, also ten, would be there for the night. Carlos, a full-blooded Apache, had been taken in by the priest after his parents were killed, and now, after four years at the rectory, he seemed more white than red. He and Mike served together as altar boys, and they enjoyed each other's company. They shared adventures, and had planned one for tonight.

The orchestra began warming up at five in the afternoon. There were two pianists, two violinists—J. L. Fonk on lead—and two flutists, Tombstone ladies who advertised theirs as the "sweetest flute music in the southwest." Jose Fernandez and his five *mariaches* had been hired to stroll about the hall and play between dances. After dinner the music would liven up when the violinists turned to being fiddlers.

By six the hall was pretty well filled, and even though Frank was doing great business at the bar, everyone stayed on their best behavior in keeping with the occasion, and also because the law was very much in evidence. John Behan, city sheriff, was there. He had cleverly commissioned Harry Jones as a deputy, and Harry was now sitting it out alone in the sheriff's office thereby, as Behan had planned, leaving Kitty Jones free to spend the entire evening with him. They drew applause with their version of the schottische, thanks to the lessons they'd taken in San Francisco.

There was another election in the offing, and when not showing off his skills on the dance floor, Johnny was all over the place shaking hands, patting backs, buying drinks, and being very much the politician. The only people he avoided were Sarah Marcus and her tall, handsome escort, Wyatt Earp. They showed up early, arm in arm, and stayed late. According to Sarah, Wyatt wasn't much of a dancer, but he went through the motions. Missing was Mattie Blalock, Wyatt's friend from Kansas days.

All the Earp brothers were there. Morgan came in with his stunning wife, Louisa. Typically Earp, he too wasn't much of a dancer. He sat most of the evening on the sidelines, puffing on a cigar, sipping beer, and marking time with his feet. He didn't object when other men asked for the privilege of taking a turn around the floor with Louisa. He'd nod assent and boom out, "Just so's you bring her back." Louisa loved the attention. She was born to dance, flirt, and captivate men.

So was her niece, Hattie, who came with her father, Jim Earp. Hattie was eighteen years old, big-breasted, vivacious, and very pretty. With her come-hither look, it was no time at all before her dance card was filled.

Virgil Earp came with his wife, Allie, who was content to stay by his side and listen as he regaled any available listener with his stories. He got the biggest laughs when he recounted the story of John Behan and the Chinese laundry.

More than a few eyebrows were raised when Doc Holliday appeared with his woman, Mary Katherine "Kate" Haroney. They were dressed to the nines, and smelled of perfume, liquor and tobacco. Despite her rather unsavory reputation, plenty of men there would have loved to take Kate for a turn around the floor, but they weren't about to ask Doc's permission. No one could predict the mood he might be in.

Although the law prohibited the carrying of handguns within the city limits, it was obvious that Doc wasn't wearing an empty holster. For that matter, neither were the Earps, John Behan, and several others. The situation in Tombstone made it almost mandatory that these men be armed.

Mollie Fly's eyebrows arched higher than a cat's back when she saw Doc settle Kate on a chair, bring her a drink, and then make a beeline for Nell Cashman. Men who had only seen Doc gambling and drinking in the saloons were surprised at the change in him as he engaged Nell in spirited conversation. None of this was lost on Kate, either. She flounced to the bar where she'd have some company, and where Frank was engaged in telling stories. The more beer he drank, the funnier and more exaggerated they became, and that suited Kate just fine.

Funny thing about Frank. There was no May. It came out that he'd left her alone at their ranch in the Swisshelms. His partner for the night, or so it appeared, was Mollie Williams, known as Blonde Mollie. She was a singer at the Bird Cage Theater, and was endowed with a voluptuous figure and a lusty voice. Several times during the evening she and Frank sang for the crowd, and everyone enjoyed their performances. Everyone, that is, except Nell Cashman.

When Frank asked her for a dance, she responded by lighting into him for leaving his wife home and openly sweet-talking Blonde Mollie. "I wouldn't have believed it if I hadn't seen it," she exclaimed. "You who always spoke of the sanctity of marriage! Now look at you! Don't be asking me for any dances. I don't care to dance with the likes of you!"

She turned abruptly and stepped to where Doc Holliday was sipping Irish coffee. She held her hand out to him and inquired, "Doctor?"

"Magnolia blossom," he replied as he stood and offered her his arm.

As they stepped onto the floor, Doc raised his hand to the musicians and called, "The mazurka, if you please."

Frank Leslie's mouth dropped open, Mollie Fly's eyebrows went to the ceiling, and a collective gasp came from the crowd.

The festivities didn't stop, but they sure stumbled a bit as Doc Holliday, deadly gunfighter, and Nell Cashman, pillar of the community, picked up the beat and abandoned themselves to that lively dance. Doc danced with skill and grace, and Nell followed his lead with ease. Bystanders picked up on the tempo and began clapping their hands; Morgan Earp's right foot was really banging away; and when the dance finally ended, Doc was bushed. But Nell was just getting warmed up.

The next dance was a Viennese waltz, and none other than big Bob Paul led Nell onto the floor. The six foot six inch, two hundred and forty pound Paul was amazingly light on his feet, and he gave the diminutive Nell a real whirl. Everyone was caught up in the spirit of the evening, and the good time just kept rolling along.

Frank Leslie knew why he'd been rebuffed, and it stung him. He went back to the bar and poured himself a stiff shot of Double Eagle Whiskey, and looked around for Kate. She was gone. She'd left for one of Tombstone's less elegant gin palaces.

Around nine that night, to everyone's disbelief, Billy Clanton, Billy Claiborne, Tom McLaury and Frank Stillwell showed up at the dance. They'd decided to come and see how the "other half" lived. Even though they were sober and reasonably well-dressed, these cowboys from Galeyville weren't welcome. They looked around, then made for the bar.

Frank Stillwell right away took a shine to Blonde Mollie, and ordered a drink for her. But Buckskin Leslie put his hand on Frank's arm and said quietly, "The lady's with me."

Claiborne piped up, "I thought you was married to May Killeen."

In the same quiet voice, Leslie said as he slid him a glass of bourbon, "Don't pursue it, Billy." Then, with a grin and in a loud voice, he added, "The folks are all having a good time, and you're welcome to join in. Have yourselves some fun." With those words he defused the explosive atmosphere.

Another disturbance that went unnoticed by most of the revelers involved handsome, twenty-eight year old Tom McLaury, who'd been silently drooling over the vivacious Hattie Earp. It took a while, but he finally worked up the courage to ask her to dance, and she accepted. Though he was more than a little clumsy, and managed to step on her toes several times, they got along well, carrying on a lively conversation between dances.

Then, out of the blue, her father confronted them. "We'll have no more of that," he said stonily. "Hattie, you go back to your aunt, and reserve your favors for honest folks. McLaury," he continued, "you keep your hands to yourself, and don't let me ever hear of you approaching my daughter again."

Tom reddened. His pals were watching. He was embarrassed, and getting angry.

"And what if I do?" he snapped.

"Yeah, we'd like to know just what you'd do, gamblin' man," Frank Stillwell chimed in as he, Claiborne, and Clanton moved toward the irate Jim Earp.

At that point, Wyatt arrived on the scene. "I reckon he'd do what we'd all do," he answered. "We'd kick your goddamn asses all the way down to Mexico, and then we'd feed you to the coyotes."

The cowboys looked the Earp brothers over and noticed the bulges in their coats. Claiborne stepped back, grumbling, "You're lookin' for trouble. We ain't got any weapons with us. Go pick on someone else. You wouldn't dare talk to us that way if we had our pieces."

A cold look passed across Wyatt's face. "Maybe next time you'd better bring them."

The boys glared at the Earps, then turned on their heels and left. They weren't sure they liked how the other half lived.

The festivities continued until the sun came up the next morning. This Grand Ball would be remembered as the best that Tombstone ever had.

In the meantime, everyone in the hall was busily engaged. Those not dancing were either watching from the sidelines, gossiping, or indulging themselves at Frank's bar or Nell's punch bowl. The Oriental and Alhambra had closed early, and Frank had arranged for a couple of their bartenders to help out at the ball, which gave him an opportunity to take an occasional breather. That's what he was doing now as he wended his way through the crowd to Nellie's table.

"Nell," he shouted over the din, "what do you say we do a couple rounds together?"

Nell gave him a withering look and replied tersely, "I've already given you my answer on that, Frank, and my feelings about it haven't changed one iota."

She turned her back on him and went on serving her customers, while Frank slowly made his way back to the bar.

Just a few minutes later, eight-year-old Theresa Cunningham timidly entered the hall and sought out her Aunt Nell. Nell looked up just as Theresa reached her table, and was dumbfounded to see her niece. This was certainly not the place for her to be, and Nell's first reaction was to give her a good tongue-lashing. Then she saw the girl's red, puffy eyes. Nell leaned down and put her arms on the girl's shoulders. "What's the matter, Teree?" she whispered.

"It's Mike," Theresa tearfully replied. "Mike is gone."

Nell drew aside one of her committee, saying, "I'll be back shortly," then hustled her niece over to the relative quiet of the cloak room.

"Where did Mike go?"

"He and Carlos went. They said they were going prospecting in the old Yanky Sam Mine."

"Where's Father Gallagher?"

"Somebody got real sick, and he had to leave."

"Didn't Mike say when he'd be back?"

"He said he'd be back in a couple hours, but that was way before it got dark. Biddy went with them."

Nell's mind was whirling. It had been dark for two and a half hours, which meant the boys had been gone for several hours, at the least. She was frightened, but took a little comfort knowing the dog had gone with them. Telling her niece to stay put, Nell hurried back into the hall and found Sheriff John Behan. After she explained the situation, he put his arm around her shoulders and said, "Nell, the boys are probably just playing with their pals and have forgotten all about the time. They'll be along any minute now. Trust me."

"Sheriff, please come with me and help me find them," Nell pleaded.

Johnny looked over at Kitty Jones, who was making time with her feet and anxious to get on with another dance. He wasn't about to leave.

"I tell you, Nell, they're just out having fun. If they're not back by morning, I'll wire Fort Huachuca and they'll send out some soldiers. We wouldn't dare go traipsing around the countryside without a soldier escort. There's Apache fires to be seen all over the mountainsides. Just keep a good thought, Nell," he told her, and walked away.

Nell was so astounded at his attitude that her mouth fell open as she watched him leave. She quickly recovered herself and looked around, hoping to find Doc Holliday or Bob Paul, but they'd already left.

She took a deep breath. "Behan's probably right," she thought, "but I'd better go and have a look-see."

She returned to the cloak room to get her niece, and they slipped quietly out the side door where she'd left her horse and buckboard. She lifted Theresa onto the seat and climbed aboard.

"First things first," she said, and headed for the church at a fast pace. Father Gallagher's faithful old housekeeper was waiting at the door, and she burst into tears when Nell approached.

"No están aquí, no están aquí," she wailed.

Nell quieted the old woman, and led her and Theresa into the sitting room of the rectory. She checked the guest room to make sure the other children were sleeping, told the housekeeper to get Theresa back to bed, and scrambled onto the buckboard.

She moved the horse along at a near gallop, down Fifth Street to Fulton, slowing only enough to determine if any lights were showing in the one house Mike might have gone to. The house was dark. She quickly concluded the boys must still be at the mine, and worried that they might have had an accident. She remembered the mine had once been considered a real bonanza, but the one silver vein had not yielded a whole lot and the mine was closed down. People were always talking about reworking it.

Nell urged the horse on toward the mine, which was a little over a mile out of town, but as she drew away from the outskirts she became more and more apprehensive. She could see the Apache fires, and raced on in a state of near panic.

She finally reached the mine and pulled up near the entrance to the shaft, calling out the boys' names. There was nothing but silence. Then, from her left, came a voice. It startled her almost out of her wits. She plunged her hand into her bag and gripped the handle of the double-barreled Remington Derringer.

"You shouldn't be out here this time o' night, ma'am. There's Injuns up there in them hills."

Nell peered into the darkness and could barely make him out. He walked closer, and she was relieved to see it was John Rittenberg, a grizzled old prospector hired by the Tombstone Mining Commission to keep an eye on things.

He threw his hands up as he recognized Nell. "Oh, Miss Nell, I didn't know it was you. You gotta' get out o' here. It ain't safe. I'll see you back to town."

"That would be most kind of you," Nell answered, "but I'm looking for two little boys and their dog. Have you seen them?"

"I did," John replied. "They came by a while back, afore dark. Said they was goin' to take a hike up toward the hills. I warned 'em to stay away from up there, but they said they'd only go a little ways. Reckon they took another trail home, 'cause I ain't seen 'em since."

"They didn't come home," Nell cried out. "Will you come with me and help me find them?"

"No, ma'am, not me. Not old John Rittenberg. I tangled with the Apache afore, and ain't about to do it again. Cost me my left arm," he said, waving an empty sleeve at her. "You'll need the United States Government army to go up there. I can't let you go on."

But Nell was determined. She laid the whip to her horse and was gone before old John realized what was happening.

She raced into the night toward the hills, now and then calling the boys' names. She was sick with worry.

Nell thought of reciting a rosary. The one she'd had most of her life was in her bag, and she reached inside for it, but instead pulled out the gun and laid it in her lap.

It was very dark and hard to see, but Nell sensed she was on a trail and kept to it. "The boys must have come this way," she cried out to the horse. And on they went.

It seemed longer, but less than an hour after leaving the old watchman, Nell saw the glow of a fire coming from inside the crumbling walls of an abandoned adobe ranch house. She was wary, but nevertheless drove her rig right up to where there had once been a door. She called out, "Mike! Carlos!" and got an answer!

Hearing Mike's reply, she grabbed her gun, jumped from the buckboard, and hit the ground running. A campfire was burning in the middle of the room, and she could make out the two boys huddled in a far corner. But something had to be bad wrong, because the boys didn't move. They sat as if paralyzed, their backs pressed against the wall.

Nell suddenly felt the presence of the two Apache warriors crouched in opposite corners of the room on either side of the doorway. They were armed with carbines, revolvers, and Bowie knives.

They rose and moved toward her, and without hesitating Nell brought her Derringer up and fired. The bullet thwacked harmlessly into the adobe wall. She fired again, and this time the bullet whistled off into the night. This was a gambler's gun, whose best shooting distance was two or three feet. Now it was empty and useless.

Nell's blood went cold, but her Irish was up and she didn't panic. She stared defiantly at the Indians as they stood looking down at her, and they laughed as one of them twisted the gun out of her hand, slapped her across the face, and sent her reeling to the floor next to her nephew and his friend. The younger Indian followed and stood menacingly over them.

Nell and the boys held each other close. Mike sobbed, "I'm sorry," and Nell hugged him tight.

Carlos whispered, "They're going to take us to Mexico."

Nell tensed. She knew about the slave trade that went on below the border. "No!" she gasped. "They can't!"

The older Indian walked over to Carlos, and reached for his arm. Then, suddenly, he stopped dead still.

Two distinct clicks were heard over the crackling of the fire.

"*Dioblito,*" a voice hissed from behind him, and the old Indian recoiled. One name flashed through his mind: Frank Leslie!

There he stood silhouetted by the fire, his long Colt revolver swinging in his right hand, first at one Indian, and then the other. His eyes were filled with loathing, as were those of the Apache warriors.

"Leslie!" was all *Dioblito* could say.

The younger Indian jerked his carbine to his hip, but before he could fire, Leslie's .45 caliber ball smashed into his face. He fell to the dirt floor and died in the blood of the dog whose throat he had slit not long before.

Frank spoke in English to the older Apache. "*Dioblito,* you and I once traveled together. You broke your oath to the United States. You are a forked-tongued bastard."

Dioblito snarled, "I talk to no United States. I talk to *Ihidman,* the Great Spirit. You, Leslie, *Has-kay-bay-nez-ntayl,*" and he went for his gun. Leslie shot him between the eyes.

For a moment, the only sound was the crackling of the fire, which cast eerie shadows over the dead Apaches. Then Nell sprang to her feet, and found her voice. "Frank!" she cried.

Still holding his gun, he went to her and drew her trembling body to his. He held her as he looked around.

To the boys he said, "Get their weapons."

The boys hesitated as they moved toward the awkwardly sprawled bodies, but did as they were told. Leslie was already hurrying Nell toward the buckboard, and the boys followed at a run. Suddenly, Mike turned and ran back into the room. He came out carrying Nell's gun.

Frank shouted "Yeehoo" to the horse, and gave it a whack with the whip. He spun the rig around and headed down the hill toward Tombstone, with his horse following behind.

Nell clung to the man who had saved their lives, and for some time was too overcome to speak. Finally she asked, "Frank, what did that Indian say to you?"

Leslie remained silent. Then, in a faraway voice, he answered, "Brave and wild one will come to a mysterious end. He was a *shaman*, a prophet. I wish he hadn't said that to me."

The boys huddled in the back of the buckboard, but as close as possible to the two sitting up front. Frank began singing an Italian aria at the top of his lungs, and Nell's spirits began to perk up. She snuggled closer to him, savoring the warmth of his body, his masculinity, and the smell of buckskin, tobacco, and liquor. She was overwhelmed with a sensation she'd never felt before.

As they hastened along the trail, Nell urged Frank and the boys to tell what had happened.

Mike spoke right up. He said they'd just gone out for a lark, and were waylaid by a party of Indians as they headed home when the sun began to set. Two of the Indians took them back to the old ranch house, where there was a campfire going, while the rest of the party continued foraging. Later, when the Indians heard the buckboard approaching, they laid in wait. Nell knew the rest.

Frank said, "I saw you speak to Sheriff Behan and leave the hall, so I asked him what was going on. He told me about your concern, but convinced me you'd only left to take your niece back to the rectory. When you didn't come back, I figured Behan was wrong. Maybe he was sincere about his assessment of the situation, but I have good reason not to trust that man. I figured it was time to come looking for you."

Nell started to speak, but was interrupted by the cheers of the boys as the familiar outline of the bell tower on the Catholic church came into view.

Father Gallagher met them as they pulled up in front of the rectory, shouting, "Hail Mary, the boys are back!"

The housekeeper came out, weeping with joy, and Nell embraced both of them.

"I'll tell you all about what's happened in a bit, but meanwhile I'd appreciate that my horse be stabled and fed and watered."

The priest directed the housekeeper to do this, and Nell then asked him to take the boys inside, saying she'd be in shortly.

Frank and Nell faced each other. She started to cry. "I don't know what to say."

She reached into her handbag for her rosary, and dropped it into his pocket.

Frank put his arms around her waist and drew her to him. Her satin dress slid smoothly against his buckskin shirt as she reached up and clasped her hands behind his neck, and she eagerly returned his long, passionate kiss. Then Frank abruptly pulled her arms away, walked to his horse, swung onto the saddle, and rode off.

Tears rolled down her cheeks and onto her dress as she watched him go.

Up in the hills overlooking Tombstone, the campfires continued to burn, and a new sound—the Apache death song—broke the stillness of the night. Two more warriors would no longer follow the trail of life. They had gone to *Ugashi*, the Supreme Being.

11

SHORTLY AFTER THE HIGHLY SUCCESS-
ful Grand Ball in Tombstone, the Tucson *Weekly Citizen* reported that the Indian problems were over:

> Our man in the field tells us that the Apache has been licked. We understand that our brave men in blue sent the bronchos skidaddling back into the Sierra Madre Mountains in Mexico. It'll be a while before they dare to confront Uncle Sam again.

A number of skirmishes, including this one, were described in quite some detail:

> In the hills overlooking Tombstone, a very successful action took place that does credit to our regulars. Without the loss or wounding of one man, our troops from Fort Huachuca engaged and drove off a large band of Geronimo's braves. We know of two hostiles who will never reach the Sierra Madres. They had been shot while forting up in an abandoned ranch. Our boys are to be commended for their fine marksmanship. Both were found shot in the head. Good shooting, men of the 6th! One of the dead was a former contract Apache scout, known as *Dioblito*. If our informant is correct, he scouted for the United States army in the late 1870s. Again we see the folly of General Crook's recruiting of Indians to scout for the army. The Apache just can't be trusted to turn against his own kind. Thanks to the straight shooting by the men of the 6th, *Dioblito* will never again betray his oath.

Everyone breathed easier but, as usual, one problem followed another. Tensions were mounting between the cowboys and the citizens of the town. United States marshal Wyatt Earp reported that one of his favorite horses, which he called Dick Naylor, was missing and presumed stolen. Wyatt had often entered Dick in sporting events.

Word reached Wyatt that the horse had been seen in Charleston, about eight miles from Tombstone, and he rode there that evening. Now Charleston, like Galeyville, was a hangout for cowboys, any or all of whom would gladly do Wyatt in, given the right opportunity. To avoid raising any hackles or arousing anyone's suspicions, he just trotted right on through the town as though he had business elsewhere, but his eyes didn't miss a thing. Sure enough, as he passed the open door of Honest John Montgomery's Livery Stable, he spotted Dick Naylor chomping down his dinner.

Wyatt circled around the block and dismounted at the magistrate's office. Jim Burnett was out of town, so he went next door to the telegraph office and sent a wire to his younger brother, Warren, in Tombstone.

Warren sought out Judge Wallace, who issued the legal papers necessary for recovery of Wyatt's horse, then he saddled up and rode all-out for Charleston.

While all this was taking place, Billy Clanton showed up. He'd been taking his pleasure in a brothel when he was told that Wyatt Earp was in the area. Billy had no doubts as to what brought Wyatt there, and knew he was in for big trouble if he didn't move his butt to the stable and get rid of the horse.

He had Dick Naylor saddled and ready to go when he heard that hated voice.

"Hold up there, Billy. I believe you're moving the wrong horse. That steed is mine."

Earp had been there all the while, watching every move that Billy made.

"No it ain't," Billy answered. "This here is my animal. I won him fair and square in a poker game."

"Let's see your papers, Billy."

Billy paused, then offered, "They ain't come in from Tucson yet. I'm a-goin'."

"I don't think you are," Wyatt responded as he put his hand on the gun in his holster.

"Well, I think I am," Billy shot back, and moved toward Wyatt. "Right, boys?"

His question was directed to Pete Spence and Frank Stillwell, who were standing in the small crowd that had gathered.

"I don't think you are, either," came a distinct southern drawl. The voice belonged to Doc Holliday. He was where nobody except Wyatt expected him to be. He'd followed Wyatt at a discreet distance, and gone directly to the stable where he picked a spot from which he could watch Dick Naylor without being seen himself.

Wyatt said to Billy, "We've got here what you'd call a Mexican standoff, which means you don't go anywhere until my brother gets here with my papers. Fact is, he should be here any minute."

Billy wasn't about to take on Doc and Wyatt. Wyatt was one thing, but Doc Holliday? Billy mumbled something about being cheated, but stripped the saddle off old Dick.

Warren arrived and Wyatt got his horse back, but he wasn't about to let the matter drop there.

"Billy, you owe me six bits."

"What in hell for?" Billy asked in surprise.

"For the telegram I sent to my brother. Pay up."

Billy reached in his pocket, pulled out some silver dollars, and said with a grin, "I ain't got six bits."

"Then I'll take a dollar. Hand one over. That'll teach you to watch who you gamble with."

Billy tried to make light of it, asking, "You got any more horses to lose?"

"Lose?" Wyatt retorted. "Not quite. From now on I'll keep them in the stable so you won't have the chance to steal them."

Billy pulled himself up and stuck his thumbs in his belt. "Wyatt," he asked smugly, "why is it you always travel with a goddamn army?"

Wyatt, Warren and Doc began to laugh. It was common knowledge that the Earp brothers always tried to back each other up when trouble was on them, or in the offing.

As he rode off with Warren and Doc, Wyatt shouted back, "Hey, Billy. Tell your brother and Frank McLaury I'd like to see them. I've got a deal for them."

⁂

"A deal with the Earps is tempting," Old Man Clanton said. "Ike, you go get Stillwell and see if he can find out what that son of a bitch has in mind. If we could get him and his bunch on our side, we'd really run this county. Just like the Evans boys did in Lincoln, New Mexico." He thought for a moment, then added, "Once we get control of the city, we can just as easy dump the Earps some dark night." He thought that was pretty clever, and gave his boys a knowing wink. "Billy, you stay here with me. Ike'll handle this one."

It took four meetings—all of them held in a vacant lot behind the Oriental Saloon—before Wyatt, Ike Clanton and Frank Stillwell got comfortable enough with each other to get down to brass tacks.

Wyatt explained his deal in language these boys understood. "You boys have got it in for my friend, Doc Holliday. You're trying to pin the Benson stage holdup and Philpot's murder on him, and you've spread ugly rumors and started a lot of gossip. I'm telling you, he didn't do it. You know, and I know, that Harry Head, Billy Leonard, and Jim Crane pulled that job. Luther King told me so, and he should know, 'cause he was there. I've got an idea you boys might just know where those men are holed up. You finger them for me, and I'll do the rest. All of that thirty-six hundred dollar reward offered by Wells Fargo is yours. Nobody'll ever know who leaked their whereabouts. I like money as much as you do, but I'm going for something else. First, I want Doc in the clear. Second, I'm running for county sheriff, and the capture of those killers will get me all the votes I need."

Wyatt even brought them a telegram from Wells Fargo's San Francisco office, verifying that they'd pay the reward for the apprehension of the Benson stagecoach robbers and the murderers of Bud Philpot and Peter Roerig, dead or alive.

Earp, Clanton and McLaury shook on it, and the deal was made. The two cowboys rode off to "Judas" their friends for thirty-six hundred dollars.

Doc was having his late morning coffee at the Russ House, and Nell had joined him, as usual. They were reminiscing about the night of the Grand Ball held the previous week. Though he'd heard it before, Doc always got a laugh out of the story about John Behan, the Celestials, and the six-shooter that wouldn't shoot.

Nell had a way of embellishing Virgil Earp's version of it, and had Doc doubled over with laughter, coughing hard, when in walked Kate. She'd been drinking, and seriously, ever since the Grand Ball, when he'd left her sitting alone and humiliated in front of all those people.

She hadn't gone back all week to the cozy little apartment in Fly's studio that she shared with Doc. She didn't remember or care where she'd spent those days and nights, or with whom. She didn't give a damn. But she'd been hurt, and that was the problem, because if she didn't love Doc so much she wouldn't have cared. She also would likely have shot him. Now here he was again with that little goody-two-shoes, carrying on like a sixteen year old.

"You bastard!" she spat at him as she swung her purse at his head. It wasn't the smartest thing for her to do in her inebriated condition. He ducked, and she missed him by a mile, walloping the wall behind him. The bottle in her purse broke, and spilled its contents all over her dress. Kate looked with disbelief at the dripping handbag, then stepped back and hurled oaths at Doc the likes of which Nell hadn't heard from anyone's mouth since the potato farmers in Ireland vented their anger.

At that point James Flynn, Tombstone's Irish policeman, got up from his table and walked over to Kate. "We'll be having no more of this blather, young lady," he said, "not here in a public place with decent folks looking on."

He encircled her waist with his gorilla-like arms and carried her, kicking and screaming, outside and off to jail, amidst the jeers and catcalls of passersby.

"She's disturbing the peace," he called out to them, and to Kate he said, "You're gonna stay in jail until you learn to behave yourself and act like a lady."

John Behan and Milt Joyce, the county supervisor and a good Democrat, were taking a siesta in the jail's office when Flynn brought Kate in. She was turning the air blue with descriptions of Flynn's ancestors, but it wasn't until Behan heard Doc Holliday's name that he took particular notice. He smelled an opportunity, and determined to take advantage of it.

"Maybe we ought to go a little easy," he said to Flynn. "A lady shouldn't be treated this way. Let's sit down and enjoy a toddy from my private stock here, and see what we can do about this."

Kate quieted right down. She'd heard the magic words: lady and toddy. Flynn turned her loose and she flopped into a chair as Johnny pulled a bottle of Old Crow out of a desk drawer. He filled a glass and handed it to Flynn.

"Shouldn't be doin' this, Jim," Behan said with a grin, "but I can see you've had a rough morning."

Flynn, a true Irishman, didn't need any urging, and emptied the glass in a few swallows. He shook his head, returned the grin, and said, "Mighty good, sheriff. Mighty good."

Behan said knowingly, "Yeah, guess there's no rest for the wicked, eh Jim? A man in your position has to keep up the good work. You just leave Miss Kate here and I'll take care of her so you can get back to your business of keeping this a safe place to live in."

Flynn was flattered. He thanked Johnny profusely and returned to the street.

Johnny filled a glass and handed it to Kate, who swallowed its contents greedily. Slurring her words, she said, "If you gennamen don' mind, I'll jus' have me 'nother glass."

Johnny set the bottle in front of her.

By three in the afternoon, the bottle was pretty much empty, and most of its contents were in Kate. All the while, Johnny was catering to the hate she was feeling right then for "that son of a bitch bastard, Doc Holliday."

He agreed with everything she said, including that Doc was a two-timing scoundrel, and a menace to society who deserved to be locked up. To make sure Kate stayed in this frame of mind, he sent Milt out for another bottle—but a cheaper one this time. Then to Kate he continued, "They say he was in on the Benson stage mess, and I'll bet you know it. Believe me, Kate, he deserves to be in jail, and I'm just the one to do it. You just tell me all about it, and I'll put him where he won't be able to insult you again. Not for a long, long time."

Behan had earlier whispered to Milt to prepare a paper stating that Doctor John Holliday had confided to Miss Kate Harony that he had participated in the attempted holdup of the Benson stage on March 15, 1881. Now he put the paper on the table, and urged Kate to sign it.

"It'll even the score for you," he said quietly. "You need to teach him a lesson he'll never forget."

"D'serve him right," she muttered as she sloshed more whiskey into her glass. "He prob'ly was in on it. He's been in trouble all his stinkin' life. Wha's a little killin' to him, anyway?"

She took the pen from Johnny and aimed it at the bottle of ink. She missed the bottle and sank the pen into her glass of Forty-Rod. Finally, with Johnny's help, she got her name signed to the paper, thus falsely accusing the man she loved of attempted robbery and murder.

Behan was elated. "When this gets out," he chortled to Milt, "Wyatt Earp won't be able to get a job as dog catcher."

Then he turned a vagrant out of the only jail cell so Kate could have it to herself overnight. He even allowed her to take the bottle with her when he locked her up.

Within the week, both the Tombstone *Nuggett* and the Phoenix *Herald* ran this story:

A warrant has been sworn out before Justice Spicer for the arrest of Doc Holliday, a well-known character here, charging him with complicity in the murder of Bud Philpot and the attempted stage robbery near Contention some four months ago. The warrant was issued upon the affidavit of Kate Elder Harony, with whom Holliday has been living for some time past. Holliday was taken before Judge Spicer in the afternoon, who released him upon bail being furnished in the amount of $5,000, W. Earp, J. Meagher, and J. L. Morgan becoming sureties. The examination will take place before Judge Spicer.

The next day, the *Nuggett* carried this little gem:

Miss Kate Elder Harony sought "surcease of sorrow" in the flowing bowl. She succeeded so well that when she woke up she found her name written on the Chief's register with two 'd's—drunk and disorderly—appended to it. She paid her matriculation fee of $12.50, took her degree, and departed.

When Kate realized what she'd done, she was horrified, and loudly proclaimed the story told by Behan was a pack of lies. The District Attorney, upon hearing Kate's account of what had transpired, didn't take long to declare that the affidavit she'd signed was null and void. He pointed out that an inebriated person is not a valid witness, and also said there wasn't the slightest evidence to show that the defendant was guilty. The case against Doc was dismissed.

Behan had made a big mistake when he made that entry in his register, because it helped in exposing the extent to which he'd go in order to attain his personal objectives.

Holliday wanted to shoot him, but Wyatt counseled otherwise. First, he suggested that Doc "send that fool woman away." Doc agreed he probably should, but he just couldn't bring himself to turn his longtime lover, confidant, and drinking companion out. Both of them realized they had a stormy relationship, but he loved her as much as she loved him. It seemed sometimes that they couldn't live with each other, but they couldn't live without each other, either. So, in spite of the Earps' antipathy toward Kate, she stayed on, and was in and out of Doc's life right up to the time she all but stood with him at the O. K. Corral.

Meanwhile, Wyatt, Doc, and Bob Paul returned to the serious business of apprehending Harry Head, Billy Leonard, and Jim Crane.

12

BILL LEONARD AND HARRY HEAD

needed some money, and fast. They'd counted on getting a bundle off the Benson stage. They knew that someone had talked, and that they were marked men. The word was that Buckskin Leslie had been asked to track them down, and they wanted to avoid him at all costs, figuring rightly that one gun in his hand was a whole lot more deadly than two in theirs.

Still, Frank Leslie wasn't their most dangerous enemy. That distinction belonged to their buddy, Joe Hill. Joe had been sent by Ike Clanton and Frank McLaury to lure Bill and Harry back home in order to kill them and collect the Wells Fargo reward. Clanton and McLaury also planned to ambush the Earp party in the process.

The plan was for Joe to tell Bill and Harry that Curly Bill and Old Man Clanton were plotting to hold up the Bisbee Copper King payroll, and that they wanted Bill and Harry in on it so they'd be able to share in the sizable heist. Once back in the San Pedro Valley, where the Earps would be waiting for them, Clanton and McLaury would bushwhack the Earps while they were distracted by the business of capturing Leonard and Head. Then they'd claim the Earps had been killed by Leonard and Head while attempting to take them into custody, and that they'd then been able to bring down Leonard and Head.

If the plan worked, they knew it would pretty much ensure the end of the Law and Order Party, and they'd collect the reward money to boot. Then they'd go after the Copper King payroll.

❧

In the middle of the isolated area in which the Hachita Mountains of New Mexico are located, just across the border from Arizona, is the little town of Hachita, which took its name from the sixty-five hundred foot Little Hatchet

Mountain which shaded it. This was not hospitable territory. It was crossed by just a few game and Indian trails. Running north and south, however, was a worn path over which contraband cows were moved up from Antelope Wells on the Mexican border to Lordsburg and Deming. Most of the folks in Hachita made their living catering to the Anglo and Mexican cattle smugglers.

Ike and Bill Haslett, brothers, pretty much ran the show in this hole-in-the-wall community. They owned and ran the store, the saloon, the flophouse, and the brothel which boasted "four of the most talented girls west of Las Cruces." Their water fees were reasonable, and they got along with everyone. They'd been chased out of Texas, but that didn't matter to the locals or transients who enjoyed their hospitality. Bill and Ike were known in these tough parts as "good old boys."

Into this brotherhood of misfits rode Bill Leonard and Harry Head. Purely and simply, they came to rob and move on. "Gone to Texas," a frontier expression, described such intentions. They considered themselves to be top guns, capable of handling anything in this hick community. They'd forgotten how badly they'd botched the Benson stage holdup.

Bill Haslett, who'd already "gone to Texas" himself, greeted the dusty cowboys with a hearty "Howdy-do, boys. Make yerselves ta home. If ya got the wherewithal, I kin set ya up with all the drinks ya can handle, an' Gracie here'll toss a coupl'a steaks on the grill fer ya. An' when ya've filled yer guts, Gracie an' Red'll give ya the best roll in the hay ya've ever had or dreamed about. Are we talkin' business, boys?"

Leonard and Head grinned at each other. No question about it, Haslett's money could wait a tad. Drinks, eats and some poontang came first.

"Hell," Leonard whispered to his buddy, "that redhead is already giving me the eye."

They cleaned up at the water pump in the corral behind the saloon, and got right into the booze. They did a job on the steaks and fried potatoes that the redhead served, and paid for them up front, just like regular customers. Some of the locals engaged them in conversation, and they responded like they were long-lost friends.

The main event of the evening, of course, was a romp in the feathers. The redhead couldn't keep her eyes or her hands off Leonard, or her mouth off his bottle.

Gracie had Head's trousers unbuttoned, and was doing such pleasurable things to him he didn't think he could hold off long enough for them to get their anxious bodies to a room.

A door at the side of the bar led to several rooms just large enough for a bed and a small table. There were wooden pegs on the wall to accommodate gun belts, pants, shirts, and whatever else might be tossed aside. A couple of tattered towels hung from the pegs.

Another door led from the room to the corral and water pump, and a three-holer located in the stables next to the animals' stalls. Haslett told the boys, "If ya gotta go, jus' follow yer nose. Ya can't miss it."

Bill and Harry compared notes the next morning, and agreed that Red and Gracie had sure enough lived up to their reputations. There'd been no other customers, and the ladies had spent the entire night with them.

"Seven hours!" Leonard gushed as he put on his chaps and buckled on his six-shooter. "I could almost feel guilty about what we're here for." Then, with a wink, he added, "I think I'm in love."

They hungrily gulped down the breakfast of bacon, sourdough biscuits, eggs, grits and coffee that the ladies prepared for them, and Leonard proclaimed, "Now I know I'm in love."

Not enough, though, to stop him from throwing down on the Haslett brothers, who'd been looking on. Harry backed him with his Colt.

"Sorry, boys and girls," Leonard said menacingly, "but about that money we gave you last night. We want it back. Now. All of it." He pointed his weapon at the cash drawer. "And everything in there, too."

He was too busy outlining his strategy to Harry to notice that neither of the brothers made a move to comply with his demands.

"We'll take your horses with us, and turn them loose a few miles down the pike," he said to the Hasletts. "You boys've been right nice to us, and we ain't horse thieves. All's we want is a good head start."

Again he motioned to the cash drawer. "Let's have it."

The Haslett brothers went for their shooting irons.

"Shee-itt, boys, we don't want that," Leonard shouted as he and Head thumbed their gun hammers and pulled the triggers.

All they heard was, "thunk thunk." The Haslett brothers weren't in the habit of trusting a couple of saddle tramps that came wandering in as Leonard and Head had, and during the night had taken the precaution of emptying their revolvers.

Bill and Harry had even less success with this holdup than they'd had with the Benson stage. The Haslett brothers' guns roared, and they died on the spot.

The Hasletts stripped them of their belongings, and their bodies were planted in the little cemetery up in Hachita Mountain. It wasn't much of a haul for the brothers: a few dollars, two Colt pistols, a Henry Brass rifle, ammunition, and two pairs of boots. Their horses and saddles, though, would fetch a pretty penny, and Ike and Bill agreed the total haul beat a kick in the ass. But they hoped for better pickings next time.

The next time came within four days. Two riders were seen wending their way through the mountain pass, and the Hasletts and the ladies prepared to give them a warm welcome.

Their anticipation of some easy money vanished when they recognized the two as Curly Bill Brocius and John Ringo, two of the most unpredictable pistoleers in the southwest.

Ike said to his brother, "I know that son of a bitch John Ringo. He shot Jim Cheyney in the back while he was taking a leak."

"Lampasas, Texas?"

"Yeah," Ike replied.

Ike picked up his shotgun, loaded both barrels, and placed it on the bar behind some sacks of beans. The muzzle pointed directly into the room.

"Mornin', gents," he hollered as Ringo and Brocius dismounted and tossed their reins over the horse rail. "Come on in outta the sun an' make yerselves ta home. Y'all hear?"

"Don't mind if we do," Brocius replied with a grin. "Texas, eh? I think I detect a little Lone Star."

"You can bet your saddle horn on that," Ringo added. "I remember you, Haslett. You were down in Burnet during the Hoodoo troubles. I hope you've changed since then."

"John, boy," Ike retorted, "that was a long time ago. Times have changed. Come on in. First one's on me. We'll talk while the ladies here stir ya up some grub, and then if ye're in the mood—and who ain't?—they'll give ya a good time afterwards."

Ringo gave him a withering look.

They sat down at the bar and hooked their boot heels over the brass rail.

Ike Haslett stepped to the back of the bar and unobtrusively realigned the muzzle of the shotgun.

"What's yer pleasure, boys?" he asked. "How about a swig ta settle the dust, an' a beer to chase it down? All ya want. Either or both."

"What I want first off," Brocius cut in, "is a place to drain my kidneys. Been luggin' this load around a mite long."

"Right behind the bar an' through the door, an' jus' follow yer nose."

Curly Bill did just that, but not because he actually needed to use the privy. He'd taken care of his kidneys a while back. He slipped into the corral and looked it over, and spotted Head's and Leonard's horses, horses he was very familiar with. A quick glance around convinced him the general area was deserted. It was late afternoon, and siesta time.

He took his sweet time going back, and as he passed alongside the back of the bar, he spotted the shotgun. Ike had made a mistake when he pointed out the shortest route to the outhouse.

Curly took a seat next to Ringo and knocked down the drink Haslett poured for him. "One don't make the man," he snorted as he shoved his glass back to Ike.

While Ike filled the order, Curly Bill jerked his thumb toward the bar and whispered to Ringo. To the chagrin of the Haslett brothers, Ringo and Brocius moved to stools farther down the bar, and Ringo settled down to some serious drinking while Curly Bill did the talking.

"You got a couple horses out there I might be interested in. They for sale?"

Bill Haslett couldn't believe his luck, and jumped right in. "They sure 'nuf are. Fella came by t'other day with a bunch of horses. Said these two were bothersome, so we took 'em off his hands. I'll give ya a good price on 'em, and even throw in a coupl'a saddles."

Brocius looked casually toward the table where three other men were sitting. They were minding their own business. He watched as Red sidled up to John Ringo and began rubbing her fingers over his back.

"You're a tall one," she cooed. "Bet you've got a big gun."

Ringo put his hand on his pistol and snarled, "This's my gun, and don't even think of touching it."

Red was startled, and glanced at Gracie, who sensed this could mean trouble. She quickly offered Ringo and Brocius something to eat. "We got some beef out back that's just fresh cut. And some spuds." To Curly Bill she added, "You look like you could do justice to a good piece of meat."

Curly Bill ignored her, and turned his attention to the Hasletts. "I'd like to know where the owners of those two horses are."

Bill Haslett looked at his brother. "Like I told ya, we bought 'em fair an' square jus' las' week."

"Don't give me no crap!" Brocius snarled, pointing a finger at him. "Those horses belong to our friends, and I want to know where those boys are!"

Ike Haslett figured he was close enough to the shotgun that he could put it into play in a couple of seconds, and this gave him confidence. So much so that he sneered, "Better get yerselves some new friends, then. Those assholes ain't around no more, an' they won't be needin' those nags."

Turning to Ringo, he said confidently, "We had a little misunderstandin', an' your friends lost. But", he added with a grin, "we didn't do 'em in the way you did in Texas. We did 'em in face to face."

The Hasletts had a good system going for them when they were conducting any kind of business. They used the soft approach: drinks, a little smoothing by the ladies, and a good meal, before making their pitch. Now Ike had broken the friendly tone of the conversation. He'd gone feisty. Bill was taken aback by this quick shift in attitude, and shot Ike a startled look. Ike should have remembered what John Wesley Hardin had told him back in Texas: "Never trust Ringo."

Ringo's Colt practically leaped into his hand, and Ike fell where he stood. The same Colt swung around to Bill Haslett, who just stood there with his mouth open.

"No!" he cried out.

"Red, you wanted a gun," Ringo sneered. "Get his and throw it away." She quickly did as she was told.

Curly Bill settled back into his jocular mood, and motioned to the three men who had remained seated at another table. "You gents there. We got a pile of shit here that's goin' to start stinkin' the place up," and with a nod toward Bill Haslett and the ladies added, "and we're going to have a lot more than that if I don't find out where my friends are."

Six mouths answered at the same time.

After chowing down on steak and onions, fried potatoes, and half a quart of Forty-Rod, Brocius and Ringo ordered the others to bury Ike Haslett next to Bill Leonard and Harry Head. They helped themselves to Haslett's liquor supply, strapped their friends' equipment onto the dead men's horses, and started back to Arizona.

The redhead came outside and stood watching. As Ringo rode past her, he sneered, "Redheaded slut."

Curly Bill, following behind him, told her, "Don't mind him. That's just the way he is."

The two men, with the extra horses in tow, worked their way through the mountain pass. Their only concern was to get to Old Man Clanton's ranch in time for his next foray into Mexico for cattle.

Bill Haslett sold out quick and cheap, and moved on. Hachita was never the same after that.

13

THE BELL OF THE MISSION *SAN ZAVIER*
del Bac called the brothers to their evening meal. Quietly, yet in spirited conversation, the monks made their way to the great hall. They knew no matter what the fare that it would be tasty. Their cook, Brother Bustamante, was from Spain. He could make a feast out of the most simple of ingredients, and had the girth to prove it.

Three of the Franciscans—Father Humberto Rodiguez; his assistant, Brother Marcello; and Doctor James Turner from Tucson—would be late getting their meal. They were in the infirmary, huddled over Louis Hancock. It had been two months since the Indians had brought him there. His life then was almost gone, and four times Brother Marcello had called for the Sacrament of Extreme Unction—the Sacrament of the Dying. Yet each time Louis had recovered, only to slip many more times in and out of consciousness. When awake, he never spoke, but was able to sip the savory chicken broth that Brother Bustamante brought to him. Louis steadily improved, and Brother Bustamante gradually added tender pieces of chicken and vegetables to the broth.

One day, as Father Humberto spooned the thick soup into Louis's mouth, his wrist was seized in a vice-like grip, causing him to drop the spoon.

A rumble welled from deep in Louis's throat, and he cried out, "Nadine, Nadine," and then he began to sob. For several minutes he wept uncontrollably, occasionally calling out, "Nadine, Juanita."

Father Humberto tried to comfort him. "Who are these people you call for, my friend?"

"My wife. My daughter. They killed them."

"Who killed them?" Doctor Turner asked. "The Indians?"

"No."

"Who then?"

Neither Doctor Turner nor Father Humberto received an answer, but they never questioned him further. They understood the man's grief, and spoke no more of it.

From that point on, Louis's progress was better than anyone had thought possible. The brothers fashioned a patch for Louis to wear over his empty eye socket, and Louis doggedly completed the therapy that Doctor Turner prescribed on his weekly visits. Louis was soon walking the halls of the mission with a crude crutch provided by the brothers.

Though Louis would always be burdened by the effects of his wounds, he nevertheless came once more to be an able-bodied man, and a strong bond was formed between him and the brothers.

⁂

The Mexicans were on the alert for cattle rustlers. The loss of the *vaqueros* in the San Bernardino Valley had put Emilio Kosterlitsky and his Mexican *rurales* in a vengeful mood. It seemed that ever since the Mexican War, the border had been plagued by impudent *gringos*, who said and did as they pleased to their Latin neighbors. But regardless of what the *gringos* thought of the "greasers," they all admitted no one could ride a horse better than a Mexican *vaquero*.

⁂

The boys had rounded up close to a hundred of Sonora's choicest bovines and started them back toward the Clanton rendezvous. The few Mexican cowboys they encountered fled and watched from afar while their stock disappeared across the border into the United States, but they did have the presence of mind to send runners to Emilio Kosterlitsky.

The international border meant nothing to either side, and when the *rurales* came thundering after the rustlers, they crossed into Arizona territory and surprised the thieves in Guadalupe Canyon. They caught them napping and shot them. All but one. Harry Emshaw was able to slip away, and eventually walked into the Cloverdale Ranch to report the ambush.

None of this was known to Old Man Clanton and Jim Crane, who were taking their ease in the shade of their wagon while waiting for the boys to come back. They were mulling over their profit and weren't alarmed by the sound of approaching hoof beats.

Through the canyon, at full gallop, came a posse consisting of Wyatt, Morgan and Warren Earp; Bob Paul; Sherm McMasters; and Doc Holliday. To their left, atop the canyon wall, Frank Leslie slouched on his horse. He had guided the posse here. They were after Jim Crane.

"Son of a bitch, Earp," Clanton croaked as the posse reined up. "Here you come with your goddamn army again."

He was more startled than perturbed by the intrusion, and sauntered over to the fire he and Crane had going. He tilted the big, enamel coffee pot and poured himself a cupful. Gesturing toward other cups hanging from the wagon, he said, "Help yourselves, boys, and then be on your way. We got nothing here for you."

Wyatt and his men knew there were others around somewhere, because every tin cup meant there was a mouth for it. Chances were they'd be coming back sometime soon. Nevertheless, after a long ride, a hot cup of coffee was more than welcomed.

"Newman," Wyatt began, "we've come for Jim here. We've got a witness says he was in on the Benson stage murders."

"Damn!" Crane gulped.

Clanton was shrewd. He hadn't lived sixty-five years without picking up a few smarts. He was outnumbered, and knew it would be futile to put up a fight.

"Go ahead and take him."

Just then, from the right of the canyon where a narrow corridor led in from the east between sheer stone walls, gunfire erupted. Warren Earp spun around and fell to the ground. Doc Holliday joined him as a .44 Henry slug ripped through his leg.

John Ringo and Curly Bill Brocius had chanced upon the scene. They'd been moving along slowly when they heard the sounds of the Earp posse galloping into Skeleton Canyon, and the steep walls had concealed their arrival from the ever-watchful eyes of Buckskin Leslie. They were in an impregnable position. Still, they were brash to believe they could win out over superior numbers, and on the face of it their actions appeared to be courageous. But they had counted on Clanton and Crane to go for their guns, and had also calculated that Clanton's other hands must be somewhere close by.

They were right about Old Man Clanton. He leaped toward the back of the wagon, drew his pistol, and got off a shot, but it drilled harmlessly into the ground. He fired again, but not in time.

Though he was down, Doc Holliday managed to swing his Winchester into play, and the old cattle rustler bit the dust right then and there.

All hell broke loose from the Earp party, and Jim Crane was a lead mine by the time he hit the ground.

Leslie spotted Ringo and Brocius. He fired shot after shot into the opening in the rock wall where the two men huddled, and they beat a hasty retreat. The shooting was over in three minutes.

Sherm McMasters looked down at Clanton and Crane. "They died game," he said. Indeed they had, by the gun, just as they had lived.

"Goddamn," Warren cursed. "They got my shoulder." The slug had gone through muscle, and although painful, it wasn't serious. Still, he wouldn't be using that arm for a while.

Doc Holliday coughed, sat up, and examined his leg. "Clean through," he marveled, "but nothing broken. That was clever shooting from way up there."

"Want to go after them?" Leslie asked.

"I don't think Warren or Doc are up to any more chasing around," Morgan replied. "Best to get them back."

Wyatt looked disgusted. "Damn," he groused. "We nearly had them all."

They poured a bottle of Clanton's whiskey over their wounds, but not before Doc first got a little inside himself. One of the men in the posse offered his shirt to wrap Doc's leg in.

Wyatt suggested they get moving before the rest of Clanton's men showed up. "With a couple lame ducks to look after, I wouldn't want Ringo, McLaury or Brocius coming up against us."

"We've just had a visit from Ringo and Brocius," Leslie piped up. "That was pretty good shooting. They've probably gone looking for the others."

The wounded men were helped onto their horses, and the posse quickly left the canyon. They escorted Warren north to the railroad station at Deming, and Morgan rode with him to the Earp ranch in Colton, California.

Leslie and McMasters rode back to Tombstone with Doc. It took them two days, and Doc never let up cursing his luck and sucking on a bottle.

⁂

The Clanton-Earp feud was out in the open. Ike and Billy knew that one of the Earps had killed their pa, but they also knew no court of law would try a United States marshal for throwing down on known cattle rustlers. Ike bellowed threats all over Tombstone, and even the oily-tongued John Behan couldn't stop him.

"That Earp bunch is askin' fer a fight, an' by God we'll give 'em one," was among his favorites.

Behan would placate him with a few drinks, and assurance that "Our time will come. Just be patient, Ike. Just be patient."

Behan was secretly hoping for a quick showdown. It infuriated him to see Wyatt and Sarah Marcus strolling down Front Street, or smiling at each other over a sundae at Banning and Shaw's Ice Cream Saloon on Fourth Street.

The Clantons and the McLaury brothers were also itching for a show-down. Frank McLaury couldn't forget the knot on his head from Wyatt's pistol-whipping right after Marshal Fred White was shot. He'd been one of those roughed up and locked up that night.

Then there was the episode involving six government mules that wandered away from Fort Rucker. It was United States marshal Virgil Earp's job to find them, and his brothers Wyatt and Morgan joined in the search. The trail led straight to the McLaury ranch.

Even though it was obvious that the brands on the mules had been altered from U. S. to D. S., both Frank and Tom McLaury insisted the mules were theirs, and always had been. Neither the Earps nor Captain Hurst of Fort Rucker, who was with them, could prove otherwise, and the matter was settled with no arrests being made.

But from that day on, the McLaurys and Earps harbored bad feelings against each other. The McLaurys even sent word to the Earps through Captain Hurst that they'd be shot on sight the next time they came their way. They said their friends would find what was left of them in the sagebrush, where the coyotes dragged them.

Wyatt's response was to tell Captain Hurst to let the boys know they'd get their chance.

Doc Holliday noticed he was getting fishy looks from the cowboys, probably because they knew he'd been with Wyatt when Old Man Clanton was done in. Cane in hand, he limped into Nell Cashman's restaurant for his usual breakfast of coffee and scones.

"Make that Irish coffee, Magnolia," he said.

"Good heavens, John, what happened to your leg?"

Doc settled back in his chair and tapped the leg with his cane. "Got to playing with guns and nicked it a bit. I need to improve my aim. It's nothing to fret about."

Nell wasn't about to be put off. "John, I've heard rumors that you and Frank were out in the hills, and that some men were killed. Why, John, why?"

He knew a flippant reply wouldn't satisfy her, and said, "Nell, it's strange, very strange, for me to admit this, but the truth is, I was on police business." He coughed, lit up a cigar, and continued. "Wyatt Earp is a United States deputy marshal, his brother Morgan wears the badge of a special policeman for the city of Tombstone, Bob Paul is the sheriff of Pima County, and they tell me Sherm McMasters is some sort of private detective. I was riding with those fellows in order to clear my name of being a suspect in the Benson stage holdup. As it turns out, those who could have straightened out that lie are gone where they can't do me any good. People are still crossing the street to avoid me. They think I'm some kind of murdering monster. Nell, if it weren't for your friend, Buckskin Leslie, right now none of us would be here. We were plain and simple ambushed. Frank was minding the store, and put down such a hail of bullets that the bush-whackers turned tail."

Doc leaned back in his chair, puffed on his cigar, and took a big sip of coffee. His explanation was finished.

Nell shook her head and brushed aside a maverick lock of hair. "John," she admonished, "all of this nastiness in town isn't really any of your business. Those men are fighting for money, power and politics. You're not like them. They're just a bunch of bounty hunters. You don't have to go traipsing in the hills with them to catch those cowboys, regardless of what they've done. And your friend Wyatt Earp! Why, he's the most cold-blooded man I've ever met in my entire life!"

"That's just it, Nell," Doc said quietly. "He's my friend. You do for your friends, and I do for mine."

The conversation wasn't the light banter he always enjoyed with Nell, and he didn't like the direction it was headed. As he rose to leave, he made a statement Nell would remember for a long time.

"Magnolia, the world has marked me as a killer. Believe me, that sticks deep in my craw. What I've done, I've done in self-defense. Unfortunately, my nocturnal habits often place me in situations where I must use my gun or lose my life, or at the least my dignity. I don't like it. Look to your friend Frank Leslie if you want to criticize someone. There's a man who enjoys gunplay. He's built a life around his gun."

Doc knew he'd carried the conversation too far, and added with a grin, "I'll be darned if I know how they missed that giant, Bob Paul, and clipped me. Hell, even I could hit a target that big."

Nell was grateful for this lighter tone and, laughing, called out to her nephew, Mike Cunningham, who was doing chores for her. "Bring the doctor another cup of coffee, please."

She turned back to Doc. "John, you really must get away from here for a while. I'd like a change of scenery myself."

Nell was known to have itchy feet.

"What do you say we take a trip back to Georgia together? The trains are running the entire distance from Tucson. You could visit your cousin Mattie. You haven't seen her since before she entered the convent, and I know you write to her faithfully. I'd like to talk to the Mother Superior of the Sisters of Mercy. I'd like to see them start up a convent out here. We need one, don't you think?"

"Nell, you've been reading my mind. I always knew you were some kind of Leprechaun. Fact is, I've promised Mattie—oops, beg your pardon, Sister Melanie—a visit soon. Let's do it! Kate's been hankering to get out of Tombstone and have a go at the tables in Tucson. She likes the big city lights. I'll take her, we'll have a week or so, and you can join me there. Then you and I can go back to Georgia. Kate won't mind. We've come to an understanding. She'd probably have a better time in Tucson without me, anyway."

Nell poured them each a small glass of Irish whiskey, they shook hands, and drank a toast to their vacation back east.

As Doc rose to leave, he heard Mike whisper to his Aunt Nell, "that man over there doesn't like your beans."

Nell shrugged. "Can't please everybody."

Doc stopped at the man's table on his way out, and introduced himself. It turns out the man was a salesman, often referred to as a whiskey drummer, and he'd heard of Doc Holliday. He went pale as Doc pulled out his pearl-handled pocket gun, and looked on in shock as Doc carefully stirred the bowl of beans with the nickel-plated barrel.

"I think you'll like those beans now," he purred, "and I mean every last one of them."

While Doc looked on, the poor man gobbled them down and scraped the bowl, proclaiming them to be the best beans he'd ever eaten.

John Holliday walked back to Fly's and his lodgings. He knew Kate would welcome the news of a change, even though it involved Nell Cashman.

On his way, he passed the vacant lot between the Harwood House and Fly's, and noticed John Montgomery painting a sign.

"Morning, John," Doc said with a tip of his hat.

"Morning, John," the painter replied with a grin as he waved his paintbrush in the air.

Doc went into his quarters, and John Montgomery finished painting the sign. It read: O. K. CORRAL.

14

IN TUCSON, OFTEN CALLED OLD

Pueblo, the Fiesta of San Augustin was at its full-blown, colorful and exciting best. It had begun as a memorial—a strictly religious event—to the original Cathedral of San Augustin in Spanish Colonial times, but over the years developed into an urban State Fair. Now there were roulette wheels, games of chuckaluck, seven up, and roll the dice, as well as shell games. Faro was played twenty-four hours a day. There was something to satisfy the desires of every gambler, but there were still plenty of *tiendas religiosas* where the devout could buy their scapulars and holy medals.

As a result of their intrusion following the Civil War, the Anglos now evenly matched the Mexican population, but the best Mexican food west of El Paso was still served there.

Doc and Kate ensconced themselves in the Porter Hotel located close to the Southern Pacific depot. After a noon breakfast, they'd stroll arm in arm through Levin Park, listening to the bands and watching the picnickers battle ants. Then they'd get into the gambling and sporting events, and for four days worked the tables with great success. Holliday would only play a short time at each table, pick up his winnings, and move on to another. No one suspected that this well-dressed gentleman with the lovely lady on his arm was a professional gambler, though few could match his skill at winning.

By the time they got into the liquor and the serious night games in the Broadway Avenue saloons, their daytime winnings would have dwindled considerably, but they didn't care. They were enjoying this little lark, and were glad to be away from the tensions in Tombstone, even for this short time.

On October 21, 1881, while "bucking at faro" in one of Levin Park's many tents, Doc was surprised to feel a tap on his shoulder and hear a familiar voice. It was Morgan Earp, who'd waited patiently until Doc played out his hand. Now he whispered in Doc's ear, "We need you in Tombstone. Better come this evening."

Doc turned to the dealer and said "I'm out." He gathered his winnings, motioned to Kate, and the three of them left.

As they hurried through the park, Doc spilled out the reason for his being there. In their haste, they failed to see a lame man in the company of two friars from the mission to the south. Doc accidentally knocked him down, and immediately stopped to apologize and extend his hand to the fallen man, who reached up and took it.

Doc was surprised at the strength of the man's grip, and his deep, resonant voice as he replied, "No harm done."

The man wore a black patch over one eye, and a deep scar ran along his cheek. It was a face Doc Holliday and his companions wouldn't soon forget.

One of the friars said in a light Andalusian accent, "We are taking the air, *caballero*. Our friend here has been ill."

"But not for much longer," the big man thundered.

Doc was anxious to be on his way, but took a moment to pull some of his winnings from his pocket and hand them to one of the friars. "Light some candles for me," he said as he hurried away, and added, "Take care of our friend here."

Morgan turned the conversation to the business at hand. "We need you, Doc. Warren's still in California and the Clantons and McLaurys are hanging around town talking fight. Ike has accused Wyatt of leaking the news that Ike was willing to sell out Crane, Leonard and Head for the reward. He's pissed to the gills, and calling for a showdown. Two days ago Ringo, Brocius, Claiborne and Stillwell tried to prod Virg into a shoot-out. They've got us outnumbered. Bob Paul's in San Francisco on Fargo business, and Leslie doesn't give a damn. The fuse is lit, and it's going to blow any minute. Wyatt wants you real bad."

⁂

The only train running to Benson that day was a freight. Doc urged Kate to stay put and enjoy the fiesta, saying he'd return soon on his way to Georgia. He emptied his pockets and handed her all of his cash, but she wouldn't take it.

"The best we can do from Benson is a buckboard to Tombstone, Kate. You're a lady. I just can't let you travel in an old cattle car, and then hours in a buckboard. My God, Kate," he chuckled, "you'd come home smelling like a cow."

"Who cares?" Kate laughed. "Sometimes you don't smell so good yourself."

Still laughing, the threesome hurried to the Porter House to get Doc's and Kate's belongings, and then to the depot.

At eleven o'clock on October 25, 1881, Tom McLaury and Ike Clanton rode into Tombstone in a spring wagon. They rolled into the Dexter stables where they knew Johnny Behan's partner, John Dunbar, would take good care of their horses and the wagon.

Tom was wearing a money belt with two thousand nine hundred twenty-three dollars and forty-five cents in it, a lot of money for a peaceful rancher to be carrying. Especially so because he and Ike walked directly to the Grand Hotel and began drinking. Not only did they lap it up at the Grand, but throughout the afternoon at just about every saloon within walking distance.

Drunk or sober, Ike Clanton had a big mouth, and he was flapping it all over town. He was indignant at being thought a Judas. It ate at him, and he protested all over the place that he hadn't volunteered to double-cross his friends and hand them over to the Earps for the reward money.

The story was no longer the secret it had been intended to be. Anyone that hadn't heard about it before now got it straight from the flannel-mouthed Ike. He said it was his intention to get the Earps out in the open so he could have the satisfaction—all by himself—of sending them one at a time to hell.

Tom McLaury, on the other hand, kept his drinking under control. He had a more practical plan for dealing with this situation. Some of the money in his belt was for paying James Kehoe, a butcher that he, as a cattleman, had done business with. The bulk of the cash was to ensure that the boys would be here when the big showdown took place. Right now he was looking for John Ringo and Curly Bill Brocius.

Toward late afternoon, Clanton and McLaury decided to go their separate ways. Tom returned to the Grand where most of his kind headquartered, thinking Curly Bill and Ringo might have taken a room there.

Ike's "curly wolf" was up. He decided that if Holliday wasn't in any of the saloons on Allan Street, he was probably slurping tea with that goody-goody, Nell Cashman. He made a beeline for the Russ House.

Nell was busy with preparations for the evening meal, and Mike Cunningham was helping set the tables. Everyone could hear, and smell, Ike even before he stormed through the doorway. A mixture of manure, sour breath, alcohol, and unwashed body permeated the dining room. He carried a Winchester rifle, and was shouting obscenities about Doc Holliday. It was lucky for him that Doc wasn't there.

"Casman," he bellowed, "where's that sonabitch Hol'day? I know he's aroun' here someplace sniffin' at yer skirts."

The few patrons who'd been lingering over coffee quietly got up and left.

"He's not here," Nell said in a stern voice.

"Hell he ain't," Ike retorted as he threw himself into a chair. "I'm stayin' right here 'til he shows his pasty face."

"Sir," Nell continued, "Doctor Holliday is in Tucson, and he's planning to go east from there."

"Damn, I hate a liar!" Clanton shouted as he waved the twenty-four inch barrel of his carbine at her. "He was in the Or'ental las' night with that slut o' his. Mebee yer jus' stupid, or yer hidin' him. Anyways, I'm waitin' right here."

Ike leaned back in his chair and put his feet on the table. He yawned loudly, and within seconds began to snore.

Nell quickly motioned Mike over, and whispered, "Go get Frank Leslie. He's probably at the Oriental. Hurry!"

Mike took off as if the devil himself were after him, and ran to the Oriental a block away. He went straight for the man behind the bar, ignoring the stares and "what's this's?" coming from the locals that occupied the bar stools.

"Mr. Leslie," Mike blurted, "Aunt Nell needs you right now."

"What for?" Leslie queried. "What's wrong?"

"There's a man there with a gun, and he's yelling at her."

Leslie grabbed his gun from beneath the bar and slipped it into his belt. He was out of the Oriental in a flash, with Mike right behind him.

As they came to the Russ House, Leslie motioned to Mike and a few curious onlookers who'd seen him pull and cock his pistol, to stay back. When he entered the dining room, Nell put her fingers to her lips and pointed toward Ike who was sprawled in his chair, still snoring like a disgruntled hog.

She didn't have to voice her thanks to Leslie for coming. The look on her face said it all.

"That man says he's looking for Doc Holliday," she said softly. "He says he knows he's here, and that he won't leave 'til Doc shows up. I happen to know that Doc is in Tucson."

Leslie shot her a curious look, then removed Ike's rifle from the table and went back to Nell.

"Let's have a cup," he said, indicating the table facing Clanton. He pulled out two chairs and laid the rifle across the table so the muzzle pointed straight at Ike's chest. Nell poured two mugs of steaming-hot coffee and they sat down.

"It's sure nice to get away from the bar and come to a quiet, peaceful place like this," Leslie said very seriously.

Even though Nell knew he was joking, she spouted, "Peaceful! The devil you say. I can't live on peaceful. That cockadoodledo has driven off my customers. He wouldn't believe me when I told him Doc was in Tucson."

"My dear Nell," Frank said as he took her hand in his, "Holliday was drinking at my bar last night, and he's probably in bed right now sleeping it off."

The moment he told her he regretted it, because he saw the look on her face go from total disbelief to disappointment as she sagged in her chair. Leslie couldn't know she was thinking of her planned trip to Georgia, and that her disappointment came from her knowing there'd be no trip, and no meeting Doc's cousin Mattie.

Frank was surprised at himself for the way he felt about her reaction. It really bothered him. More than that, even. It cut him to the quick. Though Frank Leslie was a married man, he was deeply in love with Nell Cashman.

He walked over to Ike's table and slammed the rifle butt against Ike's boots, knocking his feet to the floor. Ike awoke with a howl, but it turned into a moan as he realized he was looking down the awesome muzzle of his own .44-40 Winchester.

"God damn you, you son of a bitch!" Leslie hissed at him through clenched teeth. "Pull your pistol!"

Ike stared in amazement. His drunken slumber of a moment ago had turned into his worst nightmare. He stammered, "I got no quarrel with you, Leslie," and threw his arms up to protect his face.

"You do now," Frank snarled. "You ever come into this place again, or even think of speaking to this lady here, and I'll blow your stinking ass from here to Mexico! You got that?"

Ike stammered, "Yeah, yeah, I got it."

Leslie continued, "Hand over that hog's leg, and take your smelly carcass back to your cesspool."

Ike gingerly handed Frank his six-shooter and took off running, faster even than he knew he could.

Frank turned to Nell. "You did right to call me, but you're doing wrong when you truck with the likes of Doc Holliday. Keep away from him, Nell. Please."

Nell sighed. "Frank, I've a feeling something terrible is about to happen in this town. I just know it. There's too much hate, and too much nastiness going on.

Please try to stop it."

"It's none of my concern," Leslie replied flatly, and left the restaurant.

He felt uneasy about this encounter, especially because Nell seemed so distraught. Only Mike Cunningham was elated. He'd seen his hero in action, and knew there wasn't anything that could happen that Frank couldn't handle. He followed Frank out to the street, called to him, and waved. Leslie turned and waved back. Mike continued to watch as Leslie walked away, but didn't notice that Frank didn't turn in at the Oriental.

Frank continued walking at a brisk pace until he reached Fly's Boarding House. He stalked in. "Where's Holliday's room?" he demanded of Mollie, but instead of waiting for her answer he opened the register on the counter and ran his finger down the list of names until he came to Doc's.

He turned heel, strode down the hall, and threw the door to Doc's room open. Doc was in bed, alone. He sat up like a shot, yelling "What the hell?"

"Doc," Frank started in, "you keep yourself out of Nell Cashman's life. She's a lady, and you're nothing but a tramp. She's got enough problems taking care of her sister and raising her sister's kids. You're headed for boot hill, and right soon, 'cause if a bullet doesn't get you, the cough will."

"What's happened?" Doc questioned as he removed his hand from the cocked .38 Colt under his bed covers. He knew Leslie had just come to talk, and talk he did. He described the whole ugly scene with Ike Clanton, and told Doc he was the cause of it all. He reminded Doc of the dangerous position this put Nell, and her nephew, in. He hadn't threatened Doc, but his meaning was clear. Now he waited for Doc's reaction.

Doc reached up, scratched his head, and looked at Frank. "Frank, I'm sorry, truly sorry. I never intended to bring trouble to Miss Cashman. I never thought those damn cow thieves would bring this all into town."

Frank knew Doc was sincere, and for a fleeting moment was concerned that Doc was going to cry as he continued, "Other than Miss Nell, I only have one friend in this whole world, and that's Wyatt Earp."

"I know that," Leslie responded.

Doc continued, "I have a woman who loves me, but she's too much like me. We hang onto each other because no one else will. We both know it's got to end soon."

He coughed and reached for a cigar, and motioned for Frank to pour a couple drinks from the bottle on the bedside stand, then added, "Except for a long-lost cousin of mine, Nell's the only woman who will talk to me, and listen to me. God!" he murmured as he put his hands to his head, "if only it could be different."

He raised his head and looked straight into Frank's eyes. "If it could be, I'd have a practice, and I'd marry that woman if she'd have me. No wonder they call her the angel of the miners."

Leslie knew the feeling.

As he stood to leave, Frank took another drink and added, "Doc, do her a favor. Stay away from her."

Doc answered, "You do me a favor. Watch out for her. I'll take care of Ike Clanton."

Frank turned as Doc continued, "There's a showdown coming, and right soon. If Wyatt and I don't swing clear of it, we'll be in boot hill. And if we are, Frank, look after Nell."

Without answering him, Frank left the room.

Doc got up, reached for the bottle, and didn't bother with a glass. He upended the bottle and took a long swig, then dressed, checked the loads in his pistols, and placed one in his hip holster. The other went into his vest pocket holster. He knew Ike Clanton would likely be drinking somewhere in the tenderloin district, and if not there, then at one of his usual watering holes. He'd find him.

15

DOC HAD BUT ONE THOUGHT ON HIS
mind, and that was to find Ike Clanton and goad him into a fight. He checked out
Moses and Mehan's Saloon on Fifth and Fremont, but Ike wasn't there. As he
looked around and breathed in the familiar aroma, Doc decided to take the time
to lubricate his dry throat.

"Moses," he called as he slapped his cane on the bar, "let's have a drink."

This place was one of Doc's favorites, and Moses was one of the few
bartenders in town who knew how to handle him. He slid a full bottle of Old
Crow down the bar, and followed it with a couple of glasses. Doc liked that—no
nonsense.

Moses said heartily, "I'll have one with you, Doc, and it'll be on me."

Doc liked that even more. He always enjoyed having a drinking companion. Moses listened patiently to Doc's tirade against the world in general, and Ike
Clanton in particular. He empathized with this misguided gentleman of the old
south.

Doc took no offense when Moses would leave him alone while he took
care of other customers, just as long as he left a bottle close at hand. As the
evening progressed and the contents of the bottle dwindled, Doc mellowed. He
got to rolling the dice with the barflies, and winning small change. It made him
feel good. Then Joe Pascholy joined in.

Doc asked him if he'd seen Ike Clanton, and Joe said he'd seen him over
on Sixth Street going into Mme. LaDeau's Parlour for Men.

That was all Doc needed to hear. He looked around and gave an exaggerated flourish with his arm, saying "Gentlemen, y'all been most gracious this
evening. I'd linger longer, but urgent business draws me elsewhere." He settled
his bill, and once out the door a flurry of speculation made the rounds among
those he left behind. They all agreed there would likely be a hot time in the old
town that night.

Mme. LaDeau's Parlour for Men on Sixth Street—as were almost all the brothels—was one of a chain throughout the southwest owned by a French organization. Kate occasionally picked up a few bucks there when Doc was involved in an all-night card game, and frequently brought home more money than he did. All the ladies there knew Doc, and liked him for his gentlemanly ways when he was sober. But when he was drunk, they knew him to be unpredictable and often mean, the mood he was in tonight.

Lizette, who was called The Flying Nymph, greeted Doc as he walked in. She'd gotten that label from her daring act at the Bird Cage Theater, which she'd left to join up with Mme. LaDeau because she could earn more than at the Bird Cage.

The fragrance of her perfume trailed after her as she came up to Doc and gave him a welcoming kiss.

"How nice to see you, Doctor Holliday," she purred. It was obvious that Doc was in a bad mood, and she knew the best thing to do at the moment was to get him a drink.

"I'll bet you can use a tall, cool one," she said soothingly as she took his hand and led him to the small, stand-up bar in the parlor.

"One more won't stop me from catching Clanton," he thought, and answered with a quick smile.

Lizette poured a drink, laced it with a little sugar, and garnished it with a sprig of mint. She handed it to Doc, saying, "If you're looking for Kate, she's not here tonight."

"I'm not looking for Kate. I'm looking for a lowdown polecat named Ike Clanton. I heard he's here."

"Oh, no, no, no, Doctor," she protested, "we don't allow that man in here. He's uncouth, and he smells. He's not welcome here."

Doc knew she was telling the truth. "Damn," he growled, and pushed his glass over for a refill.

⁂

Ike had returned to the Grand Hotel and checked into a room. He'd been shaken by the encounter with Frank Leslie, but now that the danger was past his confidence was returning. He stretched out on the bed, intent on finishing the nap that Buckskin Leslie had so rudely interrupted.

"Hell," he said aloud, "I was only funnin' with that woman. Just wait'l

Ringo, an' Curly Bill, an' the McLaurys, an' Spence, an' Stillwell, an' my brother Billy, an' whoever else Tom comes up with get here. We'll make spaghetti sauce out'a those city dudes. It'll be fun. An' daddy," he added looking up at the ceiling, "we'll do them for you." Then he dozed off.

But his excitement was running too high, and real sleep eluded him. He got up after a couple hours of shuteye, feeling refreshed and cocky.

Still talking to himself, he continued, "What I need is a little action. A few hands at the Alhambra, an' mebbe a coupl'a drinks. The boys'll be comin' into town, an' mebbe we'll all get together and have some laughs. Hell, mebbe we'll run into that Earp bunch an' clean 'em all out."

He reached for his guns as he was getting ready to leave, and exploded, "Shit! That fancy asshole Leslie took my guns. Now what in hell am I supposed ta do?"

He quieted down for a couple minutes while he contemplated a plan of action. "I'll get some more at Spangenberg's, that's what I'll do." Then he brightened, pleased with himself to have come up with an even better solution. "Don't need ta do that! The boys'll prob'bly have extras."

Ike stepped into the clear, chilly night and looked up at the sky until he found the brightest star. "Daddy," he said, "it won't be long now."

He detoured over to the Dexter stables to see if any of the boys' horses were there. They weren't. Then he walked over to the O.K. Corral. Still no sign of his friends. "They'll be here," he said confidently, and continued on to the Alhambra "where the latch string is always on the outside," meaning it was open twenty-four hours a day.

The Alhambra was unique in that its bar separated the saloon from the lunchroom.

Ike was feeling a bit hungry, and decided to have a sandwich before getting involved in a game, so went directly to a table. He was half through a ham and Swiss cheese sandwich, washing it down with a mug of beer, when all of a sudden he spotted Doc Holliday sitting at the bar.

Ike got up to leave just as Doc turned in his direction. The load of booze Doc was carrying didn't slow him down one bit as he made straightaway for Clanton. Ike looked around, hoping to find any kind of help, but there was none. He knew he was in a spot as bad as bad gets when he also saw Morgan Earp sitting at the bar, talking to the barkeep.

"Shit!" Ike groaned. He knew he was in enemy territory. Even worse was what he didn't see. Finishing off a meal, hidden by a potted plant, was Wyatt Earp.

Doc shouted, "You damned son of a bitch cowboy! I hear you're going to kill me! Get out your gun and commence!"

Clanton, scared out of his wits, bleated, "I ain't got a gun. Frank Leslie took it." And to prove it he opened his coat.

"You abused Nell Cashman," Doc spat at him.

Ike blustered, "I only went there askin' fer ya."

"Yeah, and you left your stink all over the place. You want me for what? You got a booger up your nose, blow it out!"

"You been tellin' lies that I'm double-crossin' my frens!"

"So what?" Doc retorted. "The whole town knows you for the double-dealing son of a bitch you are."

Clanton was clever enough to know that without a gun, neither Doc nor the Earps would dare shoot him, at least not in front of witnesses, and it gave him the courage to smartmouth.

"Sure, Wheezie, I had a deal goin', but it weren't ta get any of my frens kilt. It was to get you bastards out in the open so's I could make coyote food outta ya."

Doc was livid, and shot back, "All it got you was your old man dead, and I was the one that did it!" He grabbed a fistful of Clanton's collar. "You hear that, boy? It was me that did in your old man!"

He pulled his nickle-plated Colt from his shoulder holster and shouted, "Here, take it!"

Clanton cringed.

"Use it! I'll use this one!" Doc added as he let go of Ike's collar and put his hand on the gun in his belt.

Clanton went pale. "Please don't shoot me, Doc," he pleaded.

Morgan Earp leaped over the bar and grabbed Doc's arm. "Not here, Doc," he said sternly, then whispered in his ear, "you're drunk. Go home and sleep it off."

Wyatt helped Morgan hustle Doc to the street.

"Wheezie," Doc grumbled, "he called me Wheezie." He coughed hard. "That son of a bitch. He shouldn't have called me that."

True to their tradition, the Earp brothers were rarely far apart, and Virgil was shortly on the scene. Clanton was trying to slip away from the Alhambra, and when he saw Virgil whined, "Don't shoot me in the back."

"Get out of here, Clanton," Virgil roared, "or I'll arrest you for sassing an officer of the law."

Virgil gave him a shove and sent him heading in the direction of the Grand Hotel.

"And you, Doc," he added in a gentler tone, "I might have to haul you in if you don't go home and sober up. We got laws, you know."

Doc weaved his way back to Kate at Fly's Boarding House. A passerby heard him muttering, "Wheezie. He called me Wheezie."

Wyatt walked to the Eagle Brewery where he'd had a faro game going. He watched as it came to a close, settled with the dealer and the saloon keeper, and stepped out into the still night. He lit a cigar. Two hours had passed since Doc's confrontation with Clanton, and Wyatt was surprised to see Ike walking toward him. He could see that Ike was now armed. There was a six-shooter in plain sight in his belt, and he was carrying a Winchester rifle. He also appeared to be carrying an extra load of "Dutch courage."

Wyatt drew back into the shadows, touching the gun in his overcoat pocket. But Clanton had spotted Wyatt, and called out, "I wanna talk ta ya."

Wyatt eased out and replied, "Talk," as he glanced quickly at the rooftops and windows of the nearby buildings.

Ike was back to his loudmouthed, belligerent self again. "When Hol'day came at me back at the 'Hambra, I wasn't fixed jes right. Now I am. In the mornin', I'm gonna have it out with him, jes me an' him. I'm tired a talkin'. I wanna finish it." Ike smirked at Wyatt. He was real pleased with himself.

Wyatt answered, "Ike, why fight anybody? There's no money in fighting. If I can avoid a fight, I will. So should you."

That was true, especially now. None of the Earps wanted a gun fight when things were going so well for them. They were on friendly terms with Mayor John Clum; they all had positions in the field of law enforcement; Wyatt's pursuit of Sarah Marcus had progressed to the point of commitment; and their various gambling interests were paying off. Life was too good to muck it up with a common and possibly deadly street brawl.

"Makes no sense, Ike. No money in it at all," Wyatt continued.

Ike moved his gun belt around so his six-shooter showed big and plain. "I aim ta make a fight tomorra' mornin' with Hol'day an' you an' all the rest of 'em. An' don't think fer a minute I won't! Me'un my frens."

"Go home, Ike, you talk too much for a fighting man," Wyatt said as he walked away. But he kept his hand on his gun.

Clanton was feeling lucky. After that bad start with Frank Leslie, he now felt he was back in control. Hadn't he talked Holliday down, took on the whole

Earp clan, and just now given that Dodge City cop, Wyatt Earp, a piece of his mind?

Talk about luck. He looked into the Occidental Saloon and saw his old pals, Tom McLaury and Johnny Behan, playing poker with another fellow he didn't know. But the real surprise was the man dealing the cards. It was Virgil Earp!

"Jeez," Ike thought, "could Tom have bought off the chief of police?"

He walked in and ordered a drink as he pulled up a chair to join the players, and spotted a fully cocked Colt on Virgil's lap. It didn't seem to matter. The conversation was light, as were the stakes. Nothing to get steamed about; yet Ike was in a steamy mood, and it wasn't long before he was back to beefing about Doc Holliday.

While he fumed, the others played cards. For all his mouthing off, no one was paying him heed. He got louder and more belligerent, and began to work the Earp brothers into his tirade, despite knowing that Virgil's pistol was at the ready. He began to gloat about what was in store for them tomorrow when he and his friends taught them all a lesson. Johnny Behan was kicking him under the table in an effort to shut him up, and Tom McLaury was elbowing him in the ribs for the same purpose. Ike wasn't the least put off, and continued to throw the drinks down and make threats.

It was six-fifteen in the morning when the game ended. The players cashed in their chips and left the Occidental. McLaury and Behan walked off in the direction of the Grand Hotel, and Virgil went west to his house. Ike followed him, still slicing the air with his foul mouth.

He called out to Virgil, "I want ya ta carry a message ta Hol'day. That damn sonabitch has got ta fight."

Virgil turned and looked at Ike with disgust. "Ike, I'm an officer of the law, and I don't want to hear any more such talk. I'm going home now and to bed, and I don't want you raising any disturbance while I'm there."

Ike thought Virgil was making light of him, and he didn't like it one bit. He lurched ahead of Virgil, shouting, "Ya won't carry my message?"

"No, of course I won't," Virgil answered, and turned away.

Ike was furious, and bellowed angrily, "Ya may have ta fight afore ya know it."

Virgil just continued walking.

Ike was really frustrated. No one would listen to him. Then he saw Ned Boyle, a barkeep at the Oriental, who was on his way home after all-night duty.

Ike staggered and swaggered up to him, and boasted, "Ned, make sure yer up an' out in a few hours. There's goin' ta be one helluva ruckus. Soon's Hol'day an' the Earps show theirselves on the street, the ball will open."

Ned reached out and closed Ike's coat, saying, "Ike, you know the law about guns. Yours are out here for all to see."

"An' tha's where they're gonna stay 'til those sonsabitches are eatin' Boot Hill dirt! Le's have a drink."

"Can't do that, Ike. I'm on my way home to get some shuteye. You do the same. Just take it easy."

"The hell you say," Ike smirked, and went on down Allen Street to Kelly's Wine House.

He plunked himself down next to Joe Stump, who was having his morning toddy, and ordered one for himself.

"You seen any o' that Earp clan this mornin'? They got the drop on me las' night when I wasn't heeled. They an' that damn Hol'day insulted me. They knew I didn't have a piece, so they insulted me."

Stump, and Julius Kelly who was sitting on a bar stool nearby, weren't looking for trouble, and just let Ike prattle on. This led Ike to believe he had an interested audience, and he warmed to his subject.

"You bet," he grinned as he tapped the revolver in his belt, "with this here li'l toy I intend ta drill all of 'em a new asshole. Shit! They'll be messin' their pants all over the place afore I'm done with 'em," and he got such a kick out of this witticism that he slapped his thigh and guffawed loudly.

One by one the other patrons at Kelly's had quietly slipped out, and when Ike finally realized his audience was gone he left for R. F. Hafford's Saloon down the street, and continued his threats there.

⁂

The citizens of Tombstone cared about their community, and helped their neighbors when they were in need. So at eight forty-five in the morning, Wyatt Earp was awakened by an excited Ned Boyle, who blurted out, "A little while ago I met Ike Clanton on Allen Street. He was waving a Winchester around and making all sorts of threats. He said that as soon as those damned Earps make their appearance on the street today, the ball will open."

"Was he alone?" Wyatt asked.

"Yes, but he said 'we're here to make a fight. We're looking for the sons of bitches'. By "we" I believe him to mean a gang of cowboys will be joining him."

Wyatt thanked him, and Ned left.

At about the same time Andy Bronk, a city policeman, woke Allie Earp and asked to see Virgil. Allie showed him into the bedroom, where he related to Virgil the talk that had been going around.

"You'd better get up," he said, "there's liable to be hell. Ike Clanton has threatened to kill Doc Holliday the minute he shows up, and he's counting you and your brothers in on it, too."

Virgil listened, but dismissed it as whiskey talk. "I'll catch a few more winks, and then come on in. I suspect Ike will be long gone and sleeping it off."

But when Joe Stump, and then Rod Safford, showed up at both Wyatt's and Virgil's homes, they knew their sleep was over. They got up, went through their usual morning rituals, and on downtown.

Around noon, Mollie Fly was tending to the potted plants in her parlor, when a loud thumping came from the direction of the reception room. She hurried in and was appalled to see a drunken man swaying in the doorway. His clothes were filthy, and he was a mess. She could see the pistol in his belt, and he was brandishing a Winchester rifle.

"I'm lookin' fer that devil's asshole, Doc Hol'day," he slurred as he weaved his way right up to Mollie. "You jus' tell me where he is, an' don' be goin' sulky on me."

Mollie stood firm, and replied in a clear, strong voice, "He hasn't come home yet. I think he's downtown."

"If that don' beat all," Clanton said to no one in particular. "Him 'n me walkin' aroun' town, an' I can't find the sonabitch!"

Mollie was surprised, but mighty happy, when Ike tipped his hat, said "Thank ya, ma'am," and lurched out.

The truth was, Mollie knew Doc was in his room, and had been most of the night. She headed straight to it, and tapped on the door. Kate opened it a little way and peeked out.

"There was a nasty man here looking for Doctor Holliday," she told Kate. "He was waving a rifle around, and didn't sound like a friend, so I told him no one was home."

"Thank you, Mollie," Kate said, and closed the door. She walked to the bed and looked down at Doc. He was sleeping—the most peaceful thing he ever did.

"Doc, wake up," Kate urged, gently shaking his shoulder. "Ike Clanton was here looking for you. Mollie said he had a rifle with him."

Doc patted Kate on the cheek, and whispered, "If God will let me live long enough to get my clothes on, he'll see me, all right."

He got up and dressed in his usual meticulous fashion, as though headed for an important social function. Then he checked his gun, picked up his cane, and opened the door. To Kate, who had stood silently watching, he said, "I won't be here to take you to breakfast, so you just go on alone."

Kate knew he wouldn't be seeing that Cashman woman, but honestly wished he was going to.

Cold air had come down from the north during the night, and the morning air was brisk, making Doc's breathing easier. He flourished his cane as he strode out, passed the entrance to the O. K. Corral, and proceeded downtown.

16

WEDNESDAY, OCTOBER 26, 1881, WAS A
cold day. People were bundled up and moving briskly as they went about their
business.

Mike Cunningham had just finished sweeping in front of his Aunt Nell's
hotel. He was burning with curiosity about the fight talk that had been circulat-
ing around town, and wanted to see for himself what was going on. All he had to
do was get Nell to agree to let him off for a while, and to do that he had to play
his cards right.

He cleaned off his shoes and went to Nell's office at the back of the Russ
House, where she was busy working on her records.

"I've got it all done, Aunt Nell," Mike said almost too cheerfully. "Think
I'll just take a walk over to Father Gallagher's and see what Carlos is doing. I
won't be gone long."

Nell wasn't fooled. "Hold it right there, young man. I don't want you poking around the saloons and gambling halls. I hear there's bad blood down there,
and I don't want any of it spilled on you. The way that dirty man talked yesterday, I do believe there could be real trouble today. You'd better stay here."

"Aw, Aunt Nell, please let me go," he pleaded. "I promise I won't go that
way. I'll keep my eyes and ears open, and stay out of trouble. I promise. Please
let me go."

Nell herself was anxious to learn what was going on between Ike Clanton
and Doc Holliday. "Oh, all right, but stay clear of the saloons and gambling
halls, like I said. And keep an eye out for Doctor Holliday. Let me know right
away if you see him."

"Okay!" Mike chortled, and headed for the door.

By noon, Ike Clanton was back at Hafford's, still going strong. He actually believed that Holliday and the Earps had been scared off by his bluster the night before, and told Roderick Hafford, whom everyone called Colonel, the insults and abuse that they had heaped on him.

"An' all, Colonel, jus' 'cause Frank Leslie highjacked my weapons. They wouldn'a dared come at me the way they did if I was heeled." He made a show of his rifle and pistol. "This ball was s'posed to open 'afore noon, an' here it's five minutes past, a'ready."

Colonel Hafford knew Ike was trying to convince himself of his own bravery. Anyone in their right mind wouldn't want to come up against the Earps or Holliday, especially if they were on the prowl for them.

He stroked his long, white beard and said soothingly, "It's ten past, Ike. You ought to go home and get a little shuteye."

Hafford couldn't believe that Clanton was still full of fight, what with his drinking and carousing all night. "Nothing will come of this, Ike. I reckon you got in the last word."

Half jubilant, half let down, Ike muttered, "Guess so," and made his way down to the post office a couple doors away. He tensed when he saw a man walking toward him, and was relieved to see it was only Mayor John Clum on his way to the Grand Hotel for lunch.

When the mayor saw Ike's guns right out in the open, he said jokingly, "Hello, Ike. Any new war?" He chuckled and continued on.

Virgil Earp had spotted Ike, slipped up behind him, and grabbed his Winchester. Startled, Ike let go of the rifle and went for his six-gun. Virgil slammed him across the head with his Colt, and Ike went down. Then Virgil wrenched Ike's pistol from his hand, and pulled him to his feet, asking, "You hunting for me?"

Ike snarled, "If I'd a seen ya a secon' sooner, I'd a kilt ya." He spoke the truth. Just before Virgil grabbed him, Ike had spotted Wyatt coming his way. The thought of throwing down on Wyatt and finishing it right then was just too much. He got so excited he was blinded to other danger, and now here he was, a prisoner of the law, and Wyatt was standing there beside Virgil.

"You'd have killed Virgil, Ike?" Wyatt asked. "Not likely."

Just then Morgan walked up.

"The whole damn Earp army," Ike groaned.

They hustled him off to Justice Wallace's courtroom a block and a half away, and Wyatt was not too gentle as he pushed and prodded the drunken Clanton.

Knowing that everyone's guns were holstered and there was no danger of a bullet coming his way, Ike began shooting off his mouth again. He bragged to Justice Wallace that if Earp had been just a second later, there'd have been a coroner's inquest in town.

"So you said," Wyatt responded. "So you said."

"Jus' r'member," Ike went on. "Fight's my racket. You boys better keep that in mind."

Justice Wallace wasn't impressed. "City Ordinance Number nine, Section one: Carrying deadly weapons within the city limits. Twenty-seven dollars and fifty cents fine."

Wyatt's jaw was tightening. Looking at Ike, he said, "You're a thief and a son of a bitch. You want shooting, you'll get all you can handle."

Emboldened now that Justice Wallace was looking on, Ike challenged Wyatt. "I'll get even with all a ya fer this. If I had a six-shooter now, I'd make a fight with all a ya."

"If you want to make a fight that bad, I'll give you this one," Morgan said and offered Ike his own revolver.

Ike started to go for it when a deputy of the court, R. J. Campbell, pushed him back. "We'll have none of that here in the court," he admonished Ike.

Ike made a big show of counting out the money for his fine, when Virgil spoke up. "Clanton, I'll pay your fine if you'll just settle with us right now."

Ike kept his mouth shut.

Morgan, tired of all the talk, told Ike, "I'll take your guns over to the Grand and leave them there until you leave town."

The proceedings broke up and Clanton left after tossing out one more threat. "I'll see ya after I get through here. I only want four feet a ground ta fight on."

Wyatt was at his boiling point. "I think I'd be justified in shooting you down any place I should meet you, but if you're anxious to make a fight I'll go anywhere on earth to make one with you, even over to the San Simon among your crowd."

Ike got in the last word. "That won' be nec'sary. My crowd is a'ready here." He left and headed for the Grand Hotel.

Wyatt watched him go, then started out for Hafford's where he could have a good smoke, get away from all this petty bickering, and calm down.

The first person he saw was Tom McLaury. He was coming on fast and was obviously steamed. "What the hell is going on around here? You have no right to toss Ike around like you have. If you want to make a fight, I'll make a fight with you anywhere."

This was not a good time to be challenging Wyatt Earp. He'd had enough.

"All right, then, make a fight right here!" As he said it, he slapped McLaury in the face with his left hand, and drew his pistol with his right. "Pull your gun and use it!"

If Tom had had an advantage, he knew he'd lost it. He just stood there with his mouth open and his hand as far from his gun as he could get it.

A disgusted Wyatt Earp hit him on the head with his Colt, and continued on to Hafford's.

Ike Clanton, left to himself, sauntered over to Doctor Gillingham's office to have his head wound tended to. The doctor told him that despite the heavy bleeding, it was just a flesh wound, and after bandaging it sent Ike on his way.

More help for Ike reined in at the Grand Hotel where Doc Holliday had just finished downing a few. As he stepped outside, he came face to face with two horsemen: Ike Clanton's brother Billy, and Frank McLaury. Doc reached out his hand to Billy, saying with a smile, "Nice to see you, Billy," and immediately went on his way.

Why Doc shook hands with the brother of the man he'd vowed to kill, only Doc knew. Perhaps he wanted to show that his quarrel was with Ike, and not Billy.

Ike came down the walk toward the Grand, wearing a scowl on his face. He'd fully expected to see a veritable army of cowboys, and was disappointed. But Billy and Frank were a welcome sight. Frank was known to be mighty handy with firearms, and was a good man to have at one's back.

"Damn, Ike, what the hell'd you run into?" Billy queried.

"Those stinkin' Earps snuck up on me an' took my guns, an' then they beat me up," Ike whined.

He needed their sympathy, and they gave it to him. Together they went into the bar at the Grand, the two riders to wash down the trail dust, and Ike to get some "hair of the dog."

Ike inquired as to the whereabouts of Billy Claiborne and Ringo. "Shit, I thought they'd be here. Claiborne said he was comin', an' Spence an' Stillwell. Where the hell are they?"

Frank shrugged his shoulders. "They should be here by now. I sent Claiborne the word, but you tell me, where's Tom?"

At that moment the sorry-looking Tom showed up. He'd also been to Doctor Gillingham to get his head bandaged. The doc was having a busy day.

Tom's story duplicated Ike's. Hate permeated the air. Then Billy Claiborne came riding in, and the odds got as good as they were going to get.

Claiborne brought unwelcome news to his friends. "Ringo's gone to San Jose in California to visit his sisters, so he won't be here. He told me he didn't think things would come to a head until Curly got back from Mexico."

Clanton didn't like that, and neither did the McLaurys. Curly Bill in Mexico, probably on some cattle deal, and Ringo in California sucking up to his sisters! Not the way it was supposed to be.

Frank, without a doubt the most level-headed of the group, shook his head. "That's it, boys. It's off. When we take those sons of bitches, I want to do it right. I want it so they won't know what hit them. A week or two more won't matter. Let's get the hell out of here."

"Shit!" Billy Claiborne retorted. "I come riding here looking for some action. We got them outnumbered. We can take them."

At that moment, Billy figured he could get away with most anything. Just the week before, he'd shot and killed James Hickey in Charleston, and had been acquitted.

Ike Clanton rubbed his head. "Do what ya want. I'm goin' after Hol'day. He's had his las' say ta me. You boys don' wanna throw in with me, so be it, but I aim ta get my man t'day."

That said, he tossed down a double shot.

Tom's head hurt. He said, "I don't feel so good."

But Billy Clanton was full of fight. He didn't give a hoot how Tom's head felt. "They kilt my pa, and I aim ta kill 'em!" he boasted.

"Believe it," echoed Ike.

Tom rubbed his head. "Okay. Guess I owe them something myself."

Frank was being voted down, but he wasn't all that opposed to a show-down. He remembered the goose egg he'd carried around for a week from a gun whipping just like his brother and Ike had gotten.

"Okay," he agreed, "but we'll do it smart-like. We outnumber them, but we'll take them one at a time. I know that Holliday comes back to Fly's before the night games. He likes to change clothes or something like that. Maybe he's filling his pockets with marked cards. Who knows? We'll wait for him next door at the O. K. He's made enough threats against Ike that nobody'll blame us. Then we'll wait and see what the Earps come up with."

Ike was jumping for joy. "That sonabitch," he chortled.

Frank took charge. "Billy, you get down to Dexter's Corral and keep an eye on Fly's. It's right across the street, and you can see when Holliday comes in. We'll pick up another pistol for Ike at Spangenberg's and get some more cartridges for ourselves. We'll meet you at Dexter's. And Ike, no more drinks 'til we're done."

Frank and Tom McLaury, and Ike Clanton, walked west on Allen and turned north on Fourth Street. Claiborne continued down Allen to Dexter's.

⚜

Wyatt Earp was standing in the doorway at Hafford's, smoking a cigar and relaxing. He said nothing as the three cowboys passed him and proceeded north to Spangenberg's Gun Shop. He was totally unafraid of them, believing they'd been subdued by the whipping he and Virgil had given them, and was partially correct.

Wyatt was actually looking for an opportunity to open the ball, as Ike had called it. He felt that he alone could collar the three of them and put them in jail for carrying weapons within the town limits. He saw an opportunity when Frank McLaury's horse, which had been following the threesome, clomped up onto the wood plank sidewalk, and stuck its head into the gun shop. Wyatt stepped up, took hold of the bridle, and backed the horse into the street.

The three cowboys came out in a hurry. Billy had his hand on his pistol, but it was Frank who did the talking.

"Not yet, Billy," he warned, and then to Wyatt, "That's my horse."

"I know it is. You know the ordinance about horses being on the sidewalks."

Frank saw that Wyatt's hand was inside his coat by his left shoulder. He took the reins from Wyatt and tied his horse to a post. With a dozen or so townsfolk looking on, Frank knew this wasn't the time to make a play.

He tipped his hat to Wyatt. "We're leaving town. Just filling up our belts."

Since the weapons ordinance didn't apply when someone was leaving town, Wyatt could only watch as the three made their purchases and left.

⚜

The two Billys—Clanton and Claiborne—watched for Holliday from the Dexter-Dunbar livery, but he was nowhere to be seen. Instead, along came the

McLaurys and Ike Clanton. The five of them were deep in discussion when their friend, Wes Fuller, joined them. The odds were getting better.

"We kin take 'em all," Ike said confidently.

They crossed over to the O. K. Corral, hoping to surprise Holliday, and were talking over their plan to kill Holliday, Virgil, and Wyatt. So intense was their discussion that they were practically upon a stranger passing by before they noticed him, and they quickly lowered their voices.

The gentleman who had chanced upon their conversation was H. F. Sills, an engineer for the Atchinson, Topeka and Santa Fe Railroad.

He'd heard enough to convince himself these men were up to no good, including a boast by one of them that, "We'll kill that damn Virgil Earp on sight." Another had chimed in, "We'll kill the whole Earp party when we see them."

For a brief moment Sills feared for his own safety, because he had observed the younger of the three men put his hand on his gun. He quickly crossed the street and hurried on toward town. Sills was new to Tombstone, and didn't recognize any of the names he had heard.

A small crowd was gathered at Hafford's corner, talking excitedly. Sills asked one of them who the Earps were, and where he could find them. They pointed Virgil out to him, and Sills got his attention right off when he told him of the threats he'd heard as he passed the Dexter and O. K. corrals. Virgil had just been alerted about his brother Wyatt's confrontation with Frank McLaury, and though Morgan and Wyatt were close at hand he had no way of knowing how many men were waiting for them. A friendly bystander had told him he'd heard talk of other cowboys riding in. Not a pleasant prospect. It was unfortunate that Wyatt's good friends and former peace officers, Bat Masterson and Luke Short, had recently returned to Dodge City. The Earps were on their own.

Doc Holliday strode up at that moment, foiling Frank McLaury's plan to ambush him that day.

Virgil slipped into the Wells Fargo office, unlocked the gun rack, and took down a ten-gauge double-barrel shotgun.

"Here, Doc," he said. "Slip this under your coat." As Doc did, he handed Virgil his cane. Then the three Earp brothers and Doc Holliday walked up Fourth Street together.

⁂

A woman's voice called out, "John, don't go down there." It was Nell

Cashman. She was standing with the curious onlookers and Mike Cunninghan, who had only minutes before brought her the news of the impending showdown.

"Don't do it, John, don't do it."

Wyatt looked over at his longtime friend.

"This isn't your fight, Doc."

He'd given Doc an honorable way out, but Doc answered, "That's a hell of a thing for you to say to me."

Nell watched the four men as they continued walking toward the O. K. Corral.

17

THE O. K. CORRAL TOOK UP CLOSE TO

half a city block. It was bordered by Third and Fourth streets running north and south, and by Allen and Fremont streets running east and west. The rear doors of houses and business establishments fronting these streets faced the corral, and several alleyways between them led from the streets into the stable area.

Fly's Gallery and Boarding House was on Fremont Street two doors west of Third Street, and W. A. Harwood's frame house was on the corner of Third and Fremont. Between these two buildings there was a vacant lot, often used as an entrance to the O. K. Corral.

It was Wednesday, a little after two in the afternoon, and six men huddled in the vacant lot deep in conversation. They were Frank and Tom McLaury, Ike and Billy Clanton, Wes Fuller, and Billy Claiborne. All were armed and dangerous. A seventh man hurried down Fremont Street and joined them. It was John Behan.

"Where's Ringo and Curly?", he asked.

"They ain't here," Ike answered, and then asked, "Where the hell are Spence an' Stillwell? They're supposed ta be here."

Behan bit his lower lip. "They're still in court in Tucson. I couldn't get them off. Shit," he grumbled, "this isn't the time."

"Any time's good 'nuf fer me," Ike boasted.

"We've got them outnumbered," Frank added.

"You can't count on me, boys," Behan said, backing off. "As sheriff, it's best I stay out of it, and give you boys the benefit of the law when it's all over."

Tom jumped in, saying "We can still take them." His head was beginning to feel better, and his fighting juices were flowing again, now that the group was together.

"I don't like it," Behan responded. He thought for a moment, then added, "I'll go talk to the Earps. I'll throw them off." He warmed to his idea. "I'll tell them you're unarmed."

This was typical of the devious Behan. He figured he'd come out on top no matter which way it went. Wyatt would either be dead or in prison, and wouldn't Miss Josephine Sarah Marcus stew over that! Likewise Virgil and Morgan. That would pretty much leave the law in Tombstone in his hands. As for Doc Holliday, he didn't care, and didn't think anyone else would, either.

"You boys stay here. I'll go talk to them."

As he started down Fourth Street he turned and called back, "Keep your guns under cover."

When the Earps and Holliday rounded the corner of Fourth Street and turned west on Fremont, they saw the cowboys and John Behan. Behan left the group and came toward them, saying to Virgil, who was in the lead, "For God's sake, don't go down there. You'll get murdered." He said it loud enough so on-lookers would later report that he tried to keep the peace.

"I'm going to disarm them," Virgil growled, and kept on walking.

As Doc, Wyatt and Morgan drew nearer, Behan said just loud enough for all four of them to hear, "I've disarmed them. There's no danger."

These words had the effect Behan hoped for. He saw Wyatt take his pistol from beneath his coat and put it in his pocket. Virgil also relaxed. He shoved his six-shooter deep into the waistband of his pants, and put Doc's walking stick in his shooting hand.

Behan figured those guns wouldn't be coming out too fast, and as Doc and the Earps continued on, he followed at a distance.

Doc expected there would be gun play, and as they neared Fly's it dawned on him that Kate would be there and could be put in danger. He whispered his concern to Morgan, who was at his side.

Morgan nodded. "All the more reason to let them have it."

"You're right," Doc replied.

This was not what Virgil and Wyatt wanted. They had too good a thing going for them in Tombstone, and wanted to stay there. Wyatt was hitting it big with his gambling ventures, and owned some promising mining rights. Virgil, as chief of police, was doing well collecting fines, in addition to being a deputy United States marshal and tax collector. He also owned mining rights and other properties. Their objective was to buffalo the cowboys, humiliate them, and run them out of Tombstone forever.

When the cowboys spotted the Earp party they retreated farther into the vacant lot. The corner of Fly's Boarding House gave them momentary conceal-ment as they backed up against the Harwood house. Billy Clanton was closest to the sidewalk. Tom McLaury was on his right, and Frank McLaury was on Tom's right. Ike Clanton had stayed at the corner of Fly's building, where he'd be the least visible to the men walking toward them.

Wes Fuller decided that now was a good time to get lost, so he moved deeper into the lot and slipped through Fly's back door. He was out of it.

Billy Claiborne—he who thought he was another Billy the Kid—conjured up a mental picture of his own death. This wasn't what he wanted at all, and he followed right on Wes's heels.

Virgil led his party into the lot and faced the cowboys. He saw immediately that Frank McLaury and Billy Clanton had their hands on their six-shooters. Tom McLaury's horse had followed him in, and Tom had his hand on the Winchester hanging from the saddle.

The seasoned lawman nevertheless stopped and called out, "Boys, throw up your hands. I want your guns."

He emphasized his demand by raising Doc's cane above his head. As a gunfighter, he was at his most vulnerable right then. There was a brief silence, followed by the unmistakable sound of six-shooters being cocked.

Now Virgil also raised his left arm, shouting, "Hold on, I don't want that." It was meant for both sides, and both sides ignored him.

Billy Clanton's six-shooter, thumbed to full cock, was out of its holster and leveled at Wyatt. Virgil, with both arms in the air, didn't pose an immediate threat to him.

Morgan was standing slightly in front of Doc Holliday, so Doc also posed no immediate threat to Billy. Wyatt was the one he wanted out of this fight, and quickly.

As these thoughts were racing through Billy's head and down to his trigger finger, Wyatt was making his own assessment of the situation. He knew that Frank McLaury was the one to deal with, because he was the best shot of the bunch. Wyatt chose to ignore Billy. He jerked the pistol from his coat pocket.

Doc Holliday had positioned himself behind Morgan where he could see into the lot as well as into the window of Room Four at Fly's. The terror-stricken Kate and the equally terrified Mollie Fly were looking out at him.

Doc literally went berserk at the sight of Kate, his lover and companion, in the center of a shoot-out she had nothing to do with. He experienced a flash of love for this woman—who had rescued him from a lynch mob, and who had put up with his ill humor and ill health for years—which burned more intensely than the flame that erupted from his double-barreled shotgun. A load of number twelve buckshot blew a gaping hole in Tom McLaury's side, and he staggered about thirty feet down Fremont.

Wyatt's and Billy's guns went off simultaneously. Billy's shot went wild, spinning off between Wyatt and Morgan. Wyatt didn't miss. His ball struck exactly where he wanted it to—square in the middle of Frank McLaury's belly.

The yellow in Ike Clanton was running down his leg. He threw up his hands and cried out, "Don't kill me! I'm not shooting!" He ran to Wyatt, who was closest, and wrapped his arms around him, keeping Wyatt from bringing his gun into play again. It went off, but the shot drilled harmlessly into the ground.

Wyatt twisted and turned to extricate himself from the grasp of the one man, more than any other, responsible for this gun battle. Disgusted, he roared at the cringing coward, "This fight's commenced. Get to fighting, or get out!"

Clanton got. He dashed around the corner of Fly's Boarding House, leaving a trail of urine and watery feces behind him, and ran into the parlor. There he collided with Johnny Behan, who also had seen the wisdom of exiting this situation.

Clanton continued on through the boarding house, into the photo gallery, out the back door, through the O. K. Corral, onto Allen Street, and through Kelly's saloon. He finally stopped two blocks away in Alfred Henry Emanuel's building on Toughnut Street, where he cowered behind a barrel of mescal, certain that no bullet could reach him there.

Back at Harwood's lot, all was momentarily quiet. Then a shot rang out from Fly's. It couldn't have come from Ike Clanton, because he was long gone. It might have come from Johnny Behan, but it was more likely to have come from Clanton's pal, Wesley Fuller. Another possibility was William Allen, a cowboy partisan with a long criminal record, who'd been in Fly's that afternoon.

Regardless of who fired the shot, it caused Morgan Earp to turn toward Fly's, exposing his back. Tom McLaury, still in the fight, put a bullet through Morgan's right shoulder, and he went down. Wyatt quickly stepped over to where Morgan lay, and stood in front of him.

This created another lull in the shooting, just enough for Frank McLaury to shake off the belly shot that Wyatt had given him, and to get to firing. His reputation as a shooter was well-deserved. His first shot sliced through Virgil's calf and felled him. His second shot walloped through Virgil's coat, just missing him. His third shot went wild as he crumbled to the ground.

Throughout all this, Billy Clanton was banging away with his gun, but Old Man Clanton's favorite and youngest son was out of his league. Though he was much more game than some, his shooting was ineffective, and for good reason. Within fifteen seconds, he'd been hit by Virgil Earp, and Wyatt's slug had torn into him. One of these shots had caught him in his right wrist, and he skillfully executed the "border shift maneuver," switching his gun to his left hand. But he'd gone down, and was hit a third time by Morgan Earp. He lay with his back against the Harwood house and attempted to load his empty pistol. He'd gotten off five shots, but wanted more.

But the fracas wasn't over. Frank McLaury, showing real grit, rose up from the dusty street. He laid his pistol across his left arm, took aim at Doc, who was facing him, and called out, "I've got you now."

Doc tersely replied, "You're a daisy if you do."

Frank pulled the trigger on his fourth shot. It ripped through Doc's holster and drew blood. Doc had dropped the empty shotgun and now had his nickle-plated .45 in his hand. His bullet struck Frank at the same instant that Morgan's did. Frank died quickly with bullets in his heart, his forehead, and his gut.

The gunfight at the O. K. Corral was over. It had taken place within a span of thirty seconds, and the firing had been so swift and deadly that no one could be quite sure who shot whom. Doc Holliday thought that Frank McLaury was the one who had wounded him.

Doc had been enraged when he fired the first shot of the fight, and he still was when he fired the last. He strode over to McLaury's body and shouted to the wind, "That son of a bitch has shot me, and I mean to kill him!" Then, realizing the deed was already done, he holstered his pistol, looked toward the window of his room at Fly's, and saw that a bullet had gone through it.

The stench of death hung over W. A. Harwood's Lot Number 2, Block 17, Tombstone, Arizona. A crowd began to gather.

Billy Clanton was slouched against the wall of the house, sitting in a pool of his own blood. He attempted one last shot, but the hammer of his six-shooter fell with an audible click. His gun was empty. He cried out feebly, "Somebody give me some cartridges."

Camillus Fly came out of his studio, a Henry brass rifle in his hand, and gingerly approached the dying boy. He grabbed Billy's gun and backed away.

Billy called out, "Give me water."

He never drank from the cup gently pressed to his lips by Mike Cunningham, who had witnessed the fight from Bauer's Meat Market. His life ended as he moaned, "Go away and let me die."

Johnny Behan cautiously poked his head out of Fly's doorway. Seeing it was all over, he straightened his tie and walked boldly over to Wyatt Earp. Wyatt was helping Morgan and Virgil into a buggy that had been brought in to take them to the doctor's office.

Behan spoke up so everyone could hear, "I'll have to arrest you."

Wyatt, whose six-shooter was still warm, and which he'd reloaded, looked Behan square in the eye. "I won't be arrested. You've deceived me, Johnny. You told me they weren't armed. You won't have to disarm them now. I won't be arrested, but I'm here to answer for what I've done. I'm not going to leave town."

⁂

When Holliday burst into his room at Fly's, he was prepared for the worst, and was flooded with relief as Kate ran to greet him. All the tensions of the past moments drained away, and he sat on the edge of the bed and sobbed, "Oh, this is awful. Just awful."

Kate comforted him, saying, "It's foolish to think a cow rustler gunman can come up to a city gunman in a gunfight."

She was wrong. John Ringo, Curly Bill Brocius, Pete Spence, and Frank Stillwell were on their way back to Tombstone.

18

THE WINDS THAT ROARED DOWN THE

Rocky Mountains from the northwest in the fall of 1881 brought a variety of weather conditions with them, and the normally bright blue sky was as change-able in hue as was the mood within Judge Spicer's courtroom where the lives of the Earp brothers and Doc Holliday were on the line.

The same weather prevailed eighty miles north in the upper Gila Valley. There the Gila Mountains dominate the landscape to the north, and to the south the eleven-thousand-foot Mount Graham rose abruptly. Within its shadow lay the ruins of *Chichilticalli*, and from that direction came deep, racking sobs and a low moaning which rivaled that of the winds which howled throughout the ruins.

Silhouetted against the setting sun, a man could be seen rising up from the ground. He was big by any standards, but under the cover of the bearskin coat he was wearing, he looked huge. He was truly a mountain of a man. He limped as he stepped forward, his moaning giving way to a discordant bellow.

He raised his arms, one of which held a .40-60 Whitney-Kennedy rifle, and cried out, "Justice, O God. For the pain I have suffered, may I see them suffer. Vengeance belongs to you, but let me be your instrument."

This had been Louis Hancock's prayer the last few months. He stood on the Indian mound overlooking the burned-out ranch house he'd shared with his wife and daughter. Now he would act upon his desire for revenge, a desire nour-ished throughout his convalescence at the Mission San Zavier del Bac.

With the aid of a sturdy, hand-hewn crutch, he eased himself through the ruins and limped to his horse—a big, black stallion. He slipped his rifle into its boot and, because of his weak left leg, pulled himself into the saddle from the right side. He adjusted the holster which held his long-barreled .44 Smith and Wesson, and rode off toward the town of Safford.

Louis Hancock had literally been saved from the grave by two people. One was the savage Apache, Geronimo, and the other the gentle Franciscan priest,

Father Humberto Rodriguez, with a notable assist from Tucson's popular doctor, James Turner. Louis, The Man of the Apaches as the brothers often called him, had made a remarkable recovery, though he was left with a stiff left leg, an empty eye socket covered by a patch, and a slight tilt of his head to the left as the result of his shoulder wound. His determination to exact revenge had given him reason to want to recover. As soon as he was able, he'd gone to work in the mission's kitchen. Brother Bustamonte, a culinary wizard, pronounced Louis the most intuitive cook he'd ever worked with. Everyone at the mission wanted him to stay.

But Hancock was determined to move on, and the day came when he informed Father Humberto that he was leaving. The good cleric took him to his "war chest" and brought out a leather pouch filled with coins.

"The Indians who brought you here gave this to us. We've never wanted anything for your care. Take it, and go with God."

Louis was deeply moved. There were tears all around when the big, black man left the mission in a buckboard driven by one of the brothers. He bade the driver good-bye in downtown Tucson.

No one from the mission knew where Louis had come from, or where he was going. But Louis did.

He knew from former forays into Tucson that he both fascinated and frightened people. Some, because of his awesome appearance, deferred to him. Some avoided him. Merchants were not inclined to haggle when Louis made an offer for goods or services, and now, at the livery stable where he bought Big Black, he got a bargain. The same was true at the gun shop next door. They even threw in a couple boxes of cartridges.

Had it not been for the grim task he'd set for himself, Louis would have gotten a hearty chuckle out of it all, but he wasn't in a laughing mood when he rode out of town.

One task remained before setting out on his trail of vengeance, and that was to pay a visit to his old friend, Pat Murphy. It was to his ranch that Louis now headed. He wanted to meet with Pat alone, away from other people.

When he reached the turnoff to Murphy's ranch, he tethered Big Black to a tree and made himself comfortable beneath his recently-purchased poncho. He rolled a smoke, lit up, and waited.

Louis knew Pat was a punctual man. At the same time every day, he closed down his faro game, turned the bar over to his assistant, and headed for home.

Arizona had very little rain and fog, but this night was an exception. At times, Pat could barely see his horse's head through the downpour which had come on suddenly while he was still more than half-way home. It was the same kind of weather that had made him—among other reasons—leave Ireland. He drew his great cloak snugly about his shoulders and thought about the stories his grandmother had told him so long ago: stories of leprechauns, wood nymphs, and little elves. He'd always been frightened by these stories, and especially when she referred to the wail of the banshee. He had no idea what a banshee looked like, but the big, dark form that suddenly loomed in front of him could well be one.

In an instant, Pat leveled his shotgun at the apparition. "Lord Jesus Christ," he shouted, "what have we here?"

"Pat Murphy, you old beer pusher," Louis chuckled, "since when have you been afraid of me?"

Pat was shaken by the sudden encounter, but instantly recognized his old friend.

"My God and all the saints in heaven preserve me," he cried out as he slid from his horse and steadied himself by grasping the saddle horn.

"You're dead, Louis. You're dead."

Louis laughed. "No, Pat, I'm not dead. Never have been. But I will be if you don't get me out of this weather."

Pat grabbed Louis's hand, and they clutched each other in a long and hearty embrace.

When Pat at last stepped back, he said, "Louis, you're not only a sight for sore eyes, but you're a sight as well. You make me want to cringe and cry for joy at the same time. Let's head on up to the house so we can talk in comfort."

"Alone, Pat. I won't have anyone see me."

"That's no problem. My wife's been dead a spell, and Luke and Sam are asleep in the soddie. Salvatore's in San Carlos."

They rode in silence the short distance to the little ranch house. Pat led the way to the lean-to stable and they unsaddled their horses. As Pat fed them, he told Louis, "I often bring home an extra horse for one reason or another. Usually," he chuckled, "because some yo-yo hasn't paid his liquor bill. No one will give yours being here a second thought. The boys'll all be out on the fences before sunup anyway, so there's no chance they'll see you."

A big, stone fireplace dominated the room which Pat and Louis entered. It was used both for cooking and heating, and above it hung a large oil painting. Thin cracks zigzagged through the paint, marring the face of a pretty colleen who hadn't lived to see the promised new world. She was buried in the churchyard of her parish in Ireland. Pat often raised a mug of ale in salute to his lost love.

Next to the fireplace was a sturdy wooden table, four chairs, and a bunk. A door on the opposite wall opened into a small storeroom. Pat went into it and brought out a bottle of his favorite whiskey.

"Louis," he said beaming, "let's loosen our tongues."

Louis declined by bending his arm at the elbow and showing the palm of his hand.

"Is it wine you want?" Pat asked.

"Lord, no," Hancock replied with a grin, "I had enough of that at the Tucson mission where I've just come from. What I'd really like is some of your good beer. Most of the saloons I've stopped in lately have turned me away. Might be because of my color, but I've got a feeling it's more likely my good looks." His hearty laugh was infectious, and Pat joined in.

Pat brought out several bottles of beer for Louis, and a bottle of Irish whiskey for himself, and placed them on the table. They sat down, and as Pat lit up a clay pipe he said, "Tell me about it."

Louis told Pat the whole story, none of which he had ever told the clerics at the mission. He hadn't wanted them to know. He knew the man now sitting before him would understand, and as he detailed the horrible deeds perpetrated by their neighbors—Fred McSween and Harry Kent, and their three friends—his voice sounded hollow. He cried bitterly as he spoke of the murders of his pregnant wife and little daughter.

Pat comforted him as best he could. He was dumfounded by Louis's account of his rescue by Geronimo, and nodded his head knowingly when Louis recounted his treatment at the hands of the Franciscans.

"They are good lads," he murmured, and looked up at the portrait over the fireplace. Then he poured himself another drink.

Louis fell silent. The story was over.

"Now what do you propose to do?" Pat inquired.

Without hesitation, Louis angrily replied, "I propose to do to them what they did to my family!"

"Well, there's one you won't have to deal with," Pat told him. "Harry Kent has been dead for some weeks now."

"No!" Louis cried.

"Yes," Pat answered. "He and McSween were driving cows to Carlos when lightning stampeded the herd, and both of them got trampled. Kent died on the spot, and was buried right on the trail. McSween might better have. He got pretty crushed up, and word is he's as good as dead. Lost another man, too."

"Where's McSween now?"

"Oh, mostly home in bed. But I heard he gets up once in a while and looks around," Pat replied.

Louis boomed, "He won't after tomorrow!"

The two continued talking for several hours, and came up with a plan. It called for Pat to go to the bunkhouse at McSween's Blue Jay Ranch and ask the cowboys for help in rounding up some dogies that had gotten loose and wandered in their direction. That way he'd get them away from the ranch house, and out in the open. The promise of free drinks in town would assure their cooperation. It always worked. Thirty dollars a month didn't buy a lot of drinks for a thirsty cowhand. Louis would then be free to do whatever he pleased. Pat didn't even want to know.

Murphy put some rugs and skins on the floor, and that was Hancock's bed for the night.

The next morning, Pat turned a few of his calves loose, and then he and Louis rode together in silence to the Blue Jay. There was nothing more to be said. When they reached the southwest corner of McSween's property, Pat held out his hand.

"Good-bye, my friend, and good luck."

Louis said nothing as he took Pat's hand and gave it a firm squeeze before letting go, and watched as Pat headed for McSween's bunkhouse.

The plan worked. Before long, Louis could see his friend and two cowboys riding off together, and seeming to be having a good time. He knew it wasn't just free drinks that encouraged them. These men led lonely lives, and they craved the companionship available at the bars. Now Hancock was alone. He guided Big Black to the stable area at the ranch, dismounted, and unlatched the gate. He led the horse through it, and warily approached the front door of the house, then slipped the long rifle from the saddle scabbard, and loosened the strap on his holster as he mounted the steps. He stepped on a loose board.

"Who's there?" a voice called out.

Louis stayed quiet.

Again, "Who's there?"

Louis moved quickly to the window at the left of the door and looked in. There was McSween, struggling to get his rifle which hung from an elk horn rack. Its strap was caught in the horns. Louis could see that he was feeble, and barely able to stand up.

Louis kicked the window in and stepped over the sill into the room. He stood over McSween, who'd fallen into a chair. Breathing heavily, he thundered, "I've got you now!"

McSween sucked in his breath and clutched his hand to his chest. "Hancock! It can't be! You're dead!"

"I'm getting mighty tired of hearing that," Louis shot back. "I'm not dead, but you're sure as hell going to be!"

"My God!" McSween groaned. "How can this be? You were burned up with your house! I saw it go. Everything! You were in it!"

"So was my wife and little girl!" Louis almost wept with pleasure as he grabbed McSween by the throat and lifted him out of the chair. Then he threw him back onto it.

McSween knew he was in for it now, and that the price he'd pay for what he'd done would be high; but he was a hard man who gave no quarter and didn't expect any. Yet he just couldn't comprehend how this man could be alive, much less in his own house, and silently damned Ringo who had told him the deed was done.

"I've come to kill you, McSween," Louis roared, "but first you're going to give me the names of the other men who were with you. And you will tell me, one way or another. Make it easy on yourself, unless you enjoy pain."

Louis grabbed a chair and slid it near McSween's. He was trembling as he sat down.

"I'm listening," he said mockingly.

McSween's mind was whirling, thinking how he'd fought with the Texans in the Civil War against just such abominations as this dumb nigger sitting in front of him; how he'd fought the Apache to get the land which was the Blue Jay Ranch; how he'd battled for everything all of his life. He wasn't about to let this black son of a bitch ruin everything now.

He could see Hancock's Smith and Wesson resting loosely in its holster, barely two feet away, and saw a chance to get out of this.

"I'll tell you," he said quietly as he leaned forward in his chair, a move calculated to bring him a little closer to Hancock.

"One of the men was Frank Stillwell. He rides with the Clantons. Another was Billy Clanton, but I read he got shot down back in Tombstone. Pete Spence was another one."

"The tall, thin Texan. Who's he?"

McSween inched closer to Hancock, who was listening intently.

"Name's John Ringo. He's a strange one."

Louis was picturing that awful night when Ringo had said to him, "You're going to hell." He asked where the men lived.

Very softly, McSween answered, "Tombstone."

Louis couldn't hear. Leaning forward, he asked, "Where?"

"Tombstone," McSween said again, even more softly.

"Where?" Louis asked once more as he leaned even closer to McSween.

"Tombstone, Arizona, you dumb, black asshole," shouted McSween as he leaped on top of Louis, sending them both sprawling to the floor. He grabbed Louis's gun at the same instant that Louis's big, black fist smashed into his mouth. McSween threw up his arm to deflect the next blow, throwing Louis's aim off. He struck McSween square in the chest, and in that instant McSween's heart stopped beating.

Louis got to his feet and stared down at his dead foe. He was breathing hard, and muttered "Sonabitch." This had been too easy for McSween. He had wanted more.

Looking around the room, he noticed a bottle of whiskey on the sideboard, limped over to it, and took a big slug from the bottle. He held it toward McSween's body.

"Thanks for the drink."

He took another slug as he contemplated the dead man, and returned the bottle to the sideboard. Then he grabbed McSween's legs and dragged him across the room, through the door, across the porch, and bounced him down the steps. He stopped, took a deep breath, picked him up and threw him across his shoulder, and lugged him across the barnyard to the outhouse.

He dropped McSween, stepped inside, and kicked the two-holer board from its base. Then he carried McSween inside, looked down into the putrid mess, and dropped him in, saying aloud, "A man like you deserves a decent burial."

Then Louis limped back to his horse, mounted up, and trotted south toward Tombstone.

19

JOHN RINGO'S VISIT TO HIS FAMILY

in San Jose, California, had gone totally wrong. Though once his sisters' favorite brother, their feelings had cooled considerably as the result of the occasional newspaper articles that mentioned his name as a participant in the brutal Texas Hoodoo War. A couple of dime novels had even portrayed him as a vicious killer. His sisters, and their husbands, didn't take kindly to such notoriety, and their reception when they met him in San Francisco was lukewarm. Still, he pleased them by dressing well for the occasion, and in spite of their reservations about him, thought he looked quite handsome.

The ride southeast to San Jose had gone well, and it appeared to John that this was going to be a pleasant visit. A week later, everything changed.

John, thinking his sisters would want his portrait for the family album, went to have his picture taken. The photographer was a refined, sophisticated man of the world, happily married, and the father of two children.

He was making the usual fuss over a paying customer, and John watched everything he did, completely fascinated. The man's artistic demeanor, and the way he moved his body, excited John.

Accustomed as he was to the no-frills, direct approach common to frontier life, John totally misinterpreted the photographer's actions. He not only propositioned him outright, but in the process actually got physical. The astounded photographer summoned the police.

The upshot of the whole messy business was that his sisters got the photograph, and John got the boot. He was on his way back to Arizona Territory that very night, and never saw his family again.

When Ringo settled into his favorite saloon in Charleston, he was in a foul mood. He not only had been totally rejected by his family, but worse yet by the sort of man he had always fancied. He began to drink, considerably more than usual. His mood soured even more when, on that very first evening home, his friend Billy Breckenridge joined him. Billy, always in a light mood, was on his tax-collecting rounds and had stopped in for a beer.

Ringo told him about his recent unpleasant experience and Billy thought it was hilarious. He shook with laughter while John scowled. Hoping to cheer John up, as he usually could, Billy broke into a song which he and Ringo had often laughed over:

> Tiddly winks, old man
> Get a woman if you can.
> If you can't get a woman,
> Get a clean old man.

John wasn't amused, and told Billy to shut up.

Billy quieted down, and with the expertise of a born storyteller began to recount the showdown at the O. K. Corral. He told of the deaths of their friends, Billy Clanton and the McLaury brothers, of the grand funerals, how people lined up for blocks to watch as the two hearses passed slowly by to the cadence of drums, and how the brass band played *We Shall Gather at the River*.

"I should have been there," Ringo said sadly.

Breakenridge continued, "Nothing you can do now, especially with Wyatt Earp and Doc Holliday in jail. Virgil and Morgan are still recovering from their wounds, and are under house arrest."

"Who shot them?" Ringo asked.

"Who knows?" Billy answered.

"How's the trial going?"

"Hard to say. The Earps hired a crackerjack lawyer. Still, the prosecution has a good case and lots of witnesses. Johnny Behan's testifying against them. A lot of people are saying it was cold-blooded murder."

"There'll be murder if those damn prima donnas ever get out of that jail," Ringo sputtered.

Billy changed the subject. "Did you ever meet Tom McLaury's brother Will?"

"No, but I heard he's from Fort Worth. Good place."

"Well, he came in right after the funeral. He's got plenty of savvy, and I hear enough money to put those boys in Yuma for a long time."

"I don't want them in prison. I want them looking down the barrel of my gun," Ringo countered as he poured down another drink.

"You might just get that chance. Will McLaury has been talking to Ike and Curly Bill. Feelings are running pretty high. If the Earps get away with this thing, there'll be hell to pay. Right now there's a twenty-four hour watch at the jail to keep anyone from getting a shot at them."

"Are you one of us, Billy?" Ringo asked.

"You're my friend," he answered. "I'll go anywhere with you. But John, you know I'm not a killing man."

Ringo was aware of Billy's feelings. He knew some men could do things other's couldn't, and respected him for being honest about it. At least he wasn't a blowhard like Ike Clanton.

"Yeah, Billy, I know," he said, looking him straight in the eye. Then he lowered his gaze.

"I'd like to go somewhere and get rid of this tickle in my pants."

They left the bar and rode off together.

William McLaury arrived in Tombstone on November 4, 1881, eight days after the shoot-out. He was a successful lawyer from Fort Worth, Texas, and familiar with frontier justice. It was he who forced the court to keep Wyatt and Doc in jail without bail, and who wrote his sister that, "I shall try to have these men hanged."

He brought plenty of money with him, so if the court failed him he'd have the wherewithal to do whatever he felt necessary. He'd been out to the McLaury and Clanton ranches where he had long, serious talks with Ike Clanton and Curly Bill Brocius.

Now that the fight was over, Ike Clanton had come out of his hole and was back to lipping off. Once again he strode belligerently up and down Allen and Toughnut streets, boasting as to how he'd see the whole murdering Earp gang swinging from the gibbets.

Sarah Marcus frequently brought Wyatt a tray of bagels, kippers, and a tureen of chicken soup. Each time, to goad Johnny Behan, she'd poke her head into his office and wish him a good day. Doc Holliday got some special attention too. Every day during the trial Mike Cunningham was seen bringing him a basket of scones and hot coffee.

Throughout, the Tombstone *Epitaph* championed the Earps, and the *Nuggett* condemned them.

The Earps' lawyer, Tom Fitch, had wisely counseled Wyatt and Virgil to testify they had fired the first shots. As accredited officers of the law, they had the right to be armed and in pursuit of peace at the O. K. Corral. This took the onus off Doc and Morgan, who hadn't been officially deputized.

The prosecution, headed by Will McLaury, insisted that the cowboys were unarmed, or if they were armed it was because they'd been planning to leave town.

The defense naturally countered by asking how it could be—if they were not armed—that Virgil, Morgan and Doc all suffered bullet wounds.

The prosecutor also claimed the Earps had been threatening the boys, while more witnesses for the defense testified they'd heard just the opposite.

It went on like that for several weeks.

The trial was finally over on November 29. Judge Wells Spicer concluded that,

> "...the deceased from the very first inception of the encounter were standing their ground and fighting back, giving and taking with un-flinching bravery. It does not appear to be a wanton slaughter of unre-sisting and unarmed innocents,...but armed and defiant men accept-ing the wages of battle and succumbing only in death..."

Two factors likely convinced the judge to rule in favor of the Earps. One was the testimony of H. F. Sills that he had overheard the McLaurys and Billy Clanton discussing plans to "kill him on sight...kill that whole party of Earps when we meet them." The other was that Marshal Virgil Earp had approached the cowboys with nothing but a cane in his shooting hand.

And so Wyatt, Virgil, Morgan and Doc were off the hook and back on the town. Their trial was the longest in Arizona territorial history up to that time.

Three weeks later, threats were received in the mail by the Earps, Tom Fitch and several of their friends, including Mayor John Clum, and Judge Wells Spicer, whose read:

> ...you are liable to get a hole through your coat at any moment. If such sons of bitches as you are allowed to dispense justice in this

Territory, the sooner you depart the better...It is only a matter of time you will get it sooner or later...

The judge, who was no marshmallow, answered in kind in the *Epitaph*, and actually challenged the writer.

By no means were these idle threats. Typical of them was the small box that Doc Holliday received, which contained a .45 caliber bullet wrapped in cotton, along with a card that read: I've got another one just like this that I'm going to give you some day—in the neck.

⁂

At eight in the evening on December 14, John Clum boarded the Concord stage for Benson. He was returning to Washington, D. C. for a Christmas visit with his young son and his parents, who had been caring for the boy since the death of John's wife some time before. He carried two six-shooters because he suspected there'd be trouble, and he was right.

Not an hour out, as the coach went by the lights of Malcolm's Well, they passed a freight stage going in their direction. Moments later, shouts were heard and shots were fired at both sides of the Concord. The four passengers riding with Clum dropped to the floor, but he pulled out his pistols. Then he, too, was thrown to the floor when the horses panicked and raced off into the night.

The freight driver, who'd been running nearly parallel with Clum's coach, sustained a flesh wound during the assault. Clum figured correctly that the innocent driver, Whistling Dick, had been shot in an attempt on his own life. He also figured the highwaymen could easily ambush them again down the line, and he had had enough. He abandoned ship, and the stage continued on without him.

Clum lost his way in the darkness, and it wasn't until early morning that he came upon the Grand Central Quartz Mill. He rested a couple hours, borrowed a horse, and rode to Benson, where he telegraphed Jim Flynn, his temporary chief of police in Tombstone, and told of his narrow escape. Then he continued east.

⁂

Virgil and Morgan were still laid up at Virgil's house. They were sharing the same bed, and being attended to by their wives.

One day, an obvious attempt was made on their lives by a man crudely disguised as a woman. He wore a dress and a veiled hat. When Allie and Lou responded to his knock on the door, he pushed them aside and made straightaway for the bedroom, just off the parlor. His hand was tucked into the bodice of the dress, apparently holding a gun.

Lucky for Virgil and Morgan, their brother Warren was there, having just returned from California. He heard the commotion and stepped from the bedroom. The intruder stopped dead in his tracks and backed off, mumbling apologies in a fake female voice about getting into the wrong house. He beat a hasty retreat.

Taking on two sick men in a bed was one thing. Standing up to an Earp was another.

The brothers spent some time mulling over the identity of the intruder. They thought it might have been Will McLaury, as they had already concluded the threatening notes were written by an educated person attempting to appear ignorant.

December 28 came, and the boys were finally on their feet. For several reasons—mainly because of the most recent attempt on their lives—they decided to take rooms in the Cosmopolitan Hotel, C. S. Bilicke, Proprietor. Virgil, anxious for some action, had later gone on to the Oriental Saloon. This account of what followed appeared in the *Epitaph*:

> At about 11:30 o'clock last night, U. S. Marshal Virgil Earp was proceeding from the Oriental Saloon from the northeast corner of Allen and Fifth streets to his room at the Cosmopolitan Hotel, and when he was about the middle of the crossing of Fifth Street five shots were fired in rapid succession by unknown men who were standing in the old Palace Saloon that is being rebuilt next door...Immediately after the firing the assassins ran rapidly down Fifth past the Combination shaft and disappeared in the darkness...two of the shots took effect on Mr. Earp, one badly shattering his left arm, and the other entered his left side...The shots were evidently fired from double-barreled shotguns loaded with buckshot...Mr. Earp walked into the Oriental and told his brother Wyatt he was shot. His friends escorted him to his room at the Cosmopolitan....

Doctor Goodfellow was summoned to Virgil's room and once again went to work on his patient. Virgil was in a daze. He looked up at Wyatt and pleaded, "Don't let him take my arm." Wyatt made sure he didn't.

While the surgeon probed Virgil's wounds, Allie cleaned up after him. It made her sick to her stomach, and she heaved a sigh of relief when he finished up.

"He'll keep the arm," he said, "but it won't be worth much."

From the bed, barely awake, Virgil whispered, "Never mind."

He turned his head toward Allie. "I've still got one arm to hug you with."

George Parsons wrote in his diary that night:

...It is surmised that Ike Clanton, Curly Bill and McLaury did the shooting. Bad state of affairs here. Something will have to be done....

The story in the *Epitaph* was:

...This further proves that there is a band of assassins in our midst, who having threatened the lives of Judge Spicer, Mayor Clum, Mr. Williams, the Earp brothers and Holliday, have attempted upon two occasions to carry out their threats into execution, first upon Mayor Clum and second upon Virgil Earp. The question naturally arises, who will be the next subject?

Doc could have been it. Billy Breakenridge related that quite late on a drizzly night he was on his way home, when at the corner of Allen and Sixth streets a gun barrel was suddenly shoved into his chest.

The man behind the gun was Frank Stillwell, and when Frank saw it was Billy he lowered it. In answer to Billy's inquisitive look, Frank told him, "Someone said he was going to kill me. Not if I see him first, when he comes down this street."

"Frank, it's late. You just go on home," Billy advised.

He figured Doc Holliday was likely Frank's intended victim, and felt sure of it when he spied Doc strolling along on his way home. Billy always contended that he had saved Doc's life, but he was nowhere around when the next attempt was made on him.

Wyatt received word from United States marshal Crawley P. Dake that he had been commissioned a deputy United States marshal, and Virgil—still convalescing—administered the oath of office from his bed.

This appointment didn't alleviate the frustration felt by the Earps and Doc Holliday. Especially Doc, who was drinking heavily, much more than usual. Neither Kate nor Nell could convince him to slow down.

On the afternoon of January 17, 1882, George Parsons wrote in his journal:

> …Ringo and Doc Holliday came nearly having it with pistols…Bad time expected with the cowboy leader and D. H. I passed both not knowing blood was up. One with hand in breast pocket and the other probably ready. Earps just beyond. Crowded street and looked like another battle.…

The story related to an incident which had taken place that morning. John Ringo had also been hitting the bottle hard the last month. The San Jose affair had shaken him. He was a man who pretty much let his gun do his talking, and he was still smarting at the constraints which he'd had to operate under while he was there. He'd had to eat crow in front of the family he had hoped to reconcile with and here, he knew, the feeling was that he'd let his friends down by not being with them at the O. K. Corral. He was tossing down the drinks and watching the boys rack the balls for a game of pool when, through the window overlooking Allen Street, he saw Doc and Wyatt talking. He'd heard Doc was hitting the bottle hard, and figured with the boys to back him up he could easily provoke Doc into pulling his pistol. Everybody knew Doc wasn't the best shot around, and Ringo was better than all of them, except maybe for Frank Leslie. The odds seemed good.

"Watch Earp," he said to his buddies, and walked out onto the street. He could see Doc was in his cups, but then, so was he. He called out, "Doc."

Doc spun around and would have tripped himself if Wyatt hadn't grabbed him.

"Doc, I hear you've been looking for me. I hear you've been calling me names."

"Ya bet yer ass," Doc slurred, and put his hand into the breast pocket of his coat.

Ringo, even more bold now that he realized how inebriated Doc truly was, needled him some more. He pulled out a handkerchief and shoved a corner of it at him, saying "Grab it and draw."

"I'm yer huckleberry," Doc chortled as he reached for it. "Tha's jus' my game."

Wyatt watched as the burly city police chief, Jim Flynn, came quietly up behind Ringo and encircled him with his arms. Wyatt restrained Doc with a hand on his shooting arm. The handkerchief duel would not take place.

Deputy Sheriff Billy Breakenridge arrived. You'll have to come with me, John," he said, almost apologetically.

"What the hell for?"

"For carrying arms on the city street where I can see them."

"Then arrest him, too," Ringo demanded as he gestured at Holliday.

"I can't see his gun, John."

As he led Ringo away he said quietly, "It'll be all right."

Wyatt helped Doc back to his room.

Once in police headquarters, Ringo grumbled, "You didn't have to take me in, Billy, not in front of those people. I've been insulted enough for awhile."

"John, you've got to abide by the law. That's the reason."

"Shit!" Johnny Behan exclaimed when he saw the prisoner. "Why aren't you around when someone needs you?"

That stung Ringo. "Next time, Johnny," he replied. "Next time."

Behan was in a foul mood. "Twenty-seven dollars and fifty cents fine for carrying deadly weapons."

Ringo counted out the money, and looked sullenly at him.

"And you'll have to leave your pistols here until you leave town."

"I'm leaving now," Ringo retorted.

"Then get your horse and come back for them," Behan told him as he stalked off.

Johnny Behan had had a bad day, starting with that morning when he received a court order to pay Sarah Marcus the money he'd borrowed from her the year before.

Ringo faced Breakenridge. "Billy, if I go out on the street without my guns, I won't last as long as a snowball in hell." He'd been involved in a couple back-shooting episodes, and fully expected this might be his fate.

Billy grinned as he opened a desk drawer and put Ringo's guns in. He gave Ringo a wink, and told him, "I've got to step out for a minute."

When he came back, Ringo was gone and so were his guns. Billy

Breakenridge was the only true friend John Ringo ever had.

Early that evening, John Ringo, Frank Stillwell, Pete Spence, and Will McLaury rode out of Tombstone for Charleston, where Ringo had a room at the American Hotel. With them was Tombstone's genial deputy sheriff, Billy Breakenridge. He thought an evening in Charleston with the boys would be just the ticket.

As they passed the turnoff to Richmond, they spotted a lone rider coming from the direction of Benson. He rode a huge black stallion.

Ringo pulled up. "Now who in hell is that?"

"Who cares?" Billy spouted. "Let's get a move on. I feel lucky tonight. The sooner we get there the better."

"Right," Ringo conceded, but he felt compelled to drop a little behind in order to get a better look at the stranger before trotting after his friends.

He could see the man was big, and black. His head was tilted slightly to the left, and that side of his face was partially covered by a red bandanna. Ringo didn't know why, but something about the man made him feel uneasy.

That night, Ringo had one of his worst nightmares.

20

"NOT AGAIN," GROANED THE CITIZENS

of Tombstone as a troop of United States cavalrymen bivouacked just outside the town limits. Such activity usually came on the heels of an Indian scare.

This time it was Nana, the recalcitrant Apache leader who'd been spotted by scouts of the Ninth Cavalry as he skulked about the Mexican border.

Buckskin Leslie was always called out when the army was on the move in the southeastern portion of the Arizona Territory. Now, to his satisfaction, his first conference with leaders of the military would be right here in his own back yard.

In a private room on the far side of the Russ House, he and Captain Tullius C. Tupper settled down to dinner, cigars, and brandy. The captain, a twenty-five year veteran, had taken a comfortable room at the hotel, while his men made do in the temporary camp outside the town. With the captain was Corporal Peterson, his orderly, and Frank's old friend and half-breed scout, Mickey Free.

Maps were spread out on the table, and the men got down to some serious work.

Guests sitting in the lobby were more than a little surprised when, through the window, they saw a big, black man dismount and tie up his horse at the hotel's hitching post. They watched as he removed his long rifle from its scabbard, and limped into the hotel.

Nell Cashman's partner, Joseph Pascholy, was behind the counter when Louis Hancock walked up.

"Sorry, but we're all filled. The Arcade on the other side of town might have a vacancy," he told Louis somewhat gratuitously.

Louis had heard this before. "I expect so," he replied, "but I'm not looking for a room. I have a letter here for a Miss Nell Cashman. I understand she runs this place."

"Are you one of the scouts for the Ninth?" Pascholy asked, while thinking to himself, "Damn! They're sure scraping the bottom of the barrel. There's already a one-eyed half-breed out in the back room, and now here comes a one-eyed colored."

"No, not a scout," Hancock answered. "Nothing to do with the army any more. Is Miss Cashman here?"

"Mike," Joe called out, "go get your aunt for me."

Mike, who was bellboy, busboy, swamper, bag carrier, babysitter, and anything else that was needed, put down his dime novel and went to get Nell.

She was looking Hancock over as she approached, and appreciated the fact that he was big, masculine and capable-looking. Also, judging by the way he held his hat in hand and bowed to her, obviously a gentleman. She liked him right away.

"I'm Nell Cashman," she announced as she came face to face with Louis.

"My pleasure, Miss Cashman," he replied. "I'm Louis Hancock. I was told you might have work for me. I can do most anything. Been a soldier way back, a rancher with a family once, do well with kids and fixing things, and can give you…"

He was cut short by a commotion coming from the open door of the back room. Captain Tupper was standing in the doorway, singing at the top of his lungs:

> Bobby and George went up the hill
> To fetch the Union army.
> We gave 'em a shot
> And routed the lot…

Louis, grinning broadly, had turned to face the captain, and finished the song for him:

> And sent them back to Virginny.

Then he boomed, "Sixty-ninth Pennsylvania!"

Tupper let out a whoop. "Gettysburg! Pickett's charge!" He strode quickly forward and grabbed Louis by the hand.

"By God, Louis Hancock, what the devil are you doing out here?"

Louis laughed. "I could ask you the same, Joe, but by the looks of the bluebellies out yonder, I reckon you're still up to your old soldiering tricks."

Frank Leslie and Mickey Free came into the room and watched as the two men bear-hugged each other. When they finally separated, Free pointed to Louis's eye patch, then to his own. "Bear?" he asked.

"Man," Louis answered.

"Same thing," Mickey replied, and they both laughed heartily.

The captain, with help from his orderly, pulled a couple tables and some chairs together, and then he called for drinks all around.

Nell, who had watched amused at the display of friendship, knew the captain from his previous visits. She asked, "Captain, whom do we have here?"

"Miss Nell, this here's Louis Hancock, formerly the water boy for the Sixty-ninth Pennsylvania at Gettysburg. He was big for his age then, and he's a helluva lot bigger now, as you can see," he laughed. "He helped us boys stop Pickett's charge. Hell! I've always believed that was what finished off the rebs."

Nell shook Louis's hand, and said politely, "You old warriors probably have a lot to talk about. I'll be out of your way."

As she turned to go, Louis handed her the envelope he'd kept in his shirt pocket. Nell thanked him and left. Back in the kitchen, she opened it and removed a paper bearing the letterhead of her friend, Doctor James Turner, of Tucson. The note read:

Dear Nell:

It's a pleasure to write to you. It always gave me pleasure to be associated with you.

The bearer of this note is Mr. Louis Hancock. He has been living at the mission for several months. As you can see, he was severely used, but now, except for a lame leg, he's back on his feet and fit as a fiddle. None of us at the mission knows what happened to him. None other than Geronimo and a couple of his warriors carried him in one night and left him in the care of the brothers there. We did our best for him, but Louis played a big part in his own recovery with his strong will to live. Father Marcello, of course, claims it was his prayers. Perhaps. Louis is a good man of high moral standards. He'd be an asset to any endeavor or community.

He told us when he left that he would probably be settling in the south-

east, here in the territory. Here's where you might be able to do another of your good deeds.

If you don't already have a really excellent cook, you'll find none better than this man Hancock. I know you'll remember Brother Bustamonte, who cooks at the mission, and who brings trays of his superb delicacies to the fiestas and bazaars in Tucson. He took Louis into his kitchen and, after only a couple months, acknowledged he had found a cook who might even surpass himself. Remember, Bustamonte trained in Paris and Madrid.

Nell, I know you served the finest meals in Tucson, but if you'd like some really good help, please consider Louis. He'll never let you down.

We all miss you up here, and would enjoy a visit."

> *Your friend,*
> *James Turner*

Nell read the letter again. It brought back memories of picnics in front of the great mission, and she could picture the rotund chef as he moved about the tables serving a wide variety of tasty and well-prepared dishes. Smiling, she thought, "If this man is anywhere near that good, he might be just what I need to corner the market on the Sunday afternoon diners. He could be helpful in other ways, too. Besides, I like the man."

As it turned out, the Indian scare was just that—a scare. Nana and his renegade Apaches apparently decided the army was just a bit too vigilant at this time, and they disappeared.

Frank Leslie missed out on one of those periodic adventures he always enjoyed, and went back to work at the bar.

Captain Turner and Louis talked away most of the night and much of the next day. Then the army moved on.

Louis went to work for Nell in her restaurant at the Russ House. She had simply announced to Joe Pascholy that she wanted her friend put up in the room by the kitchen, and that he'd be working for her. Joe shrugged and shook his head. "Whatever you say, Nellie."

Nell told Louis she couldn't pay him much to begin with, but promised if business picked up, particularly on Sundays, that he'd get more. She also told him about catering services he could make money on. "Room and board is on me," she concluded.

The only thing Louis Hancock never told anyone, including Nell and his old army commander, was why he'd come to Tombstone.

⁂

Early in March, Will McLaury called a meeting with Ike Clanton, Frank Stillwell, and Pete Spence at the Grand Hotel. Its purpose was to plan the murders of the men who had killed his brothers.

Frank insisted that Billy Breakenridge be kept off the street to keep him from butting into their business.

Will responded that he'd already talked to Johnny Behan about that, and John had agreed to send his man off on business any time Will felt he could catch the Earp bunch off guard. He went on, "Ringo wants in on this. He's burned that he missed out being here the last time. When the time comes, I want him and Claiborne informed. I know you boys know which end of a gun the bullet comes out of, but we'll all be safer with Ringo shooting too." He looked over at Stillwell and added, "He doesn't miss."

"Hell, Will," Stillwell said belligerently, "how'd we know Clum's horses would bolt like that? We'd have got him sure if we hadn't had to re-load and go chasing after our own nags."

"That's exactly what I'm getting at, Frank," McLaury continued. "We need a real pro to do this right; somebody who won't have to re-load."

The opportunity they were hoping for came on March 18, and sure enough, Billy Breakenridge wasn't around to interfere.

Wyatt and Sarah, and Morgan and Lou, decided to have a night out. They were joined by George Parsons, and Mayor Clum recently returned from Washington. They were going to see Tombstone favorites, Mr. and Mrs. William H. Lingard and their troop, direct from the New York stage, who were performing in the musical comedy *Stolen Kisses* at Schieffelin Hall.

The show was a big success, and the Earp party left the hall in a happy mood and headed to Banning and Shaw's for their favorite hand-churned ice cream.

Wyatt and Morgan decided that before going home they'd like to finish the night with a game of pool. The ladies, who'd already been out as long as they cared to be, didn't object, and were taken directly home. Sarah was escorted to her home first, and then Lou to hers. Morgan planted a loving kiss on his wife's lips, and assured her they wouldn't be long.

Morgan and Wyatt strode on over to Campbell and Hatch's Billiard Parlor on Allen Street, where they joined several other men and got into a game. Wyatt did well, and made a few bucks on side bets.

Virgil was making out okay, too. Just before eleven that night, he chalked his stick and broke the rack, then bent down to line up on his next ball.

Suddenly, gunshots crashed through a window with startling and everlasting effect. One of the shots splattered into the wall just above Wyatt's head. The other tore a hole in Morgan's right side, passed through his spinal column, and into the room, ending up in bystander George Berry's thigh.

Morgan collapsed onto the floor. Wyatt went to his knees to help his younger brother, knowing that he presented a perfect target to the shooters.

Several men were heard running off into the night.

Morgan died within the hour. His last words were, "Boys, I've played my last game of pool." And Lou had had her last kiss.

The handsome Morgan Earp had always been a welcome addition to the socials and dances, which he attended with his devoted and beautiful wife. He enjoyed singing any time with anybody, and could give anyone a run for their money at the pool tables. But it all ended for him that night.

Wyatt was devastated. He couldn't accept that such a tragedy could befall him and his kin. Somehow, he had come to believe the Earps were invincible, that they were not at risk from the jaws of death. Look how they'd come out of that nasty business at the O. K. Corral, and lots of other scrapes. He wasn't beyond accepting that they'd sustain some wounds from time to time, but die?! Never! Never!

Virgil was more of a realist. He was older, had come through the Civil War, and accepted that any time guns were brought into play, chances were good that someone would die. As a veteran town sheriff, he'd come to terms with the danger to himself. It was his business. But to lose his brother to such a cowardly act! He was beside himself with anger, and it ate at him that the injuries he'd received during the recent bushwacking would prevent him from joining his brother in tracking down the killers.

It was decided that Allie and Virgil would take Morgan's body to California for burial. Though terribly saddened by the loss of her brother-in-law, Allie was relieved that Virgil would soon be away from this miserable, murderous town.

Lou was inconsolable. She'd come from a fighting family, and had married into one, but never in her wildest dreams did she picture the day she'd be taking her beloved husband home in a pine box.

Wyatt went about the business of making all the necessary arrangements with the mortuary, and for transportation of the body and its escorts.

All day long he could hear the bells. They sounded from the churches, the schools, the fire station, and from many homes. Morgan Earp had been a popular man.

⁂

In the American Hotel in Charleston, Will McLaury, John Ringo, Ike Clanton, Frank Stillwell, and Pete Spence drank toasts one after the other.

"Beautiful!" Will shouted, pounding Stillwell and Ringo on the shoulders. "You did right good!" He stood back and looked at them with unabashed admiration, and added, "Tomorrow we'll do even better. When Wyatt takes the old buzzard's carcass to Tucson, we'll be there to finish him off." That called for another rousing toast.

They seriously underestimated Wyatt Earp.

21

NELL TOOK THE BUCKBOARD TO THE
open air market just outside Tombstone three times a week to pick up fresh fruits,
vegetables, and dairy products for her restaurant, and Mike always rode with
her.

The past few weeks she'd also been taking Louis Hancock along. She liked
having him with her, and he had easily gained the respect of the merchants at this
busy, noisy marketplace.

Louis had already proved his worth to Nell with his cooking. People were
requesting certain dishes, and repeat business was increasing. Even though Nell
was one of the premier cooks in southeastern Arizona, as time went by she relin-
quished more and more of her kitchen duties to Louis. She enjoyed having more
time to spend with her ailing sister, and her sister's children. The only cooking
she retained sole responsibility for was the scones for which she was regionally
famous. She never tired of the compliments they inspired.

On one particular morning, she and Louis had finished the marketing, and
Mike was helping him load the supplies onto the wagon when all of a sudden
Louis dropped a boxful of eggs. He made no move to do anything about it, but
instead stood transfixed as several cowboys came riding by, heading northwest.
Most likely to Benson.

Nell came running up, and saw that Louis was trembling.

"What's the matter?" she asked anxiously as she laid her hand on his arm.
"Do you know those men?"

"Yes, I do. One of them."

Nell frowned. "They're not a good lot."

"The one on the cayuse," Louis asked, "what's his name?"

"That's Frank Stillwell," Mike piped up. "He's a bad one. They say he
robbed the Bisbee stage. One of these days, he'll get his," he added as he aimed
and fired an imaginary rifle at the departing men.

"Hush, Mike," Nell admonished. "Is Stillwell the one you know, Louis?"

Louis didn't answer. That face had been burned into his memory forever, along with the words that came out of it: "Never had it so good. I just had me the sweetest piece of meat you ever did see."

Louis muttered a curse. This wasn't the right time, or the right place, to go after him. Besides, he didn't want to be rushed when he confronted him. Not for him the quick, almost accidental way McSween had gone. Louis wanted much worse than that for Stillwell.

He turned to Nell. "I don't really know him, Miss Nell. I only met him once."

That same day, March 19, Sarah Marcus brought a battered Marietta, the Mexican wife of Pete Spence, to the clerk of the Superior Court of Cochise County, and filed the following statement:

On Sunday morning, Spence told me to get breakfast about six o'clock, which I did; after that we had a quarrel, during which he struck me and my mother and during which he threatened to shoot me. My mother told him he would have to shoot her too. His expression was that if I said a word about something I knew, he would kill me, that he was going to Sonora and would leave my dead body behind him. Spence didn't tell me so, but I know he killed Morgan Earp. I think he did it because he arrived at the house all atremble and both the others that came with him. Spence's teeth were chattering when he came in, and I asked if he wanted something to eat and he said he didn't. Myself and my mother heard the shots, and it was a little after when Spence came in with Indian Charlie.

She indicated that Indian Charlie was the scout who kept an eye on the Earps, and who informed Spence and the others that Wyatt and Morgan would be at the pool parlor.

Marietta had had enough of Pete's beatings, and when he turned on her mother as well, that was the last straw, and she had sought help from her neighbor, Sarah Marcus.

※

It was a sad group that left Tombstone. Virgil was able to handle the lines of the buggy that carried the coffin. Morgan had been laid out in a new suit bought by Doc Holliday.

Allie, Lou and Hattie rode with Virgil. Wyatt, Warren, Doc, Turkey Creek Johnson, and Sherman McMasters rode close behind. They were heavily armed. Occasionally they spotted horsemen riding parallel to them, just out of rifle range.

They stabled their horses at a livery in Contention, and boarded the train.

As the train slowed on its approach to Tucson, United States marshal Joseph Evans swung aboard. He informed the Earp party that Frank Stillwell, Pete Spence, Ike Clanton, and a half-breed had been seen in town that afternoon.

"Wyatt, this is a civil matter. I can't be of any use to you. It's out of my jurisdiction. Bob Paul can't help you, either. He's out of town. You're on your own." Then he stepped off the slow-moving train.

Wyatt didn't care. He was going to do as he pleased anyway.

The sun had set and night was upon them when the train finally pulled into Tucson. They would remain there several hours while it took on coal and water.

Because the run through Arizona and on into California would be long and dusty, with few stops along the way, it was decided that Virgil and the ladies would take dinner at the San Zavier while Wyatt and Doc stood guard inside, and the rest of the boys stood guard outside the restaurant.

The dinner was good, and the ladies asked for box lunches to take back with them to the train. All of them relaxed in this pleasant atmosphere until it was time to re-board, then they proceeded cautiously back to the station.

A heavy cloud cover had rolled in while the Earp party was at dinner, and now the almost total darkness was broken only by occasional shafts of moonlight which came through breaks in the clouds. It was during one of those breaks that Wyatt caught a glimpse of movement from a flatcar idled on an adjacent siding. He gave Virgil's hand a squeeze. There was no need for words. Virgil got the message.

The men assisted the ladies onto the station platform, and Wyatt watched as Virgil led them to their seats opposite a large window in the passenger car. Hattie looked out at Wyatt and mouthed the words, "Take care of yourself, Uncle Wyatt."

Wyatt motioned to Doc, and they dropped down from the platform. After quickly briefing him as to what he'd seen, they crouched low and made a wide circle, coming up behind and at opposite ends of the flatcar. In a flicker of moonlight, they saw two men with guns aimed at the approaching train. The window opposite which Virgil and the ladies were seated would soon be passing by.

Wyatt fired from the hip. The shot skimmed the bed of the flatcar, and the gunmen took off at a dead run. They raced right into Doc, who was as surprised as they were. Doc went down, and one of the gunmen landed on top of him. As one, they yelled "Shit!"

The gunman scrambled to his feet just in time to see Wyatt Earp closing in. Wyatt recognized him.

He had already rammed another shell into his scattergun, and now he shoved the gun into Frank Stillwell's belly. In stark terror, Stillwell stared into Wyatt's face and shouted, "Morgan!"

"Wrong! Wyatt!" And Wyatt let loose with both barrels. As the buckshot cut into Stillwell's body, so did two slugs from Doc Holliday's six-gun. Stillwell hadn't stood much of a chance, but it was better than the one he'd given Morgan and little three-year-old Juanita Hancock when he raped her on the kitchen table.

Wyatt turned to Doc. "We're going back."

They hopped a freight to Contention, where they retrieved their horses, and slipped back into Tombstone during the early morning hours.

It was a while before Frank's body was found and taken to Jenkins Funeral Parlor. Ike Clanton had laid low until he could confirm that the shootists were gone, then came forward and identified himself to the authorities. They took him to the funeral parlor, where he confirmed that the body was that of his friend, Frank Stillwell. He insisted that a warrant be issued for the arrest of Wyatt Earp and Doc Holliday, and that it be served by Sheriff Bob Paul in Tombstone.

Paul was fully aware of the problems brewing in Tombstone. He didn't like anything about Ike Clanton, and he particularly didn't like the way he smelled. Nevertheless, it was his sworn duty to wire John Behan to hold the two for questioning. Once done, he made haste for Tombstone.

Fortunately for Wyatt and Doc, the telegrapher who received Paul's wire was a friend. He hurried over to the Cosmopolitan Hotel and informed them of the telegram, adding that he could hold onto it for a couple of hours.

They realized that they'd have to leave town, and with it their dreams of a long and happy life there. They had to go, and now. The fat was in the fire.

Doc went off to make his peace with Kate.

Wyatt gathered his legal papers and, with a couple of his men, walked to Sarah Marcus's house. He told her he had to leave the Arizona Territory forever.

"When do we leave?" she asked without hesitation.

"We don't. I do," Wyatt answered. "I have to leave before Bob Paul comes, as I know he will. He's a good lawman."

Wyatt paused. "How different it could all have been," he said quietly.

Virgil, Morgan and me here together."

He clenched his teeth, knowing it could never be.

"Paul's my friend," he continued, "but if he demands my guns I'll have to give them to him. In all good faith, he'd have to put me in jail. Just how long he could protect me in there, I don't know. Not long, I think."

Sarah began to cry.

"The path I intend to take these next weeks has no room in it for you," Wyatt said as he held her close. He handed a paper to Sarah. "Here's the deed to the house Virgil left me, with my written authorization for you to dispose of it. Right now I'm going to the Mining Commission to sell a couple mines that I own. Some of the boys I know will buy my faro games at the Oriental."

Sarah's sagging spirits were restored by Wyatt's act of taking her into his confidence just as though she was his wife. She wiped her tears.

"I am my father's daughter. If I learned anything from him, it's how to make a deal. I'll get you more for it than you ever could."

They laughed heartily, and then Wyatt prepared to go. His time was precious.

"Wells Fargo has promised me money for my work in breaking up this gang of stage robbers. It'll be enough to do me 'til I can get settled. How would you like Colorado?"

"Oh, Wyatt," Sarah answered, "I'd go anywhere with you. I'd even live with you in my mother's house." She giggled at the look on his face, and added, "Well, maybe I wouldn't go quite that far."

Wyatt kissed her and left.

⁂

Bob Paul's telegram was eventually delivered to Johnny Behan, and he was elated.

"That son of a bitch won't get away this time," he crowed. "I'll bury him in Yuma forever, or put him in Boot Hill—preferably the latter."

He gathered a posse from among the locals. There wasn't time to go to Charleston for the men he'd really like to have with him. Nevertheless, among the ten men he did gather were the tried and true Billy Breakenidge and Jim Flynn.

When they arrived at the Cosmopolitan Hotel, he knew they hadn't come a minute too soon. Six horses, in full gear, were tethered to the posts in front of the hotel, along with a mule loaded with supplies.

Behan marched into the foyer and demanded that Chris Bilicke's son, Albert, go fetch Wyatt.

"I have a warrant for his arrest," he boasted, "and I and these gentlemen here aim to serve it."

Albert's services weren't needed. Wyatt had been upstairs conferring with his attorney, Colonel Herring, when he heard the commotion, and he descended the staircase. With him were Warren Earp, Texas Jack Vermillion, Turkey Creek Johnson, Sherman McMasters, and Doc Holliday. Except for Doc, they were all carrying double-barreled shotguns and wore their six-shooters in plain sight. Doc's gun was concealed beneath his coat.

Johnny pompously approached Wyatt and said, "I want to see you."

Wyatt glared at him, then brushed him aside as he strode by.

"You just did," he sneered.

Wyatt and his men mounted their horses and rode out of Tombstone. Johnny Behan's posse slowly dispersed.

Three women watched as the Earp party rode away. They were Sarah, Kate and Nell.

The Tucson *Star* reported:

> The sheriff made a weak attempt to arrest the Earp party, but Wyatt Earp told him he didn't want to see him. The Earp party then got on their horses and rode slowly out of town. There is an uneasy feeling among the outlaw element, as Wyatt Earp is known to be on the trail of those who attempted to assassinate Virgil, and who murdered Morgan in cold blood.

Will McLaury left Tombstone and never returned.

In a letter written to his father, he admitted his presence there had resulted in the death of Morgan, and the crippling of Virgil Earp. He wasn't about to stay around and face Wyatt, should Wyatt ever return.

⁂

Nell Cashman walked up to Louis Hancock in the kitchen of the Russ House where he was preparing the evening meal, and handed him the *Epitaph*.

"Louis," she said quietly, "that man Stillwell you said you'd met. According to the paper, Wyatt Earp shot him to death last night in Tucson." He took it and began to read, then stopped, took off his apron and his chef's hat.

"Miss Nell, I'm sorry, but I won't be cooking any more tonight. I can't." Nell was so surprised that she could say nothing, and watched as Louis went into his small room off the kitchen and closed the door. He felt cheated.

22

"I'M YOUR MAN," JOHN RINGO TOLD
Behan, who had gone to Charleston to form another posse. "I'll go anywhere to
get that wheezing son of a bitch, Doc Holliday."

"Johnny boy," Curly Bill Brocius said as he slapped Ringo on the back,
"you take the good doctor and I'll take the Dodge city slicker, Wyatt Earp."

"Not if I get to them first," Ike Clanton bragged.

These were but three of the honest ranchers, as the *Epitaph* sarcastically
called them, that Behan recruited. The others were Phin Clanton, Pony Deal,
Rattlesnake Johnson, and the Hicks brothers, who'd just been released from
Behan's jail. Billy Breakenridge was not there. They all wanted to see Wyatt
Earp dangling from a rope, or dead of lead poisoning.

Behan took this bunch of ruffians back to Tombstone where he could show
off his power by deputizing them. He sent for Bob Paul, who was headquartering
at the Cosmopolitan Hotel.

Paul had a duty to perform. As sheriff of Pima County, he had a warrant
for Wyatt's arrest. He was pretty sure why Stillwell had been shot, and pretty
sure that Wyatt could beat the charges, but in Tucson—not here in Tombstone.
He wanted to talk to Wyatt and square it all away, but the law is the law, and as
a lawman he was sworn to bring him in.

He hurried over to Behan's office, and was appalled to find Ringo, Clanton,
and Curly Bill there.

"My God, Johnny! This is supposed to be an inquest, not an execution!"
he exclaimed. "I only wanted help in tracking down the Earp party so I could talk
to them."

"Earp said it all when he last saw me," Behan replied vehemently. "He
said he wasn't talking. So, with the help of these honest ranchers, I intend to
teach him some manners."

"What legal grounds do you have for pursuing Wyatt and Holliday?" Paul asked. "They were tried and cleared in the McLaury-Clanton affair."

"They killed a former deputy of mine, Frank Stillwell," Behan snapped back.

"You have no witnesses to that," Paul countered.

"Well," Behan retorted, "we'll just bring him back and see how many witnesses we can round up. I don't think he wants to come back, so we'll have to deal with that when we find him."

"You'll be in a hell of a lot of trouble if you do find him, Johnny," Paul reminded him, "because he won't go anywhere with you and this gang of cutthroats. And let me tell you this, Behan. Frank Stillwell was killed in Tucson, which is in Pima County. I am the sheriff of Pima County, and you are the sheriff of Cochise County. It's out of your jurisdiction, Johnny. Let it be."

"Are you coming with us or not?" Behan sputtered.

"I won't ride with you and that bunch," Paul said firmly, and walked away.

⁂

As Wyatt and his men began to saddle up after a night of camping out not too far from the town limits, a familiar rider approached. He'd come straight from Sarah with a note for Wyatt.

She outlined the statement made by Marietta Spence, which the court had accepted as the truth, and it gave Wyatt what he needed: names. Specifically, Pete Spence and Indian Charlie.

The Earp party rode off with renewed purpose, all the while keeping the towering Mount Glenn in sight until they arrived at the south pass of the Dragoons.

Doc said to Wyatt, "This is heavenly—the quiet, the mountains, the trees, the little brook, the blue sky." He paused, took a deep breath, and continued, "That son of a bitching, back-shooting Spence isn't fit to walk in this God's country."

"God's country?" Wyatt exclaimed, looking over at Doc. "Since when are you getting all fired up about God's country?"

"Wyatt, riding through all this beautiful country, not seeing a living soul other than ourselves, and thinking back to town with all its miseries, it just makes me wonder. Makes me wonder what life is all about."

A coughing fit put an end to his philosophizing, and Wyatt reached over to give him a gentle pat on the back.

They arrived at Pete Spence's lumber camp at eleven in the morning. Ted Judah, who was Spence's foreman, approached.

"What do you boys want way out here? Won't be doing any cutting 'til Pete gets back."

"He's not here?" Wyatt asked, dismayed. "Spence isn't here? Damn!"

Just beyond a large wagon standing by a pile of downed timber, Wyatt saw a man making a run for it.

"Hold up there," he called out, and the man ducked behind a tree.

Sherm McMasters, a crack shot with a rifle, put his Winchester '73 to his shoulder and sent a .44 caliber bullet crashing into the tree. The man came out with his hands in the air, pleading *"No mas. No mas."* It was Indian Charlie.

He warily approached the six mounted men. *"¿Por qué?"* he asked.

Indian Charlie spoke no English, but Sherm was fluent in Spanish. He questioned Indian Charlie, and Charlie sang like a canary. McMasters interpreted for both men as Wyatt continued the questioning.

When asked about Morgan's murder, Charlie spilled so fast he almost ran over his own words. He swore he'd only held the horses for Curly Bill, Frank Stillwell, Ike Clanton, John Ringo, and Pete Spence.

"They're my friends, you know. They paid me twenty-five dollars."

Wyatt almost choked. "Did I or my brothers ever harm you?" he asked, hardly able to believe what he'd just heard.

"No," Charlie answered.

"Then why did you do this?"

Charlie got the feeling he might be able to weasel out of this situation. After all, these *gringos* were talking, not shooting. They were just after a few facts.

"Curly Bill, he gave me the money. He said I had to shoot anybody who got in the way of him and the boys while they was shooting the Earps. I just held the horses. I didn't shoot nobody."

"For twenty-five dollars you held the horses and stood by while they shot my brother?" asked the incredulous Wyatt.

"That's right," Charlie answered smugly. "You just take me to Sheriff Behan in Tombstone. You got no business talking to me. It's his business."

Wyatt, who had been fighting to control his rage, lost it. He screamed at Charlie, "For twenty-five dollars you allowed my brother to be shot down! Draw your gun!"

Indian Charlie had been in confrontations before. He had once cleared out a bar in Naco, Sonora, on the Mexican border, in a situation just like this. He didn't carry two guns for nothing.

"He stepped back, saying, "I don't fight all of you."

"You fight me!" Wyatt thundered. "It wasn't their brother you helped kill. It was mine! You do it now! Go to shooting!"

Indian Charlie drew.

"An eye for an eye, eh, Wyatt?" Doc said as they rode away from Spence's lumber camp.

"He was my brother, Doc."

"I know. And he's going to eternity in the suit I bought for him. Damn those bastards!"

"Behan would have let him run, I just know it," Wyatt commented. He felt just a little guilty about the odds Indian Charlie had faced. He knew Doc and the boys would never have let him lose that fight.

"Still," he thought, "it was an even contest."

"I gave him a chance, Doc. You saw that. It could have gone the other way."

"Don't sweat it, Wyatt," Doc replied.

He returned to his earlier reflective mood, and quoted from Numbers in the Old Testament. "Blood pollutes the land, and no expiation can be made for the land, for the blood that is shed in it, except by the blood of him who shed it."

"Morgan would have liked that," Wyatt told him.

"Yeah," said Doc.

And they rode on.

⁂

Ted Judah didn't dare approach the grove of trees until the next morning, when he was sure the six riders were long gone. The day before, he'd counted twelve shots, and when he found Indian Charlie's body, it had twelve bullet holes in it.

"It wasn't my business," he told the court in Tombstone, "and I didn't want to make it my business. Charlie had his gun halfway out of his holster when he was hit. After he was down, I guess everybody took a shot at him. I kind of liked him, but he was a hard case. Tell those Earp people I didn't have anything to do with their brothers. I just work out there. As a matter of fact, I think I can probably do better in Tucson."

He moved there the next day.

.⚜.

One of the six men galloped hard to Tombstone. He went straight to John Clum, and the two of them gathered members of the Safety Committee. They insisted on a meeting outside of town, because if Wyatt came in and Bob Paul were to see him, it would mean trouble. Wyatt would either have to defy the law or be taken in, and if that happened, Behan would be the winner. The county would be his.

The meeting took place in a sheltered cove in Walnut Gulch, where Clum handed Wyatt twenty-six hundred dollars.

That was a lot of money. It had come from Dake's headquarters at Prescott.

"He wants you to clean out the rustlers and outlaws around these parts. He really wants Bill Brocius out of here. We all think you're the only one who can do it."

"I've got nothing left to do in this territory," Wyatt responded bitterly. "I can use the money to pay the boys here for the time they're losing on my behalf. John, you know it's not the money I want. I'm after Morgan's killers."

"I know, Wyatt," Clum said. "Those men right now are over in the Whetstones looking for you. I've got ways of knowing what's going on. Brocius is with them. They are one of two posses out looking for you. Behan's heading the other one. They've gone to Fort Huachuca to get Apache guides to track you down. Frank Leslie won't be a part of it."

"Whetstone mountains?" Wyatt repeated.

"Yes," Clum replied. "Wells Fargo has put up another thousand for you or anyone else that brings in those stage robbers. They want the lines running smooth and safe again. Folks are afraid to use them, what with all the holdups going on. I'll get a couple of my boys to bring the money to you. Are you familiar with Mescal Springs in the Whetstones? They'll meet you there."

Texas Jack Vermillion spoke up. "I know it. I'll take us there. It's a good place to spend the night. Plenty of water and trees."

They talked a while longer, then the six men mounted up and resumed their hunt for Spence, Ringo, and the rest.

Wyatt looked at the envelope which Clum had pressed into his hands. It was a letter from Sarah.

It was a good twenty-five miles of open, rough country from Walnut Gulch to Mescal Springs, and that was about all the men and their horses could take in one days' travel under the hot Arizona sun. They'd stayed vigilant, and saw no signs of any other horsemen along the way. Texas Jack, who prided himself on his scouting abilities, rode the point.

"I think it'll be safe to camp the night there," he told them. "No one's around, and the boys with your Fargo money can catch up with us. We'll keep an eye out for Brocius and Behan. We'll see them before they see us. I sure hope Behan doesn't get any Apache scouts, though. Kinda nice that Buckskin wouldn't have anything to do with Johnny."

That was about as windy as Texas Jack ever got. He'd used up his ration of words for the day.

They entered a narrow gorge defined on either side by sheer rock escarpments. It was the only way into this side of the Whetstone Mountains.

Wyatt said to Jack, "Tonight, we'll put a man here. Nothing can get to us from the east without being spotted."

He relaxed, loosened his gun belt, and the scarf around his neck.

Sherm trotted up alongside. "I'll be glad for a good cup of coffee and a little Forty-Rod. This has been one long day. I'll go back and tell them to hurry the mule. I can almost smell the coffee."

"Hold it a minute," Wyatt whispered urgently. "I smell coffee now."

He motioned for Sherm to follow and, with guns at the ready, rode cautiously around an outcropping of rock. Just beyond, they saw a primitive shack surrounded by a dense grove of trees.

"My God!" Sherm whispered. "It's Curly Bill!"

Sure enough, there he was—the object of their search. He and his posse had entered the mountains from the west. He was sitting on a log, holding a skillet over a small fire, and a pot of coffee was brewing nearby. A Wells Fargo shotgun was laying next to him.

Behind Brocius, eight men stopped what they were doing and stared in disbelief at Wyatt Earp.

Curly Bill looked up, shouted "I'll be a...." and left off as he brought his shotgun up and pulled both triggers. His aim was off. The double charge of buckshot merely tore into Wyatt's coat, blew his hat off, and put some holes in his trousers.

Curly never had a chance to finish what he'd started to say, because Wyatt's scattergun roared at the same instant. Eighteen buckshot from both barrels nearly cut Curly Bill Brocius in half.

Wyatt's gun, going off as it did almost in its ear, caused his horse to buck and rear back. Texas Jack reached over and grabbed the reins as Wyatt leaped off.

Curly's men opened fire with their six-shooters. Their rifles, fortunately, were all tucked into the scabbards of their saddles some distance away. Their aim wasn't good, but it was good enough to bring down Texas Jack's horse. Jack went down with it.

Wyatt had one of his six-shooters out and banged off five quick shots. One struck Pony Deal. He fell, and was dragged away by his friends.

"Let's get out of here!" Wyatt called to Texas Jack; but Jack, who had paid dearly for his horse's equipment, shouted back, "Ain't no one getting this!"

Ignoring Wyatt, he took the saddle off his horse and backed away. A couple of slugs had torn through it. Texas Jack's saddle had saved his life. Protected by his dead horse, and using the saddle as a gun rest, he began some serious shooting.

While this was going on, Doc and the rest of the boys rode in. The action was heating up, and the sharp crack of Winchester rifles could be heard above the din.

Wyatt straightened up. "Damn! I'm hit!" he cried out. "Let's go!"

Doc, who was miffed at having missed a good scrap, shouted, "No! Let's go in and get them!"

Wyatt was hobbling about with his gun belt hanging down to his knees, all the while firing away with his other pistol and trying without success to re-mount. He stopped long enough to pull up the gun belt and unsheath his Winchester.

He finally managed to get back on his horse, and hollered at Doc, "They've got their long guns now. We'd never get across the hollow. We've gotta go!"

And go they did—through the gorge and out of the Whetstone Mountains. What they didn't know was that with Curly Bill shot to pieces, and Pony Deal bleeding away, the others had lost their fighting spirit.

Wyatt examined his leg, and saw that his good fortune had held again. The heel of his boot had been blown off. Nothing more.

Having missed meeting up at Mescal Springs with the messenger bringing Wells Fargo's thousand dollars, Wyatt and his five saddle-weary men had turned north toward the Sierra Bonita Ranch. One of the largest ranches in southeastern

Arizona Territory, it was owned by Colonel Henry Clay Hooker, a tall, well-built man with a pot belly brought on by years of the good life.

As president of the Arizona Cattlemen's Association, he was a friendly ally. Hooker was well-liked. He played it straight with all comers, and boasted that he could judge a man by the way he throws his saddle on his horse.

"A man is what he is, not what he was," was his motto. This open-mindedness—which did not extend to cattle rustlers, whom he loathed—had made him famous.

Colonel Hooker's ranch was beautiful, as its name indicated. It was different than the usual spreads of the time with their sod houses, lean-to barns, and makeshift bunkhouses. His was a baronial estate boasting elaborate corrals, a blacksmith shop, a windmill which pumped water into a twenty thousand gallon tank, and great herds of blooded stock. He took pride in his animals, which were often the target of rustlers.

Knowing they were in no danger of being served with warrants in this area, the six riders relaxed as they approached the ranch. They marveled at the beauty of the setting, which they likened to a picture on a calendar.

Wyatt and his men had been observed for some time by a group of well-equipped horsemen known as "Hooker's Army." Through their binoculars, they had recognized Wyatt and a couple of his men, so when they met up they took Earp and his party directly to the Colonel.

The Colonel's greeting was hearty and sincere. His hospitality also extended to the horses, which were fed, watered, and rubbed down before being taken to stalls in the barn. The Colonel, seeing that Texas Jack was without a mount, offered him one.

Jack responded laconically, "Won't need a saddle. Got one."

They were served a meal as good as any of them could recall, and after they'd eaten they were served coffee, fine whiskey, and cigars on the long, shady porch of the main ranch house. They settled into congenial conversation.

"Wyatt," the Colonel stated, "I heard all about your doings down in Tomb-stone. That O. K. Corral affair must have been a dandy. You sure did us out here a favor, putting down the McLaurys and the Clanton boy. Too bad you couldn't have finished them all right then and there."

Doc spoke up. "I told him he should have potted Ike while he had the chance."

Wyatt shook his head. "I just couldn't get him to draw his gun. He just wouldn't go to fighting."

"The world is full of "should haves," the Colonel responded. "If I'd stayed in the army after the war, today I'd be a General. A poor General," he laughed. "Now I'm a rich rancher. No, "should haves" around here."

He changed the subject. "I heard you put down Old Man Clanton. Is that true?"

"I was there," Wyatt answered. "He went down all right, but I didn't do it. Doc did."

"Is there no way you can stop Behan?" Hooker asked. "He's given the rustlers a powerful boost. When you get a crooked lawman, you're really in a pile of cow chips."

"Can't shoot him," Wyatt continued. "He's got too many politicians on his side. If we did that, we'd have to go to Mexico. I don't want to do that."

Doc chimed in again. "Shame him out of town. That's what you've got to do with boomers like him. Get him laughed out of town. I always got a boot out of old Virg telling how those China boys took after Johnny. After that, he was finished in Prescott for good."

He followed this pronouncement with a coughing jag, a puff on his cigar, and a sip of whiskey.

"Might have something there," Hooker nodded. "With the McLaurys out of the picture, the Clantons busted up, and Curly Bill across the great divide, old Johnny boy doesn't have much of a hand to play any more."

"He's still got John Ringo," Sherm McMasters put in.

"I don't think Ringo can do much any more," the Colonel stated. "He's a loner, not a leader. Somehow that reminds me. Did you boys have anything to do with—or know anything about—the doings not too far from here at the Blue Jay Ranch?"

"Never heard of it," was the reply.

"Just wondered. A couple of lowlifes, Fred McSween and Harry Kent, owned a place up beyond me not too far from Safford. They did a lot of loose branding, and I swear they got ahold of one of my prize breeders, but never could prove it. Kent got his due when the bovines stampeded and trampled him to death. McSween disappeared for a while, but someone got to poking around one day and accidentally found the old coot—or what was left of him—taking a perma- nent siesta in the outhouse behind his ranch. They figured he'd been in there about a month. I always said he smelled like a privy, but the mystery is how he ended up in there, and why."

"I sure wouldn't have wanted to fish him out," Doc said, laughing so hard it brought on another coughing jag.

They all drank a toast to Mr. McSween's private Boot Hill, and then Hooker stood up.

"We usually dress for dinner here at the Bonita, but seeing as how you boys aren't toting your Prince Alberts with you, we'll just have Ming Ling bring some victuals right out here. He's one hell of a find. Not many good cooks in these parts. The best one I know of out this way is a big, fat fellow over at the Tucson Mission. I'd give anything to get him here on the ranch, but I guess he wouldn't be too keen on turning Protestant and coming to live with honest folks like us."

Everyone had a good laugh, including Doc Holliday, who added, "Nell Cashman told me about those *padres*. They do some right nice things."

"Ah, yes, Nellie," Hooker said softly, and raised his glass. "A toast to the Angel of Tombstone."

"I'll drink to that," Doc said, and he and the others raised their glasses.

Bedding was being brought out for the visitors when a ranch hand came pounding in at full gallop.

"They're a ways off yet, but they're a comin'! It's the Behan posse. They'll likely be here tomorrow. They're setting up camp right now at north gap in the Winchesters. There's a whole lot of 'em."

Doc groaned, and lamented, "And I was just mellowing out. There's no rest for the wicked." Colonel Hooker told the men to relax. "Look, I'll just stop them a ways out and tell them to get lost. Behan's out of his county. He doesn't carry any weight here." They all looked to Wyatt, who was shaking his head. "No, Henry, you'd only get into some sort of legal squabble. You don't want to be going back and forth and explaining yourself to the politicians in Prescott. We'll just slip out quiet-like, and find us a nice campsite. We've done it before, and it'll keep you clean."

"I'm really sorry about this," Hooker said sadly. "I've been enjoying myself. A fellow doesn't get much real friendly company out here, and you boys have sure livened up this day for me. I was looking forward to hearing more about Nell. I was pawing the ground for that woman when she lived in Tucson."

"Next time," Doc said with a grin.

When you carry all of your essentials in a bag behind your saddle, it doesn't take long to pack up and move on, which is just what the Earp party did. Later, at their camp on a hill overlooking the valley, they discovered to their surprise that each of their saddlebags held a bottle of good booze and a handful of cigars.

From their vantage point they could look down on the Sierra Bonita, and with his field glasses Wyatt was able to follow Sheriff Behan and his posse as they approached the ranch. Sure enough, John Ringo, Pete Spence, and Ike and Phin Clanton were among the posse.

"It'd be a hell of a battle if we went after them," Wyatt said to his men. "I want Spence more than anything I can think of for killing Morg and wasting Virg's arm. And Ringo, too. I'm sure he was in on it. But we just don't have enough men to go after them right now."

Doc was feeling frisky from his morning toddy. "Hell, we can do it! Let's just ride on down and teach them a thing or two."

"No," Wyatt said emphatically. "We're going to trot down the far side of this hill and ride off. I seriously doubt that we could take them, and besides, I don't want to get Colonel Hooker in any trouble."

The Colonel was waiting when Behan and his men rode up. He'd dealt with petty politicians before, in the army as well as in the cow towns.

"Colonel Hooker," Behan began, "I'm looking for Wyatt Earp, Doc Holliday, and four other fugitives from the law. I've cause to think they've come this way."

"You don't say," Hooker snorted.

Behan continued, "It's the truth. We ran into Tony Crocker a ways back, and got it out of him. He was pretty sure they'd be coming this way."

"Even if I knew, Behan, I wouldn't tell you. Not when you're riding with this murdering bunch of bandits. Johnny, you ought to be ashamed of yourself."

Behan flinched, then snapped back, "I'm going to charge you with protecting and harboring outlaws and murderers. Last October they murdered in cold blood…"

Hooker cut him off. "You just shut your mouth, and go chase your own tail, Behan. You've got no rights in this county. I know the Earps. They've always treated me fair and square, and everyone else, too, so far as I know. And I know you, too. I know your kind of law."

Behan just stood and gaped as Hooker warmed to his subject. "Damn you and your kind, and damn your so-called posse! They're nothing but a bunch of horse thieves and outlaws."

Ike Clanton nodded to Ringo and the others, and cut loose. "Damn that son of a bitch! He knows where they are. Let's make him tell. We can do it."

He moved forward, then noticed none of the others were following.

No less than twelve rifles and shotguns in the hands of Colonel Hooker's "army" were pointed at them. Someone from within that group warned, "You'd better squeeze your bunghole, Ike. You can't come here into a gentleman's yard and call him a son of a bitch. Now, you skin it back! Skin it back! You came here looking for a fight, and you don't need the Earps to get one. You can get it right here."

Ike backed away and shrunk himself into the middle of the pack without saying another word.

"You've certainly surrounded yourself with a bunch of cutthroats, Johnny," the Colonel admonished. "It's not going to look good for you when I bring it up at the next cattlemen's meeting. You're riding with mustangs when you should be riding with thoroughbreds."

Behan felt sick. He knew he was in the wrong place at the wrong time, and with the wrong companions. A voice was screaming inside his head, "Back off! Make it right. Keep your good name."

He urged his horse close to Hooker, and out of earshot of his posse. Harry Woods joined him.

"Colonel," Behan began in a voice barely above a whisper, "they're really not our associates. They just happen to be with Harry and me on this occasion. The boys mean no harm. They had a bad day yesterday. We can keep this to ourselves, can't we? No use bringing in the Cattlemen's Association. I intend to take the boys back right after breakfast. Be in Tombstone tomorrow."

Hooker was surprised, but glad, to win so easily, and replied, "Well, if they're not your associates, I'll have a couple places set for you at the table. They can eat by themselves."

And so they had breakfast. Behan's men smarted at being shunted off, but filling their bellies was more important to them than where they sat to do it.

After breakfast, while the men were getting their horses, Johnny sidled over to the ranch foreman. He didn't know that Hooker was close behind. Thinking no one was watching, he slipped a diamond stud from his shirt and pressed it into the foreman's hand, saying in a low voice, "Look, this is worth over a hundred bucks. You didn't see or hear anything that went on here."

As the foreman pocketed the stud, he looked straight at Behan and gave him a wink. "Nothing happened here that I know of." Johnny looked down, and in that moment the foreman caught Hooker's eye and gave him a wink as well. The Colonel nodded and smiled, and silently returned to where Behan had left him. He chuckled to himself, "This just might be the laugh we need to embarrass Behan. My man said he wouldn't tell, but I didn't get a diamond stud to keep me quiet." He chuckled again. "With that big-mouth Ike Clanton around, I probably won't have to say a thing. He can't quit talking even when he doesn't have anything to say. But he will now."

Tensions had eased, and a friendlier atmosphere prevailed as Behan's posse mounted up to leave. The ranch hands and the riders were exchanging pleasantries as Johnny called to the Colonel, "Has there been any Indian sign around here lately? Do we have to be on the lookout?"

"Not recently," Hooker called back. "Last year, though, we had some burnings. Not far from here they burned down a ranch and murdered a man and his wife and kid. Haven't heard of any since."

Ringo and Spence reined up when they heard this exchange, and listened intently as the Colonel continued, "Strange thing. Do you know the Blue Jay Ranch?"

"Heard of it," Behan replied, "what about it?"

"Pete McSween was the owner. He disappeared a couple months ago, and they found him rotting in his own privy. No one knows how he got in there. A man usually doesn't lay down in his own shit to die."

Hooker thought about what he'd just said, and it made him laugh. He never had liked McSween.

All of the men laughed with him, except Ringo and Spence.

Ringo spoke up. "I knew the man. Met him once. Any suspicions as to who was responsible for it?"

"No," Hooker answered, "but I heard tell that one of his ranch hands was mending fence the day McSween came up missing. He claims to have seen a weird-looking man poking around. He kept himself out of sight, then took off, 'cause he didn't want to have a run-in with him."

"Weird-looking?" Ringo asked. "In what way?"

"Well, for one thing, he said he was real big, and swore he was colored. He said he wore a patch over one eye, and walked with a limp."

"One eye?" Ringo exclaimed.

"Yeah, and that he had a scar on his face. We think the cowpoke had been nursing a bottle. No coloreds out here. Last one we had owned one of the ranches that was burned out. No, you boys won't have any Indian trouble going back. Might have a little Earp trouble, but none with the Indians."

Again, Hooker had amused himself with his own joke, and laughed. No one else did.

"Shit! Can you beat that? Buried in shit! That takes a lot of imagination,"

Ike Clanton chortled.

John Ringo and Pete Spence had nothing to say as the posse rode back to Tombstone.

That night, Ringo had another bad dream.

23

WHEN JOHNNY BEHAN RETURNED TO
Tombstone following his failed attempt to apprehend the "murdering Earp gang,"
people began to question their sheriff's ability to bring law and order to their
community.

George Parsons spoke for the town when he wrote in his journal:

> ...Mileage still counting up for our rascally sheriff. He organizes pos-
> ses, goes to within a mile of his prey, and then returns...

The story of Johnny's bribe to the foreman to keep the doings at Hooker's
ranch quiet, had been leaked to the press.

In southeastern Arizona, Colonel Henry Clay Hooker was looked upon as
a paragon of honesty, and he was the hero of every law-abiding rancher. When he
or his close associates had something to say, everyone paid attention. Therefore,
since the leak had originated from Hooker's ranch, no one doubted the story. The
idea that the "Pride of Tombstone," as Behan's campaign posters proclaimed him
to be, had come crawling home with his tail between his legs, didn't set well with
the community. There were those who considered the Earps and Doc Holliday to
be a tough bunch, but they recognized that they stood up to the thieving likes of
Curly Bill Brocius and the Clantons. Furthermore, they were fully aware that
Bob Paul, another man of impeccable credentials and reputation, rode with the
Earps, not with Behan.

Johnny's star began to fall, and John Clum's editorials kept digging in as
he wrote about Behan's posse of so-called honest ranchers: Ringo, Spence,
Claiborne, Stillwell, and Brocius, to name a few. All were under indictment or
under suspicion of dastardly crimes against the state. He wrote:

> ...We understand that the taxpayers of Cochise County will be called

upon to pay $3000 for the employment of cowboy deputy sheriffs in a fruitless endeavor to capture the Earps. Add to this the ten per cent for collection ($300), and a diamond pin, and you'll see how dearly we pay for the whistle.

The mockery continued. Each one of the Behan posse became the butt of innumerable jokes. Some laughed it off. Others, like Ringo's friend William Claiborne, were more thin-skinned, and resentful.

Claiborne went strolling into the bar at the Oriental one afternoon, wearing his six-guns low on his hips in imitation of John Ringo. With Virgil Earp away, the ban on wearing side arms in town was poorly enforced.

He strutted up to the long bar, banged on it with his fist, and in a loud voice called out, "Let's have a shot and a beer for Billy the Kid here."

Buckskin Leslie was behind the bar that afternoon, and he had never liked Claiborne.

"Well, well, well, well, well," he sang out in his loudest baritone so that everyone could hear. "Here we have one of Johnny Behan's brave men. Here's the lad who chased Wyatt Earp and Doc Holliday all over the territory, probably scared to death he'd find them. Now here he is demanding a drink, and those "miserable outlaws" are still somewhere out there, on the loose. Well, I guess if he's got his allowance, we'll have to accommodate him. Here you are, Billy," he said, and poured four fingers and a tall mug of beer.

Some of the patrons laughed out loud, and a few at the bar tittered and moved away.

Always a show-off, Billy knocked down the four fingers in one gulp, and followed with a hefty swallow of beer.

"You boys got it all wrong," he exclaimed. "Those Earps were running so fast we jus' couldn't catch up. We wanted a gun fight, but it seems they wanted a horse race. I guess they won." He laughed uproariously.

"Bullshit!" said Leslie from behind the bar. He was getting irked.

Claiborne's drink took hold in a hurry. He deliberately turned his back on Frank and faced the men in the room. He was armed and ready for bear, but he could see that no one there was interested in a confrontation, and that gave him courage.

"Any o' you boys got anythin' ta say? I'm ready ta back up my words. You fellas out there want ta get fiesty 'bout it, jus' say so."

No one made a move, and Billy fancied that he was in control of this crowd and this situation.

Frank had had enough. He picked a full spittoon off the floor and lifted it over Billy's head, then tipped it upside down and jammed it over his ears. Spittal, cigar butts, and slime oozed over Billy's face and onto his shoulders. A string of unintelligible words sounded from beneath the spittoon, and Frank gave it a good rap with his six-shooter. Then he knocked on it with his knuckles, singing out, "How you doing in there, Billy Boy?"

By this time, everyone in the bar was doubled over with laughter, and they began singing, "Oh, where have you been, Billy Boy, Billy Boy?" Some came up to bang on the spittoon.

Even the dedicated poker players came up to have a look as word quickly spread about the boy wearing a brass crown.

"Shtop that!" Billy yelled. He was flailing away, trying to get the spittoon off his head, shouting, "Get this sonabitch off me!"

He tried to lift it off. He banged, he thumped, and he tugged, but the spittoon was on to stay.

"Get him out of here," Frank ordered. "I've had enough of that asshole. Billy the Kid. Unbelievable."

Several of the patrons led Billy through the saloon, out onto the boardwalk, and left him there. The would-be terror of Cochise County sputtered and raged, and pleaded and begged for someone to help him rid himself of the miserable headgear. A few men walked around him, howling with laughter and taunting him.

Some ladies felt sorry for Billy and attempted to twist the stinking pot off his head, but it wouldn't budge. Eventually, several of them—against the advice of their husbands—led Billy over to Doctor Goodfellow's office. There the doctor lived up to his name. It took a lot of grease, and a lot of twisting and tugging, but he finally managed to get the offensive pot off Billy's head.

The day after his humiliating experience in Tombstone, Billy was at the American nursing a beer when Ringo, Spence and Breakenridge walked in. Billy hoped that word of yesterday's misfortune hadn't reached Charleston, but one look at his friends' faces and he knew better.

The boys sat down, and Breakenridge opened the copy of the *Epitaph* that he had with him, and laid it out for Billy to read.

This afternoon your correspondent was treated to a sight never seen in our fair city. Like a diver fresh from the depths of the ocean, an apparition appeared in front of the Oriental Saloon. It was dressed as we all dress, with shirt, pants, and shoes, but instead of a Stetson it wore a brass pot which covered the head completely, right down to the shoulders. There were no holes for it to see out of.

Several of our more bold citizens rapped on this contraption. One of them said, "I say, anybody home?" Strange noises came from inside. Your correspondent stepped up for a closer inspection, and was immediately assailed by the smell of stale beer, cigar butts and spittal. He recognized it immediately as a spittoon recently at use in the bar at the Oriental. The offending pot couldn't be budged from the head of the poor unfortunate, who was inside making a lot of noise.

We followed some compassionate ladies as they led the potted man to Doctor Goodfellow's office. There, using the skills which he had learned at our prestigious medical schools, the good doctor succeeded in removing the spittoon from the head of none other than Mr. William Claiborne.

Mr. Claiborne is a driver for William Herring's Neptune Mining Company. He refused to divulge why or how he came to be sporting such an unusual headpiece. We understand that Mr. Claiborne was one of Sheriff Behan's "honest ranchers" who spent much of last month playing hide and seek with Wyatt Earp and company. Maybe the reason they came up empty was that they were all wearing brass hats and couldn't see where they were going.

Billy the Kid Claiborne was totally disgraced. He stared at Breakenridge with his mouth wide open. Breakenridge, who always enjoyed a good laugh, could hardly contain himself.

"Hell's bells," Ringo said sourly, "that's nothing to get yourself all tickled over, Breck. Spence and I were in that posse, too. I don't like the way they're making fun of us."

He turned to Claiborne and asked, "Who did it to you, Billy?" Though he spoke softly, his voice had an edge to it.

"Frank Leslie did it, that's who," Billy blurted. "The son of a bitch caught me when I wasn't lookin'. He couldn'ta done it if I'd been lookin' at him. He's just a big mouth when it comes to fightin', and he's not so good with his guns, either. I could've taken him easy if he'd a fought fair."

Claiborne went on to tell the whole story, but with plenty of embellishments as to the role he played in it. In his version, he held off the whole Oriental crowd with his six-guns. He didn't know when to shut up, and planted some serious doubts in his friends' minds when he added that everyone was afraid to draw on him even though he couldn't see a thing. That went way beyond being taken with a grain of salt.

Regardless of the truth of the matter, Ringo was angry, and the more Breakenridge laughed, the hotter Ringo got.

He'd been slugging down the booze for days before this, and his hostility against Frank Leslie turned to red-hot fury. He liked Billy Claiborne, the first friend he'd made in Tombstone. He was convinced that Leslie had taken unfair advantage of the young Texan.

He leaped to his feet, and in an ice-cold voice commanded, "Let's go get that son of a bitch!"

The other three were out of their chairs before he finished saying it, and the foursome headed northeast to Tombstone. It was dusk when they trotted into town, where lights were being lit and people were gearing up for another night's activities.

Breakenridge had talked like a Dutch uncle to Ringo the whole way back, trying to avoid a showdown. Over and over he repeated, "It's a no-win situation. There'll be too many people around, and some innocent bystander could get hit by a stray bullet. Then there'd be hell to pay. They've had enough shooting there already."

Billy realized his pleas were falling on deaf ears, and finally said, "I can't be a part of this, but I'll stand by you and make sure you get a fair play if you're stupid enough to go through with it."

As they rode up to the Oriental, Breakenridge noticed that Ringo had begun to sober up. They tied down their horses and walked into the bar. Ringo sized up the room and decided he liked the look of things. He motioned to Spence to cover his rear, and to Claiborne to join him at the bar. Breakenridge sat alone at a table.

"I want to see Leslie," Ringo announced in a loud voice, "and I want to see him now." Everyone within earshot sensed that trouble was brewing.

Breakenridge heaved a sigh of relief as the barkeep answered, "He ain't here."

"Where is he?" Ringo demanded.

The bartender looked around, then back to Ringo. "He left a little while ago."

Ringo picked up a pool cue that had been left leaning against the bar. He raised it over his head and slammed it down on the bar so hard it broke in half.

"I said, 'Where is he?' you pisswilly!"

The bartender wasn't looking for trouble, and he answered quickly, "He went over to the Russ House to see Nell Cashman."

"You sure about that?"

"Yes."

Ringo and his buddies left the Oriental and headed down Fifth Street toward the Russ House just a block away.

He pushed the door open and walked boldly in. A quick look around told him there were no pistols in sight—just locals having their evening meal. Ringo was pleased.

Nell Cashman was sitting at a table near the door to the kitchen, and opposite her, with his back to Ringo, Buckskin Leslie was drinking coffee.

Ringo loosened the pistol in his holster, pulling it halfway out and letting it slip back in. Breakenridge put his hand on Ringo's arm, and whispered a warning: "No backshooting, John."

"I don't need to backshoot that son of a bitch," he snarled, and quickly strode around Nell's table so he stood facing Frank Leslie.

Nell jumped to her feet, and knocked over the cup of coffee she'd been drinking.

"Stay where you are," Ringo demanded. His gun was out of its holster and pointed at Leslie.

Frank knew this was real trouble, and he wanted to know why. "What's this all about?" he asked.

"Leslie," Ringo said menacingly, "you've stepped over the line once too often. Your free-wheeling days are over. You can buffalo Ike Clanton and shoot his dad..."

"Hold it, Ringo!" Leslie interrupted. "I never shot the old man."

"Well now, looks like we've got the great sharp-shooting Indian scout trying to weasel out of a scrap. Lying won't get you out of this one, Leslie. I was there in Skeleton Canyon. I saw it all."

"I figured that was you," Frank answered blandly.

Frank was in a bind, and he knew it. It didn't get any better for him when

Billy Claiborne came alongside Ringo and drew one of his revolvers.

"How do you like looking at me in the face for a change, you smart-ass tinhorn? You old fart!"

Leslie had a few years on these men, all right, and he had also learned from past experience. He remembered the time Old Man Clanton had said, "If you pull a gun on a man, shoot him!"

These men were talking, not shooting, and Leslie decided to try and turn that to his advantage.

"So," he teased, "here's Kid Spittoon. Didn't that nice clean bath teach you anything at all?"

Claiborne was trembling with excitement. "Le's do him now, John. Le's turn him into a lead mine!"

Pete Spence joined his friends, even though he was apprehensive about this encounter. He'd grown up listening to stories about Frank Leslie. He positioned himself a little behind Ringo and Claiborne, and pulled his pistol.

Leslie continued, "And now we've got Pete Spence, the wife beater. Hell, you beat up old ladies too, I hear."

The barb stung Spence. "Let's do it," he snapped.

Leslie's expression hardened. Nell had seen that look once before, when he'd faced down the two Apache warriors.

"No!" she cried out. "No! Don't do it!"

Louis Hancock was busy in the kitchen, and wasn't aware of the drama unfolding in the dining room just a few feet away until he heard Nell cry out. Without a moment's hesitation, he grabbed the double-barrel, ten-gauge shotgun that hung on the kitchen door, swung the door open, and stepped into the restaurant.

Three men were standing with their backs to him, and he could see they all had guns in their hands. Leslie and Nell were facing the men, and likewise facing Louis. Most of the diners were scrambling to get out of there.

"Anyone pull a trigger here," roared Louis, "and I'll cut him in two with this scatter gun. You hear me?" He pulled back the hammers on both barrels.

Ringo could feel the blood draining from his face the moment he heard that voice. He'd only heard it once before, but he'd never forget it. Nor would he forget where he'd heard it. He was afraid to turn around and look, but he had to. If ever a prayer passed Ringo's lips, it did now as he slowly turned: "Don't let it be." But it was.

His pistol fell from his hand and clattered on the floor. He staggered backwards, grabbed a chair, and hung onto it.

Louis, who'd been looking at Ringo, gasped, "My God!" His heart was beating so hard it pained him.

He saw Leslie draw his pistol and level it at Spence, who'd turned ashen just like Ringo.

Claiborne had watched his two friends turn to jelly. "What in hell's going on here?" he stammered, knowing full well the game was over for him and his pals.

Turning to Leslie, he spouted, "We was jus' hurrahin' ya, man. It didn't mean nothin'!"

Then he turned to Louis. "Don' go shootin' me! I was jus' walkin' with 'em."

Louis found his voice. He waved the muzzle of his gun toward the door. "You run along, sonny. I've got no quarrel with you."

"Billy the Kid" Claiborne got out of the Russ House faster even than he had exited the O. K. Corral.

Then Nell spoke up. "Do you know these men, Louis?"

"Miss Nell," he replied, "I've known them every hour of every day of my life for some time now. And they know me."

But that damnable, nagging thought was going through his mind again. "This isn't the time. This isn't the place. 'Specially with Miss Nell here in her nice restaurant." Still, his finger continued to caress the triggers of his gun.

Deputy Billy Breakenridge came up and laid his hand on Louis's gun. He turned it aside, saying in a steady, even tone, "Enough trouble for the day. Let's not have any more. I'll take these men along with me. A little time should take care of any misunderstanding."

He retrieved Ringo's six-shooter and led the shaken Ringo and Spence out onto the street. Spence had soiled his pants.

As they neared the front door, Spence groaned, "Breck, that man is dead. I tell you, he's dead! It ain't possible!"

Leslie made sure they went on down the street, then returned to Hancock, and with a broad smile said, "I don't know what you did, but you sure took the sand out of those two!" He grabbed Louis's hand and shook it vigorously.

Louis asked, "They live around here?"

"They do," Frank replied.

"Where?"

"After what you did for me," Leslie answered, "I'll tell you anything you want to know."

"Just so I see them again."

"I'll draw you a map tonight," Frank told him.

"Thank you, Mr. Leslie. Now, please excuse me. I've got to tend to my cooking."

He returned to the kitchen and closed the door.

Frank looked at Nell. She shrugged her shoulders.

"You owe us a coffee, Nell," he said lightly, and sat down at the table.

⁂

The federal authorities were taken aback when Pete Spence came in that week and voluntarily gave himself up as a participant in the Bisbee stagecoach robbery. They were even more surprised when he practically demanded that he be taken immediately—that very day—to the Yuma State Penitentiary.

Marshal Dake commented that he thought Spence was running away from something—something that only the prison walls could protect him from. "Sure beats me," he laughed.

Meanwhile, "Billy the Kid" Claiborne vowed that he wasn't through with Frank "Buckskin" Leslie. Not by a darn sight.

John Ringo returned to the American Hotel in Charleston, and that night took two bottles of whiskey to bed with him. He had another nightmare. It would be his last.

24

TURKEY OR MORSE'S HILL CREEK
14ᵗʰ July, 1882

Statement for the information of the Coroner and Sheriff of Cochise Co. A.T.

There was found by the undersigned John Yoast the body of a man in a clump of Oak trees about 20 yards north from the road leading to Morse's mill and about a quarter of a mile west of the house of B. F. Smith. The undersigned viewed the body and found it in a sitting position, facing west, the head inclined to the right.—There was a bullet hole in the right temple, the bullet coming out on the top of the head on the left side. There is apparently a part of the scalp gone including a small portion of the forehead and part of the hair, this looks as if cut out by a knife. (These are the only marks of violence visible on the body.) Several of the undersigned identify the body as that of John Ringo, well known in Tombstone. He was dressed in light hat, blue shirt, vest, and undershirt torn up so as to protect his feet. He had evidently traveled but a short distance in this foot gear. His revolver he grasped in his right hand, his rifle rested against the tree close to him. He had on two cartridge belts, the belt for the revolver cartridges being buckled on upside down. The undernoted property were found with him and on his person.—

1 Colt's revolver Cal: 45 No. 222,—containing 5 cartridges
1 Winchester rifle octagon barrel Cal: 45
   Model 1876 No. 21896, containing a cartridge in the breech and 10 in the magazine.
1 Cartridge belt containing rifle cartridges.
1 Do—2 revolver Do
1 Silver watch of American Watch Co. No. 9339 with Silver Chain attached.

Two Dollars & Sixty cents ($2.60) in money.

6 Pistol cartridges in his pocket.

5 shirt studs.

1 small pocket knife.

1 Tobacco pipe—1 Comb

1 Block matches—1 small piece tobacco

There is also a portion of a letter from Messrs. Hereford & I. Zabriskie, Attorneys at Law, Tucson to the deceased John Ringo.—

The above property is left in the possession of Frederick Ward, teamster between Morse Mill and Tombstone

The body of the deceased was buried close to where it was found. When found deceased had been dead about 24 hours.

Thomas White	James Morgan
John Blake	Robert Boller
John W. Bradfield	Frank McKinney
B. F. Smith	W. J. Darnal
W. W. Smith	J. C. McGrager
A. E. Lewis	John Yoast
A. S. Neighbours	Fred Ward

"ENDORSED"

Statement by citizens in regard the death of John Ringo

Filed Nov. 13/82

W. H. Seamans, Clk.

By Louis A. Souc, Depy.

John Ringo died exactly one year to the day after Billy the Kid was shot down by Pat Garrett at Fort Sumner, New Mexico.

This man Ringo, who died in such a strange and mysterious manner, was born May 3, 1850, in Indiana. When he was fourteen, he and his family did what so many enterprising midwesterners of that time did: they went west.

In two well-stocked Conestoga wagons drawn by oxen and mules, their little party—sometimes in company with other immigrants, sometimes alone—headed for California, picking up guides along the way. They crossed the Missouri River at Leavenworth, Kansas, and entered the real west: the west of seemingly endless plains, majestic rock formations, vast herds of buffalo, and Indians.

John's mother kept a journal of this adventure, and it is full of stories about the Indians, some relating to killings, and some about scares. These Hoosiers had their share of adventure, both good and bad.

About two weeks after passing Chimney Rock, that lonely sentinel and signpost of the Oregon Trail, the wagon train corralled for the night.

The following morning, John's father, Martin, walked ahead to scout the trail and look for signs of Indians. He took John with him, and they both carried shotguns.

Some time later a shot was heard, and a number of men from the wagon train hurried to investigate. They found John on the ground, and his father's body a short distance away, his brains scattered all over. John was incoherent. They brought him back to the wagons, and eventually a determination was made that his father's death was accidental.

John never spoke about the incident to a living soul. Consciously or unconsciously, he blotted the incident from his mind, and had absolutely no recollection of what had taken place in the early morning hours of July 30, 1864. Even his intimate friend Billy Breakenridge had no clue as to what it was that ate away at John, causing him to have horrendous nightmares, and to try and drown his demons in a bottle. But they wouldn't go away; not, that is, until July 13, 1882.

The reappearance of Louis Hancock, returned from the hell where Ringo thought he had sent him, unleashed all that Ringo had buried in the deepest recesses of his memory; and everything that had happened that day out on the prairie with his father came flooding back to him.

Martin had accused John of mistreating his younger brother, Martin Albert, and committing "unnatural acts" on the little boy. John vehemently denied it, shouting, "I didn't! That's a lie! That's a lie!"

"Don't you lie to me!" his father shouted back, and advanced toward him with his arm raised.

And then John shot his father's head off.

⁂

John Ringo, the pride of the rustlers and the best of the gunfighters, sat up in his bed and wept until dawn, when Billy Breakenridge heard him and came in to comfort him. Ringo refused to tell Billy what his personal agony was all about.

In the light of day, Ringo realized his real problems weren't with the past. They were here, and now. He knew the big, one-eyed black man would be coming after him, and searched his memory for a safe place to hide. Galeyville, the outlaw stronghold. He'd be safe there among his own kind, and after a while he'd drift on down into Mexico.

"Breck," he said, "ride with me."

"Where to, Johnny?"

"Galeyville."

"I can't. I'm due in court this afternoon, and I've got to be there. I'll go as far as Tombstone with you, though."

"No!" John said emphatically. "I intend to avoid that town."

"We can ride together as far as the outskirts, and then you can go around it."

They went to Montgomery's livery for their horses. As they saddled up, the stable boy came up to John and asked, "You're Mr. Ringo, aren't you?"

"Yeah," John replied. "What's it to you?"

"Fellow was in here looking for you earlier this morning."

"Did he say who he was?"

"No," the boy answered, "he didn't. I never saw him before."

"What'd he look like?"

"He was a big, black man with one eye. And he's got a bad leg too. He limps."

To Breakenridge's surprise, Ringo just looked at the boy and continued to cinch his saddle. Finally he said, more to himself than anyone in particular, "Reckon if he wants me, he'll find me."

They rode east toward the Dragoons.

⁂

Nell Cashman wasn't too surprised when, early that morning, Hancock told her he'd be gone for a couple of days, and possibly more. She watched as he brought Big Black to the Russ House and packed his saddlebags. He took three full canteens of water, a bag of hard biscuits, a pair of field glasses, a Bowie knife in a beaded leather scabbard, his Whitney-Kennedy long rifle, and a Smith and Wesson revolver holstered on his belt.

"Miss Nell," he said, "I'm borrowing your shotgun, if that's all right with you."

"Go ahead, Louis. Are you going hunting?"

"You might say that, Miss Nell," he answered.

She sensed—correctly—that he didn't want to be questioned further, so merely watched as he mounted up and rode off toward Charleston.

In Louis's pocket was a hand-drawn map, detailed as only a professional army scout would likely make it. It showed all the places that John Ringo was known to frequent. Louis was pleased with Frank Leslie's map.

At the time he first encountered Ringo back in Safford, Hancock had thought the only way he'd ever be able to best him would be to bushwhack him, but he didn't like the idea. He'd always fought fair and square, but knew he was no match for Ringo. All the same, he was determined to do whatever it took to avenge the deaths of his wife and children, no matter how much it might go against his grain.

He was on guard as he approached the mill town of Charleston, where he went first to Montgomery's livery stable. He rode Big Black up to the gate, dismounted, and used the horse as a shield as he entered the corral. There was no one there but the stable boy.

"Any of these horses belong to John Ringo?" he asked the boy.

"Yessir, that Bay over there is Mr. Ringo's. He'll be taking it this morning. Said he'd be going to Galeyville today."

Hancock thanked the boy and left the stable thinking "A lot can happen between here and Galeyville."

He turned his horse east toward Tombstone, and then continued on the trail to the south pass of the Dragoon Mountains. He didn't waste any time. Once at the pass, he dismounted, settled down behind a big boulder, and brought out his field glasses.

It wasn't long before he saw someone coming. It was John Ringo! But there was another rider with him—deputy sheriff Billy Breakenridge. Hancock took a sip from his canteen, and kept the glasses to his eyes. He laid his long rifle on the boulder. "Like waiting for Pickett's boys to come to us at Gettysburg. Like a turkey shoot," he thought. He cringed at the memory.

Louis looked at his map and came to a decision. He wanted Ringo alone. So he gathered his things together and spurred Big Black on through the pass and eastward along the trail.

A gradual climb of several hours brought him to Turkey Creek, which was a popular "nooning" spot. He reined up beneath the welcome shade of the tall oak trees, and once more pulled out his field glasses.

His heart skipped a beat. Ringo was coming, and he was alone. This ambush was perfect.

He made a three hundred and sixty degree sweep of the area through his glasses. There was no one else in sight. He took a pull on his canteen and waited.

Ringo was drunk. He knew he was drunk, and what's more, he didn't care. He tossed an empty whiskey bottle against a rock and heard it break, then reached into his saddlebag for another. There was still a good hour or more to go before he reached Turkey Creek.

All of a sudden his horse balked, and lifted its foreleg. Ringo dug in his spurs, but the horse refused to go.

"Damn!" Ringo muttered. "She's gone lame. Shit!"

Then he did—for Ringo—a surprisingly humane thing. He dismounted and examined the horse's leg. He found it had thrown a shoe, and that a sharp stone had become embedded in its hoof. Ringo knew the horse wouldn't be able to carry his weight the remaining distance.

"Damn!" he exploded. "Damn, damn, damn, damn, damn."

To his horse, he said with uncommon compassion, "Missie, I'll get you as far as Turkey Creek, and I'll fix you up. Meanwhile, I'll do my own hoofin'."

He knew the B. F. "Coyote" Smith ranch was not far from Turkey Creek, and slightly off the trail. If the horse could make it that far, he knew he could get it shod there, and that he could probably spend the night.

He took a long drag on his bottle of Forty-Rod, hitched up his gun belt, and true to his word did the worst thing a cowboy can imagine doing: he walked. With one hand on the saddle horn, and the other clasping a bottle, he hiked on beneath the hot sun.

It was a long, tiring walk that took more than two hours, and though he was plumb tuckered out, Ringo stayed off his horse. His feet hurt like sin. Those Texas boots weren't meant for all that walking.

He drained the contents of his last bottle of whiskey as he reached Turkey Creek. He was so bleary-eyed that as he glanced around he looked right at where Louis was hidden, but never saw him. Louis watched, fascinated, his rifle at half cock.

Ringo staggered down to the river and splashed water onto his sunburned face. He thought nothing on earth had ever felt so good.

He sat down, but his holster got in the way, and his six-shooter gave him a sharp poke. "Damn," he yelped. He took the gun belt off and laid it on the ground beside him.

After a bit, he worked his way to his feet and limped back to his horse, which was grazing not far away. He took off his boots, tied them together by their straps, and looped them over the saddle horn. Then he wrestled his Winchester out of the saddle holster and staggered back to the river bank. As he passed the oak tree, he leaned the gun against the trunk.

He sat down again and stuck his swollen feet into the cool water. He yearned for a strong drink. Soon he began to doze off, and caught himself. "Shit, this's no good," he said aloud. "I'd be better off back at the oak."

He laboriously pulled himself to his feet, but this time they rebelled, and he had to sit down again.

"What the hell now," he muttered.

Then he got an idea. He took off his shirt and undershirt, ripped the undershirt into two pieces, and soaked the pieces in the water. He wrapped each piece around a swollen foot. It felt mighty good, and he congratulated himself for having come up with such a clever notion.

Then he got another idea. He soaked his shirt in the water and put it back on. The evaporation would keep him cool.

He slung the gun belt over his shoulders and crawled on all fours back to the oak tree, where he settled into a natural seat formed by its roots. He'd used it before when he and Curly Bill and the Old Man had stopped here.

Ringo was pleased with himself. He still had a hankering for a strong drink, but he was too tired to care whether he had one or not.

He closed his eyes, and within minutes began to snore.

"You!"

The voice seemed to come from far away. Ringo stirred. "Must be dreaming," he thought.

Then it came again. "You!"

Ringo couldn't rouse himself enough to make the effort to find out what this "you" business was all about.

"Hell with it," he mumbled.

Then he felt something pushing at his head above his right ear, and reluctantly opened his eyes. Louis Hancock was standing over him, holding a gun to his temple.

"I've been waiting for you," Louis rumbled.

"I'm not surprised," Ringo said, a note of resignation in his voice.

For a moment neither spoke, then Ringo broke the silence.

"I never touched them."

"But you stood by and watched them killed!" Hancock shouted.

Again Ringo said, "I never touched them. It wasn't my doing. It was theirs."

"But you were enjoying it!"

"Yeah, it excited me."

"You piece of shit!" Louis exploded. "You enjoy watching someone die?"

Ringo answered simply, "Must be I do. I shot my own father's head off."

"My God," Louis groaned, "what kind of a man are you?"

Ringo didn't answer.

Louis crouched down next to him and stared into his eyes.

"Tell me!" Louis roared at him. "What kind of a man are you?"

"More of a man than you are, nigger!," Ringo spat back, and went for his pistol. He swung the muzzle toward the big man and pulled the trigger at the same instant that Louis fired his own gun. His bullet ripped through Ringo's right temple, and continued out the top of his head. Ringo's gun never fired. It's hammer had caught in the watch fob at his waist.

Ringo was a dead man.

Louis stood up. "Now you go to hell," he said as he stared down at the limp body.

This had been almost too quick, just like with McSween. But it was over.

Louis's final act of revenge was to take out his Bowie knife and cut a piece of scalp from Ringo's head. As he tossed it into Turkey Creek, he shouted, "This is for you, Nadine!"

He gave Ringo's horse a slap on the rump, and it took off down the trail. The next morning Louis was back in Nell's kitchen, preparing breakfast.

25

WHETHER A PERSON LIKED JOHN

Ringo or not, he was the subject of every discussion held over morning coffee in Tombstone.

"How did it happen?" was on everyone's lips.

Louis Hancock went about his business, and kept his own counsel.

Nell Cashman had an inkling that Louis was somehow involved, yet the bad blood she'd witnessed between Ringo, Frank Leslie, Pete Spence, and Billy Claiborne hadn't seemed to involve Louis. She knew, though, that something had transpired between the Texas gunman and her prize chef, and felt it was more than just coincidence that Louis was gone who-knows-where when John cashed in. But she'd also lived on the frontier long enough to know it was better not to ask too many questions.

Ike Clanton was among the first to expound on a theory, and to demand action. "Those damn Earps did it!" he proclaimed loudly up and down Fremont and Toughnut streets. "They sure as hell did it," he'd blabber to anyone who would listen, and even to those who wouldn't. He demanded a new posse, but Tombstone had had enough of posses, especially those of Johnny Behan.

No one took Clanton seriously anyway, because the Earps were in Colorado. Legal problems had followed them from Arizona and New Mexico, and into the courts there. Ike finally had to admit they couldn't be in two places—particularly in two states—at the same time.

Billy Claiborne set his sights on blaming Frank Leslie, because he saw it as a chance to get even with him for that bit with the spittoon. Plenty of others had witnessed or heard about the confrontation between Leslie and Ringo in Nell's dining room. But Claiborne had no proof, even though some said Buckskin had left his post at the Oriental long enough to ride out to Turkey Creek and back. Others said they hadn't even seen Frank at the bar during that time.

Frank just went about smiling, doing his job, and keeping his mouth shut.

If he had bested John Ringo, he'd have been the first to broadcast it. He'd have come up with a humdinger of a good yarn.

Someone even suggested that Billy Breakenridge was in on it. He'd been spotted riding with Ringo that day, headed east, but Billy had an ironclad alibi. He was in court. With genuine tears in his eyes, he asked, "Why would I kill him? He was my best friend."

Other names were brought up as suspects, and all the while Louis Hancock just kept on flipping flapjacks and minding his own business.

⁂

Doc Holliday had come up with the right solution to the Johnny Behan problem. It was his flippant remark to Henry Clay Hooker that the way to shut Behan up was to get him laughed out of town. The diamond stud incident had started the ball rolling, and even his own cronies weren't taking Johnny seriously any more. There weren't many of them left. His closest friends—the McLaurys, Curly Bill Brocius, and John Ringo—were all gone. There was no leadership, and the rustling business was in decline.

Behan was a politician, not a hard, fast-riding cowboy. With his standing in Tombstone souring on a daily basis, he decided not to run for re-election as sheriff. He knew he couldn't win.

Shortly after the election, he was accused of mismanaging his office and taking public funds. This wasn't exactly laughable, but it forced him to turn to other endeavors. Sheriff John Behan was history.

But "Billy the Kid" Claiborne just wouldn't give it up. His friend Ringo would have to be avenged; even more, he was determined to get back at Frank Leslie.

On November 18, 1882, Billy walked into the Oriental Saloon. At seven in the morning, most of the gamblers were home rejoicing over their good fortune, or licking their wounds. The bars were being cleaned, the night's receipts were being tallied, and the night shift was looking forward to a good day's sleep. Buckskin Leslie was one of them. He was anticipating a full day and night off to relax and re-energize. He hadn't counted on Billy Claiborne.

Billy had been on the town, and he missed the companionship of his old buddies. His social life had taken a distinct downturn. He wandered from the Alhambra to the Crystal Palace, to Hatch's, and to the Grand Hotel—his favorite—spewing invectives everywhere. The object of his venom, of course, was

Frank "Buckskin" Leslie.

"You know damn well that son of a bitch shot John Ringo when John wasn't lookin';" or "That asshole Frank Leslie lured Ringo out to Turkey Creek and back-shot him while Ringo was dismounting;" or "Only a yellow-bellied coward like Leslie would have shot Ringo in the back;" were repeated over and over at every bar.

At the Grand, he vowed the end of "that scum of the earth, that so-called scout of the plains, Mister Shitpants Buckskin Leslie."

George Munk, who was having a morning toddy, was tired of hearing it, and finally said, "Kid, why don't you just go on over to the Oriental and tell him to his face?"

A barfly chimed in, "Yeah, do that, Billy, but look out for them spittoons," and followed with a lusty laugh.

That did it. Billy downed a shot and called for another. He gulped that one down, and chased it with a beer. Then he stomped out of the Grand.

He went straight to the Oriental, and putting on his most menacing manner approached Frank Leslie, who was behind the bar. Strong words were exchanged, and Leslie picked up a spittoon and threatened Billy with a repeat performance.

Claiborne backed off, growling, "I'll see you later," and left the bar.

Frank called after him, "You can see me any time you want to."

It wasn't long before Claiborne came back and again accosted Leslie, who was talking to some friends. Leslie warned "Bill, don't interfere here. These people are all friends, and they don't want you around."

Then, in an effort to calm Billy down, he added, "There's no use of you fighting me. There's no occasion for it."

He turned back to his friends, and Billy began shouting obscenities at him.

Frank grabbed Billy by his coat collar and gave him the bum's rush out the door, exclaiming, "If it weren't for having to pay for it, I'd give you another spittoon hat!"

Billy was in a rage. He straightened his coat and went to get his gun. Otto Johnson saw him at the corner of Fifth and Allen, carrying a Winchester in his right hand, the barrel pointing down.

"Hello there, Billy," Johnson said amiably, "where are you heading?"

Billy drew himself up, and snarled, "I don' allow any man to spit on me, an' if he don' come out I'll go in an' make him fight!"

"Who, Billy? Who do you want to fight with?"

"That sonabitch Frank Leslie, tha's who."

"You don't want to do that, Billy. There's no future in fighting. Let's take a walk down the street and talk about it."

"If you interfere, I'll turn loose on you," Billy shouted.

Johnson wasn't about to antagonize an already agitated man, so he walked away and into the Oriental Saloon, where he informed Frank Leslie that Claiborne was coming after him with a Winchester. He cautioned Frank to be careful.

Frank reached under the bar, brought out his gun belt, and removed his pistol from its holster. To the men he'd been talking to, he said, "Please excuse me for a moment."

They could hear Claiborne out on the street talking to Henry Brush, Tombstone's simpatico bootblack. Billy was loud, and his "curly wolf" was way up. Brush tried to calm him down, but Billy shouted, "I'm gonna kill Frank Leslie!"

Always a peaceful man, Henry stood in his way. "Don't go over there, Billy. Give me your gun."

Billy growled, "Get outta my way you black bastard, or I'll kill you too!" Henry beat a hasty retreat.

Frank Leslie stepped out the side door of the Oriental and onto Fifth Street, and heard the shouting coming from up the street and around the corner. He called out, "Billy."

Billy was cocking his rifle as he came around the corner. Frank yelled, "Billy, don't shoot. I don't want you to kill me, and I don't want to kill you!"

Billy raised his Winchester and fired. He missed, but Frank didn't. His .45 caliber slug entered the left side of Claiborne's body, beneath his raised gun, and exited through his spinal cord.

Leslie advanced on the downed Claiborne. This was one fight he wouldn't be able to run away from.

Billy cried out, "Don't shoot again. I am killed."

Billy Claiborne died later that day.

The *Epitaph* made fun of the last of the cowboys to intimidate the town. It headlined its story in bold type:

LESLIE'S LUCK
Billy the Kid takes a shot at Buckskin Frank. The latter promptly replied and the former quickly turns up his toes to the daisies.

That night, George Parsons penned in his diary:

...Frank shot and killed the notorious Kid...making as pretty a center shot on the Kid as one can wish to see...Frank didn't lose the light of his cigarette during the encounter....

That shooting put an end to the violence in Tombstone, but other problems were to come. For a while, round-the-clock operations continued at the mines, and everyone prospered. But one by one the silver lodes played out, and the miners lost their jobs. Businesses began to feel the pinch as more and more of the residents pulled up stakes and headed for greener pastures. They appeared to be following the example set by Bat Masterson and Luke Short back in '81.

It looked like there were good pickings at Utah's Silver Reef. In addition, Bodie had a re-awakening, and Tonopah was just getting started. The Cananea mines south of the border in Sonora prospered, went broke, then really came to life with the discovery of copper, and many of the miners went there. Others went to nearby Bisbee when the Lavender Pit opened.

Yet times went from bad to worse. A couple of mine shafts in Tombstone were filling with water, and as often happens, the money to pump them out came from the miners' own pockets. The price of silver slipped badly on the world market, and wages of four dollars a day dropped to three dollars and fifty cents. The miners struck.

They targeted one of Tombstone's first mining moguls, E. B. Gage, for lynching, but Nellie Cashman saved his life by whisking him out of town in her buggy.

The town that boasted it was too tough to die was dying.

Geronimo and his Apaches went at it again. It was during the Indian uprising in 1886 that Frank Leslie was called up by General Crook. The campaign ended with nothing resolved, but Frank garnered many commendations.

When the scouts disbanded and were saying farewells at the El Paso railroad station, Frank again began to feel the loneliness he had escaped while in the Sierra Madre Mountains of Mexico with his friends, Tom Horn and Mickey Free.

The west was changing. Where once the horse and stagecoach reigned supreme, the railroad now was king. Distances were shrinking. The hustlers, adventurers and free spirits had had their best chance during Tombstone's heyday when the silver mines prospered.

Law and order had taken such a hold on the community that to an old-timer like Buckskin, life had become one big bore. The only place he could use his gun was outside the town limits, and he spent more and more time alone in the Swisshelm Mountains, banging away at anything and everything for hours at a time. Eventually his drinking got to the point where he just wasn't getting enough of a kick from his favorite, Old Crow, and he turned to that mind-bending, blood-boiling mescal. Mae became increasingly afraid of him, and their marriage was rapidly disintegrating.

It finally collapsed altogether when Frank took to leaving Mae alone at the ranch while he snuggled under the sheets with another woman. That was more than Mae could tolerate. The little Irish colleen, who had so dearly loved her man in buckskin, filed for divorce in 1886, naming as co-respondent one Mrs. Birdie Woods.

The court found in favor of the ill-used wife, and Frank was made to pay the piper. But it didn't seem to bother him at all. If anything, he relished having the freedom to pursue his profligate lifestyle.

Mollie Fly, Bob Paul, Father Gallagher, and a few others, concluded that the decline in Buckskin's morals was directly connected to Nell Cashman's departure.

In 1883 Nell had succumbed to itchy feet and, with a group from Tombstone, went exploring for gold in Old Mexico. They took the Modoc stage and headed south for Guaymas. It took the party four days to cross the Gulf into Baja, California, then they hiked another ninety miles into the desert. The maps they carried, and all the information on them, proved to be erroneous. They had not one nugget to show for months of back-breaking labor, and so returned home with nothing but a good story for Nell to tell over coffee and scones.

When Nell was around, Frank Leslie seemed more stable. In her he had found an adventurous, kindred soul. With his marriage dissolved, it was Nell to whom Frank now turned for camaraderie.

⚜

Some years after the Ringo affair, Nell made the mistake of pointing out to Louis an article in the *Epitaph* which read:

…Yuma, Arizona Territory.
The gates of the Yuma Territorial Penitentiary will open next May 18 for one of the oldest of the territory's stage robbers, Pete Spence. He

was involved in the Tombstone-Benson holdup and had been suspected of complicity in the murders of Bud Philpot and Peter Roerig who were on that stage. At the time of the mysterious demise of the colorful John Ringo, Spence turned himself in for his participation in the Bisbee stage robbery. It appears our Mr. Spence had developed a conscience....

Two days later the *Epitaph* ran the following story:

It is with great regret that we report the departure on May 10 of Tombstone's master chef, Mr. Louis Hancock, an employee of Miss Nell Cashman. Miss Cashman said he gave no reason for leaving, but feels he must have just cause. We will surely miss his mouth-watering culinary masterpieces, and we wish him well.

Nell told friends that she had offered to double his salary if he'd stay. She said she'd even threatened to hog-tie him, but he couldn't be dissuaded. Many of her friends had found it hard to understand—much less accept—the deep bond of friendship that had developed between Nell and Louis.

Nell reluctantly helped Louis settle his affairs and pack up. All she knew of his plans was that he intended to ride Big Black to Benson. Only Louis knew that he had purchased tickets for himself and Big Black as far as Yuma, Arizona Territory.

Once Pete Spence left the walls of the Yuma Territorial Penitentiary, he was neither seen nor heard of again.

After Nell lost her prize chef, she developed the same restlessness that possessed Frank, and in time pulled up stakes. Her sister had died, and her nieces and nephews were of an age that she could leave them, though they still needed her financial support. She placed them in one of the finest Catholic boarding schools in Arizona.

She followed her nose to Hillsboro, New Mexico, where she stayed briefly in order to help an old Irish friend establish a restaurant and bar. It was none other than Pat Murphy, late of Murphy's Bar in Safford.

Nell eventually settled in Kingston, about fifteen miles farther up in the Mimbres of the Black Mountain range. But she got gold fever, and before long returned to her first love—the far north. In Nome, Alaska, she found a number of old friends from Tombstone who had preceded her there.

Following Nell's departure from Tombstone, Frank had literally fallen apart. In his mescal-inflamed brain, he recreated over and over the night of the big ball in Tombstone, the night he had saved Nell from the Apaches; the same night they had hungrily shared a long, passionate kiss. Once more he turned his attention to the voluptuous Blonde Mollie, the prostitute who had been the cause of Nell's anguish that night. They created quite a scandal.

Frank was working less and less at the Oriental; his own drinking was a hindrance to his job. So it was that he spent the majority of his time at his ranch in the Swisshelms with Mollie.

They became a joke around town with their drinking, and some of the die-hard gamblers took bets on which one of them could drink the most. It looked like Frank had met his match when it came to emptying a bottle.

Frank wasn't interested in working the ranch, so he hired James Neal, a young man who took over practically all of Frank's responsibilities. Frank liked James, and so did Blonde Mollie.

On a day in July of 1889, after a week of non-stop drinking, the Leslie household ran out of all liquor except for Frank's favorite—mescal. It was the only drink that could get Nell out of his mind, and it energized his lust for Mollie. But she wouldn't touch it, and demanded "the good stuff." To keep the peace, such as it was, Frank rode to the closest ranch where he was able to get Mollie something more to her liking.

Upon his return, he found his woman and young James together on the porch, sharing a chair. Frank became enraged. He knew what Mollie had been, and the sight of her on James's lap was too much. He snapped.

He reached for what he always called his friend, his long-barreled six-shooter, and commenced firing. James was hit, but he managed to get away and hide. Mollie tried to escape, but was hit hard and died on the spot.

Frank, insane with jealousy, mescal, and self-recrimination, roared around the ranch, yelling and shooting, until he finally collapsed on the ground in a stupor. At that point, James Neal fled to the nearby Reynolds ranch, and the law was summoned.

Frank didn't resist arrest, and when he sobered up claimed he couldn't remember a thing that happened. It was no doubt true.

No lawyer would represent this relic of the frontier, and a quick, two-day trial was held. Frank had nothing to say in his own defense, and pled guilty to the shootings. He was sentenced to a life term in the Yuma Territorial Penitentiary.

Always a good yarn spinner, Frank talked freely to the reporters who occasionally came by to interview him. As the story of his service to the United

States government came out, recommendations for clemency started pouring into Yuma. They came from army officers, prison officials, and private citizens from various walks of life. Particularly gratifying to Frank was a letter from his old scouting pal, Tom Horn, who offered him a job as range detective in Wyoming.

On November 17, 1896, Governor Franklin granted Frank a full pardon, and he walked away a free man after spending six years in the hell-hole that was Yuma Territorial Penitentiary.

Back in Tombstone, Billy Breakenridge got the surprise of his life one night when he opened his door to a sun-blackened man wearing a buckskin shirt.

Frank had come back for one reason, and hadn't been altogether sure that he'd be welcome. Billy recovered quickly from his initial surprise and invited Frank in for a bottle of beer, which Frank eagerly accepted.

The two men sat down and reminisced about the good old days. Billy said he'd tried a little ranching, but was glad to once more be wearing a deputy marshal's badge. Frank gave a quick account of what he'd been doing, and finally got around to asking the question that had caused him to come here in the first place.

"Bill, do you know where Nell Cashman went?"

"She went to Alaska, Frank. She and half the frontier moved up there. It's California in '49 all over again. The Klondike Gold Rush is on, and that's where our little Nellie has taken herself off to."

"That's a ways away," Frank said quietly. Then he broke into a smile. "You know, Billy, could be I've been soaking up this damn Arizona sun a bit too long."

Frank finished his beer, stood up, shook Billy's hand, thanked him for his hospitality, and stepped out into the night.

26

IT WAS 1900. THE GOLD STRIKES IN
the Klondike, at Skagway, and farther north at Dawson, had begun to play out
when Wyatt and Sarah Earp arrived in the area. The harbor at Nome, known as
the Golden Strand, became the jumping-off place for gold-seekers going to the
Koyukuk gold fields.

When Wyatt and his Josie, as he called Sarah, saw the crowds camped on
the beach in tents and makeshift shacks, they intuitively knew that this was the
place for them. Let the sourdoughs rough it in the mountains. They would make
their fortune right there on the Strand.

As time went by, the tents and shacks gave way to business establishments, stores, banks, and houses. Few there knew mining camps better than
Wyatt. While others mined their fortunes from the earth, he mined his from them
in the newly-created town of Nome. He built and managed the Dexter Saloon,
and for a while it was the only two-story building in the town. It was an immediate success, and during the years gold came in from the interior, the Earps made
themselves a tidy fortune.

It was here that their friend John Clum, former mayor of Tombstone and
editor of the *Epitaph*, came to visit. He was in and out of their lives for two years
while he worked for the United States government. They had a lot to talk about.
And when Tombstone's diarist, George Parsons, joined them briefly, they spent
many nostalgic evenings poring over Parsons' old journals.

John Clum was at the pier on a day in July when the *Seattle Queen* steam-
ship dropped anchor in the roadstreet. He watched intently as passengers were
ferried ashore in the flat-bottomed shuttle boats. The great majority were men,
miners all: big, rough Finns and Irishmen from the copper mines of Michigan's
upper peninsula, placer miners from California's gold fields, and silver miners
from Tombstone and Bisbee. They all had gold dust in their eyes. The sparkling
eyes that John was looking for belonged to a dear old friend.

She finally was brought ashore with the others. Her boots were soiled with mud, and her big, floppy hat was water-stained. Nevertheless, she stood out from the rest of the crowd, maybe because of her diminutive size, maybe because everyone deferred to her, or maybe because of the hundred thousand dollars she'd made in the Dawson gold rush. She was a winner, and everyone knew it. She was the most famous woman in Alaska, the woman the *Yukon Midnight Sun*, Alaska's premier newspaper, called "the pioneer woman of this country."

John was waiting for her as she stepped onto the dock. "Nellie! You're here! You're here!" he shouted as he clasped her to him.

"That I am, John," she laughed, returning his embrace, "but not for long. I'll only be here one night, and I'll tell you all about that later. Right now I want to get somewhere where I can clean up."

John had a boy and a cart waiting, and once her bags were located they pushed through the mass of humanity that clogged the streets of this boom town.

As he signed her into the Cosmopolitan Hotel, he apologized, "It's the best we have here, but knowing you, I'll never hear a complaint."

"It's just fine, John."

Later, as they were enjoying coffee in her room, John said, "Now tell me. Why such a short stay? You said you'd just be here this one night."

"That's a fact, John," Nell answered. "I've leased a boat called the *Sitka*, and at noon tomorrow it'll take me and my men along the coast to Norton Bay. We'll go ashore at Kayuk, then overland by sleigh to the Yukon River, then up the river in another boat I've commissioned and on into the Kayukuk River gold district. I'll be going a hundred miles north of the Arctic Circle. That's why I'll always look back on this hotel with fondness," she finished with a laugh.

"Nell, I don't know why I should be so surprised, but I am. You always were full of surprises. I'll be honest with you, I'd do almost anything to hold you here; even marry you, if you'd have me."

They both laughed as Nell kissed him on the top of his head, saying, "That's a great idea, but it's too late now, John."

They finished their coffee and went out on the town. He took her back to the docks so she could finalize her plans for the next day. The little open-air, steam-powered *Sitka* was there, and her men were busy loading the supplies that they'd taken off the *Seattle Queen*.

The excitement and a spirit of adventure were pervasive, and John saw the sparkle in Nell's eyes as she gave orders and saw to the stowing of her equipment.

"My God, you really love it, don't you?" he said to her.

"It's my life, John. It's my reason for living."

John changed the subject. "I have a surprise for you."

"You mean Wyatt, Sarah, and George? I knew I'd be seeing them tonight. Remember, you wrote me they were here."

"That I did. Yes, they're here and waiting anxiously to see you. We'll all go back in time tonight. Catch up, you know."

That evening, John Clum slogged through the muddy streets to the Cosmopolitan, where Nell was waiting. Together they made their way to Wyatt Earp's Drexel Saloon.

The place was jammed, as usual. It was considered the best establishment of its kind in town, and many of the most respected citizens were seen dining there on the "best meal in town."

The long, mahogany bar was crowded with men, and a few ladies. A band was playing lively music as flashy women sang and danced on the little stage, lustily cheered on by the lone men. When the curtain came down, the sourdoughs clomped onto the dance floor. What they lacked in grace, they made up for in enthusiasm, and the painted ladies who partied with them didn't seem to care. It was a big, noisy, smoke-filled, masculine world, and Nell Cashman loved it.

She asked that they be seated in the main area rather than in the seclusion of Wyatt's private room because she wanted to be close to the activity. "I want to see everything," she exclaimed, as she tapped her feet to the rhythm of the music.

To accommodate Nell, Wyatt cleared a corner of the main room, had some tables placed together, and stationed one of his bouncers close by. Then he called for their dinner to be served.

Nell observed that he still had that grim look about him, but he was warm and cordial to her. As a matter of fact, he seemed delighted to have someone else from his past here. He'd become somewhat of a celebrity because of his involvement in Tombstone's affairs, and he considered it a real pleasure to be with people who were a part of them. It was hard to believe that over twenty years had gone by.

Josie-Sarah positively doted on her guest. There weren't all that many ladies of quality in Nome, and at least for this one night she had someone she could really talk to. She and Nell got along famously.

George Parsons, always the journalist, didn't miss a story that went around the table that evening. "Catch up" was the phrase John Clum had used, and catch up they did.

The younger crowd at Dexter's was amused at the sight of these dignified, middle-aged people talking and laughing, and obviously having themselves one heck of a good time. The men were well turned out: their frock coats were neatly pressed, their white shirts virtually sparkled, their cravats were perfectly tied, and their boots were spit-and-polish shined.

Josie-Sarah was wearing the latest fashion to come by boat from San Francisco. Her graying hair was pulled back and rolled into a tight bun, and she wore exquisite, oriental-looking jewelry. She exuded class.

But it was Nell who garnered most of the admiring glances. She always had one party dress with her no matter where she traveled. This night she chose the Gibson Girl look, from her hair to her pale-blue satin, bosom-exposing gown, cinched waist, and fashionably-shod feet. Nell looked—in a word—gorgeous.

The talk during the early part of the evening centered around Tombstone.

Wyatt told of his brother Virgil's job as sheriff back in Prescott, and his brother Warren's job as a lawman in the Benson-Wilcox area of Arizona.

"Doc avenged himself on Billy Allen when he ran into him one day in Leadville," he chuckled. "He gave him a lead souvenir to remember him by. We all thought it was Allen who'd taken shots at us while he was hiding at Fly's during the O. K. Corral shoot-out."

"You know," Nell added, "John corresponded with me until he died. He treated me just as he treated his cousin Mattie—like a sister. She, as you may know, is a nun."

Nell reflected for a moment, then continued, "John had a strange sense of humor, but I must have too, because he could always make me laugh. The coughing finally got him in 1887. I heard his last words were, 'This is going to be funny.' What 'this' was, is that he'd asked both a Catholic priest and a Presbyterian minister to officiate at his funeral, and neither knew about the other."

That got a laugh from everyone at the table, including Nell, but she finished on a melancholy note, "That was Doctor John Holliday."

George Parsons had the story on Ike Clanton's final days. "Ike and Phin were caught rustling cattle in Apache County in 1887. They got themselves cornered and, as you might expect, Ike made a run for it and was shot down."

The stories came and went throughout dinner, which was over by eight o'clock. Sarah ordered champagne to be served all around, and the men fired up their cigars.

The music was at its best, and the Dexter was alive with happy sounds.

Clum glanced at Sarah, who excused herself and disappeared into the crowd. She re-appeared at the bandstand, and spoke directly to the conductor. He led his musicians to the final notes of the reel they'd been playing, and the dancers gradually returned to their tables.

When the floor had cleared, the conductor raised his baton and the band began to play *The Blue Danube Waltz*. Nell leaned back in her chair and sipped champagne. She was truly enjoying this night.

She smiled at Sarah and remarked, "It sounds as though you're trying to bring a little elegance to the land of the midnight sun."

Just then she felt a tap on her shoulder, and someone asked, "May I have this dance?"

She turned to see who it was, and her mouth fell open. There stood Frank "Buckskin" Leslie, with his arms outstretched.

Frank's blue eyes danced as he smiled down at her, and Nell looked back in stunned silence. She was speechless.

Nell rose slowly to her feet, and shot a look at John Clum. He winked at her. This was the surprise she had erroneously guessed at when Clum picked her up at the dock.

Leslie led her onto the floor and paused briefly to catch the beat.

Curious onlookers saw a man with silver hair, wearing a buckskin shirt belted at the waist. His black trousers were narrow in the leg, California style, and there wasn't an ounce of excess fat on him. His face was tanned to a deep brown—unusual in this north country—and the lines on it merely served to enhance his good looks.

He was extremely confident. He was in charge.

He bowed to Nell, then to the onlookers, and bent to whisper something in her ear. Whatever it was made her smile.

They were off and dancing like no one had seen in these parts before. They went dipping and spinning, whirling and gliding around the room. An enraptured audience let them have the entire floor to themselves.

When the music stopped, Frank called for one more, and away they went again. The ladies couldn't keep their eyes off Frank, or the men theirs off Nell.

The dance ended, and Frank and Nell just stood and looked at each other. The place erupted. People were applauding and stamping their feet so hard the floor shook. Catcalls and whistles pierced the air. Frank and Nell, in the spirit of the moment, took a bow. Then they headed for their table, and the band struck up *Turkey in the Straw*. Just about everyone poured onto the floor, and if a man lacked a female partner he'd just grab another man and off they'd go.

Wyatt, Sarah, John and George stood and gave the twosome a round of applause as they approached. Nell reached over and gave Clum a light punch to his shoulder.

"You sly old fox," she laughed, "you knew it all the while."

Someone brought a chair up for Frank, and he sat down next to Nell. Sarah observed that they hadn't let go of each other's hands since leaving the dance floor.

Nell, a little out of breath, asked, "How long have you been here, Frank?"

"Just got in early this morning," he answered. "I came in on the *Star of Alaska*. She's one of the last square riggers still making the Alaska lumber run. We had to sit out in the bay for hours, because the wind quit and the lighters wouldn't come out to us. Your *Seattle Queen* passed us by, and you were ashore before we even got moving again. I didn't actually get ashore until a couple of hours ago, and went straight to Wyatt's. I've had one hell of a time getting myself together for this party tonight," he laughed.

Nell was astonished. "You knew about this before, Frank?"

"Sure did," he said with a grin. "Sarah let me know you were going to be here. I've really been looking forward to this, Nell. I've got a lot to talk to you about."

Nell was obviously distressed as she replied, "But Frank, I'm leaving tomorrow. I'm going to the Arctic Circle, and all the arrangements are made."

Now it was Frank who looked distressed. "Oh, God, no," he whispered. He couldn't believe he'd come all the way to the Yukon to see Nell, only to have her leave after a few hours.

"Can't you stay just a few days? For an old friend?"

"I'm sorry, Frank, I truly am, but no, I can't. I'm going on a government mail boat, and they don't wait for anybody. I can't even be a few minutes late in my connections or it may be weeks before I can get up the Kayukuk."

Frank covered his deep disappointment by quickly making light of Nell's ambitious plan, and only Sarah understood his reason for doing it. "Looks like you've got gold fever, Nell. But I guess you've got to follow those itchy feet of yours no matter where they take you."

Nell didn't respond.

Frank went on, "Seeing as how you'll be leaving so soon, I reckon I'd best give you this right now."

He reached into his watch pocket and brought out a small bag, pulled something out of it, and pressed it into Nell's hand.

Nell cried out, "My rosary!" Her voice broke and she sobbed, "The rosary I gave you that night, the night of the Apaches."

She stared at it, and ran her hands lovingly over it. Then she clutched it to her bosom and looked at him.

"Frank," she whispered.

"The night of the Apaches?" Parsons asked. "When was that? What's that all about?"

"A long time ago," Frank answered, laughing. "Too long."

He lifted Nell's chin with his finger and said, "Dry your tears, little one, and let's have ourselves another go-round."

Nell did as she was told, holding tightly to Frank's hand as he led her onto the crowded dance floor.

Contrary to his nature, Clum didn't pursue an answer as to what was behind Nell's statement, but remained forever curious about it.

※

The six friends met the following noon on the busy pier at Nome. They had come to say good-bye to Nell, who didn't look anything at all like the lovely lady who'd been partying with them. The change in her appearance was nothing short of dramatic.

She wore wide, black suspenders to hold up the Levis tucked into stained leather boots, which were laced from ankle to knee; a Sam Brown belt over a gray, homespun shirt, and over that a checkered mackinaw. A holstered Colt revolver hung from the belt. It was Frank Leslie's gun. Her long hair was pulled back and held at the nape of her neck by a colorful ribbon, and she carried a wide-brimmed campaign hat with a feather sticking out of the headband at a jaunty angle.

It was obvious to all of them that Nell was both eager to be on her way, and reluctant to leave the man in the buckskin shirt beside her. It seemed to Sarah that they'd held hands all morning long. Frank helped Nell onto the deck of the *Sitka*, and they stood in silence.

One of Nell's men, a big, burly fellow sporting a red beard, called out, "We've got a head of steam, Miss Nell."

Nell had been lost in thought, and it took a few seconds before she responded, "Yes, of course. Thank you, Tom."

She looked up into Frank Leslie's eyes. "Frank, oh Frank," she said wistfully.

Frank pulled her close and kissed her full on the mouth, then released her and stepped back. Nell was trembling.

Once more he reached out, gathered her to him in a tight embrace, and kissed her fervently. Then he dropped his arms to his sides.

He gazed down at her for one brief moment before stepping onto the dock. "Be seeing you," he said.

Nell watched from the deck of the *Sitka* as it pulled away, and Frank disappeared in the crowd.